SENTEN

CW00409869

DEA...

BY

A. P. MARTIN

Table of Contents

Chapter One

Some way below me, the bright moonlight glints magically on the calm water, as its laps gently against the bank. As always these days, I am alone. Distracted, I turn away from the stunning view and leave the spacious balcony of the roof-top flat. I glance at the large decorative mirror which adorns one wall and notice that, in the subdued light, my shaded eyes look unnaturally dark. I turn and stare, unblinking, at the huge LED television which, even when switched off, dominates one corner of the room.

I feel suddenly on edge, perhaps even wired. I have come to realise that tonight, everything that I have gone through in the last few weeks has led me to reach a shockingly irrevocable decision. Of course, all the detailed research and preparation remains to be completed. But, somehow, I know that I have sufficient time. For now, I allow myself to relax and to savour the anticipation of what lies ahead.

With a practised movement, I press the remote control and the sound system leaps into life. How soothing it has been to my troubled soul, this glorious music which swells and surges as the inspirational scene begins to play out. Tonight, however, even though this is the only part of the whole performance that really matters to me, I am all too aware that I'm feeling little true emotion. Over the last weeks, all of my emotion has been exhausted and drained. Now, a ruthless determination to fulfil my dream is all that remains.

I stare at the smiling face in the framed photograph, which, instinctively, I have picked up. There's no doubt that it is complemented perfectly by the gleaming white teeth and the shining, fathomless blue eyes. A casual observer may think this a charming reminder of a partner, or a lover. I smirk at the ordinariness of so many people, as I reflect that such an observer may well feel a creeping sense of unease at the sight of the hundreds of different photographs of the same smiling face which cover much of one whole wall of the room. Such banal sensitivity is of no concern whatsoever to me. I am all that matters and I find the images both intensely arousing and, simultaneously, wonderfully soothing.

'We will soon be together forever, my one true love,' I promise the smiling face, before I replace the frame on the coffee table.

Chapter Two

Monday July 4th 2016, Geneva Airport, Switzerland.

Olivia

The sun's already high in the clear blue, Alpine sky, as my taxi approaches Geneva Airport. I've spent the past twenty five minutes listening to some middle eastern radio channel which is obviously the favourite of the silent driver. How different he is from the garrulous Geordie cabbies back home, I think. They're always keen to chat about anything and everything. A sudden pang of excitement rushes through me and I realise with a little jolt of surprise, that I am actually looking forward to going home.

The scene at the drop-off point looks like something out of one of those old Merchant-Ivory films, set in late Raj India. People are bustling about in all directions, carrying, pushing and pulling all kinds of luggage and children. As I allow myself to be carried with the flow of people into the Check In area, my heart sinks, as I catch sight of the enormous queue, snaking its way towards the two solitary Easyjet desks which are staffed. Irritation is replaced by anger with myself, as I notice that only half a dozen people are waiting at the bag drop.

'Oh, shit!' I say out loud, without really meaning to. I don't like swearing and I really try hard never to fall into such lazy language. But, this time, it's out before my conscious mind can intervene.

'I know exactly how you feel, ma'am,' says a voice to my left and I turn to see a tall, rangy man, probably in his fifties. He's smiling as he asks innocently, 'You forget to check in online, as well? I've never been much of a forward planner. Don't know what your excuse is though,' he adds with a rueful smile.

He seems a perfectly pleasant man and normally I wouldn't be so rude. But today, I just can't be bothered with such mundane small talk. I respond with a shrugged, 'Something like that, yes,' and turn away from him, pretending to study my mobile phone, which remains steadfastly switched off. As soon as I'm sure that he's got the message, I survey the crowded Check In hall. There are dozens of busy desks, each of which seems to be the setting for some kind of domestic drama or crisis. A family group that must be separated on board, a man that has turned up the day after his booked flight, an older woman, worried that she will be given a seat too far away from the toilet. Whatever.

My mind tunes all this out and goes back to an equally hot day a month previously. Then, it was my eighteen year old son, Sebastian, standing here waiting to check in for his flight to the USA. He was, of course, very excited to be setting off on his gap year travels, before taking up the offer of a place to study at Imperial College in London. But I remember, wistfully, the way he kept reaching for, and then releasing my hand, as we stood side by side in the queue. That instantly told me that he was a bit nervous as well.

And so, if I'm being totally honest, was I. In my mid forties, always careful to be well groomed and dressed, I may look every inch the attractive and confident professional woman, which all the glossy mags talk about endlessly. In fact, I'm just coming to the end of that rite-de-passage, endured by many women of my age, who have struggled to create and develop a successful career - an acrimonious divorce. Anyway, the legal battle I've been fighting for the last three years has taken a heavy toll on me, both emotionally and financially. But, with Sebastian now happily enjoying his first placement with Camp America in Santa Barbara, I felt the time was right to spend a few weeks with my sister and brother-in- law in my hometown, Gateshead.

But this situation with the queues is absolutely infuriating. I have to admit that it is unusual, because I've always found Easyjet to be at least as efficient as standard airlines. And the fact that it flies direct to Newcastle is a real boon. I remember having a conversation with an irritating little man at work, who thought it incredibly funny to suggest that these planes must fly almost empty. He'd obviously bought into the prejudice of the online British press, which never fails to imply to foreigners that anywhere north of Watford is an economic and cultural wasteland. I thoroughly enjoyed putting him in his place, by pointing out that they routinely fly at almost full capacity. But today, I ruefully admit that I wish he'd have been right.

I'm one of the last to board and, peering past a fussy old man who is taking an age and a day to pack his hand baggage securely in the overhead locker, I can see that the plane will be all but full. The irritated voice of a member of the cabin crew crackles loudly from the speaker system, exhorting people to take their seats as quickly as possible, 'otherwise there is a real chance that we will miss our take off slot.' This threat, coupled with the meaningful stares of those passengers already seated and belted, finally galvanises him into decisive action and he pushes his small bag as far into the locker as possible. As he sits down, he keeps casting anxious glances above his head, as if he fully expects it to leap out of its own accord and hit him on the head.

Finally, I reach row seventeen and am desolate, when I realise that my assigned seat is the middle one of three cramped seats. Incomprehensibly, the man already happily occupying the window seat is the American from the queue. How the hell did he get a better seat? I fume inwardly. He was behind me in the queue! To make matters far, far worse, I see that the man in the aisle seat embodies everything I dread about flying. He's hugely overweight, with long, greasy hair tied into a lank pony tail and, worst of all, his upper body is clothed only in an extremely grubby looking, black singlet. Relax, Olivia, I tell myself. The flight's only a couple of hours. Just buy a bottle of red and chill.

Rescue is at hand, however, as the American obviously recognises the look of consternation on my face, as I stand, desperately checking in vain for any other empty seat. With a frustrated grunt,the fat man almost wrenches the seat in front into a horizontal position, in a bid to lever himself upright. Just as I'm thinking to myself, what right does he have to be angry? At least I'll only use up my own space on board, the American climbs nimbly out of his seat, saying, 'What a coincidence! May I offer you this window seat? I'm sure you'd be much more comfortable there. It's no problem. I'll just take yours.'

I'm mortified by my previously offhand behaviour towards him, but I'm in no mood to look such a welcome gift horse in the mouth. So I smile sweetly and gush, 'Thank you very much. That's really very kind of you.' Once we're all seated and belted up for take off, I turn to him and say contritely, 'Look, about earlier in the queue...'

He seems to read my mind, as he replies in a charming accent that still has a little of the west coast about it, 'It's OK. I know what it's like when, sometimes, you just, you know, don't really want to engage in chit chat with other folk. Forget it. It's nothing.'

However, I'm British and not quite ready to excuse myself so effortlessly. 'No really,' I say, 'it was unacceptably rude of me. And I'm not normally rude.' Having gone this far, I decide that I have to offer him my hand, adding ' I'm Olivia by the way, Olivia Clavel.'

He seems uncertain at this development and replies quickly, 'Well, it's very nice to meet you, I'm sure. You sound English, but Clavel? That's surely a French name isn't it?'

'That's right.' I say with little enthusiasm. 'I was married to a Swiss man for more than twenty years.' The use of the past tense to describe my marriage is still a novelty, but, I'm pleased to say that I find it a pleasant novelty.

'I see.' he replies, although I doubt he sees the half of it. 'I'm John Paul Kerrigan, by the way. Back in the sixties in Los Angeles, my parents were real Beatles fans. Mom adored Paul, but Dad thought Lennon was the best ever. So, I guess that's why I ended up sounding like some kind of pope.'

For what seems like the first time in several weeks, I burst out in spontaneous laughter, to be greeted by Kerrigan's anxious expression. 'Gee, I never thought. You might be a Catholic, or something, and take offence.'

This causes me to laugh even more and I struggle to get out my next words, 'No, you can relax on that score.'

As the cabin crew goes through the universally ignored ritual of the safety instructions, I take the opportunity, surreptitiously to look at my recent saviour. He's comfortably above average height, medium to slim build

11

with an open, perma tanned face and short, steely grey hair. He's dressed in a black lightweight suit with an open neck shirt. Looking at him, in fact, he could easily be taken for one of my university colleagues. I realise with some surprise that, before the interruption of the safety drill, I had actually enjoyed very much talking to this friendly American. So, I'm not in the slightest disturbed when, as soon as the initial ascent has been completed, he asks, 'Have you ever been to Newcastle before? It's my first time and I've no idea what to expect?'

'What do you mean?' I say in mock horror. 'Do you imagine it's like the Wild West?'

'Now you're joshing me, ma'am.' he replies defensively. 'No, it's just that I've only ever been around London, the South Coast and Scotland. The stretch in the middle, I usually just fly over. I travel mainly on business, as I work for one of the private banks in Geneva. We've quite a few clients based in London and Edinburgh. It's kinda weird, at one time I'd have never travelled on July 4th.' At this point his eyes seem to to focus on something way in the distance, outside the plane somewhere. 'We all change, I guess.'

I really like the way he pronounces Scotland's capital as 'Edinburg' and I reply with a smile, 'I see. Well, it so happens that 'the Toon', as we Geordies call it, is my home town and, while I've not lived there for more years than I care to remember, it's still a 'canny' place.'

''Canny.' he asks in confusion. 'How'd you mean 'canny'. Is that good?'

Amused by this, I reply with a smile, 'Oh, yes, John Paul. It's good. I'm sure you'll have an unforgettable time on Tyneside.'

The American fixes me with a curious expression, before saying, 'I do hope so, ma'am. Because, you see, it's a special, kind of bittersweet, journey for me.'

'Really? How so?'

'Well you know, I'm pretty much a Wagner fan. Or, more accurately, I should say my wife, God rest her soul, and myself were great fans . We went all over the world to performances of 'The Ring.' My Maisie, she particularly liked the productions which did all four operas in a week or two. 'Recharging her emotional batteries,' she used to call it. We saw productions all over the world. Edinburgh in the summer of 2003, Copenhagen in 2006, Melbourne in '13 and, of course, Bayreuth many times.'

'Oh, I'm so sorry to hear that. Is this the first time you'll be on your own?'

'That's right, ma'am. Y'see my Maisie, she sadly passed on last December. Cancer finally got her.'

I place my hand over John Paul's in a gesture of simple sympathy. 'Oh, that must have been awful.'

He looks at me through moist eyes, 'Thanks very much. But it's OK now, ma'am ...'

'Call me Olivia, please.'

The American nods and smiles, 'It was very, very hard. But I'm adjusted now and this trip, it's kind of for her, if you know what I mean? Anyways, you'll be visiting your folks, I guess?'

'That's right,' I confirm. 'But, by coincidence, I'm also going to all four productions of The Ring Cycle at The Sage.'

'Wow! Really? That is a coincidence,' he says brightly. 'Maybe we should meet up, exchange notes, y'know? It'd be fun.'

'Well, I'm not sure..'

'Oh, go on,' he urges, before slapping his thigh with his right hand, thereby waking up the already snoring fat man in the vest. ' Say, I've got an even better idea. I've signed up for a kind of discussion group, before each of the operas.' Alarmed by my evidently dubious reaction, he immediately adds reassuringly, 'It's run by Opera North. So it should be OK. Oh, go on. Say you'll come. At least to the first one. I've never been to anything like it before and, as I said, it's my first solo Ring, so you'd be doing me a real favour.'

I'm not so enthusiastic, but on the other hand, it would be bordering on the rude to turn him down flat. He obviously recognises my wavering, and skilfully plays his trump card. 'And, y'know? It'd be great to have a friendly face in the group, right from the start. If it's no good, I'll buy you a drink and we'll forget about the rest of them. How's that?'

Helpless in the face of his charm,I find myself saying, 'Agreed.'

'That's wonderful, Olivia. Here's the details...'

Chapter Three

Olivia

'I think I've just about had enough for now, Christine,' I sigh as my elder sister finishes rifling through yet another rack of sale items. 'There's nothing I like the look of. But I could kill for a cup of tea.'

Christine looks with faux compassion at me, 'I can see you're out of training, sis. Do you never go to the shops in Geneva?'

As I look at her, her pale complexion stands clear testimony to the time she wastes indoors, looking for non existent bargains. I immediately think that I should insist that she comes for a holiday to Switzerland, where I could make sure that she got some fresh air, exercise and, above all, some sun on her face. I read somewhere that rickets is making something of a comeback in Britain and looking at my older sister, I can readily see why.

I realise with a start that she's still waiting for my answer, so I fire back, 'Only when I absolutely have to. You want to see the prices there.' Without waiting for a reply,I march determinedly towards the restaurant in Marks and Spencers. Unilaterally, I have decided that we'll have a slightly early lunch. Christine, affecting health consciousness, chooses a Salmon and Scrambled Egg Bloomer, whereas I go the whole hog with the Cumberland Sausage Bun, each served with a pot of tea.

'What time do we have to be back?' asks my sister, as soon as we've found an unoccupied table for two, among all the young mothers with pushchairs and senior citizens, who constitute the majority of the clientele. 'I believe these Wagner epics can be pretty lengthy.'

'Oh this one's the runt of the litter... only three hours. But no interval.'

'So, you'd best be out in plenty of time. Stock up with wine beforehand eh?' suggests Christine, through a mouthful of her lunch.

'Well, that's the thing.' I hesitate, unsure whether I should say more. In the end, I decide that talking it through may help me decide what to do. So I add,'I didn't tell you about the chap on the plane, did I?'

Christine's face immediately freezes, a mixture of salmon and scrambled egg clearly visible in her open mouth. I laugh and reach for my iPhone, 'Just you stay like that. It'll be perfect on Facebook.'

Christine brushes away the suggestion and, though chewing, manages to ask, 'Was he that rather good looking guy you said a couple of words to, just before you caught sight of us, yesterday, at the airport?'

Aware of my older sister's insatiable interest in my private life, which dates back to when I was a stick thin twelve year old at the local grammar school, I had studiously ignored the raised eyebrows and quizzical look, with which I had been greeted in the Arrivals Hall at Newcastle. Now, in a moment of weakness, I've gone and piqued her interest massively. What on earth was I thinking? I moan inwardly, before replying. 'That's right. Anyway, the thing is, he's going to The Ring Cycle as well..'

'Oooh! That's nice...'

16

'And, he's also going to a pre-performance discussion group. He wants me to go to it as well.'

Predictably, Christine says, 'Hmmm, that doesn't sound the most romantic of invitations, does it?' Having taken early retirement from school teaching, my sister has recently reinvented herself as a self published author of romantic fiction. Infuriatingly, she is increasingly viewing the world through a rose tinted prism of dashing, romantic heroes and superficially feisty, but actually, traditionally needy females.

Regretting having opened my mouth, I try to shut down the conversation. 'Seriously, Chris, I'm not sure I should go.'

Big sister, however, is having none of it, and she replies, as if to a nervous teenager. 'Don't be ridiculous! It'll be interesting. And I've no doubt he'd be grateful to know someone in the group.'

Before I can stop myself, I mumble, 'That's just what he said.'

'There you are then,' Christine concludes triumphantly, as if she has just resolved a problematic plot issue in her latest bodice ripper. 'I'm sure it'll do you good.'

'We'll see,' I reply in glum defeat, while trying in vain to enjoy the last sip of my now lukewarm tea.

***

'What time does it start tonight?' Christine's husband, Joe asks me, as I sit leafing through the latest edition of Cosmopolitan. 'Only, if you want a lift into town, I could easily run you in.'

Joe's approaching retirement now, having been a civil servant all his working life. As I look up from my magazine into his ageing, kindly face, it strikes me, as it always does,that he's a perfect example of a rather old fashioned, unassuming gentleman.

I politely decline his kind offer, saying, 'That's kind of you, Joe. But it's just as easy to go down on the bus, especially as there's a stop very close to The Sage. I would like to borrow one of your mobiles though. It's much less complicated to reserve a taxi for the return trip using a British mobile. You know, they always ring to let you know they've arrived and I've had problems in the past using my Swiss one.'

'Sure,' says Christine immediately, taking her phone out of her handbag and leaving it on the large wooden coffee table. 'You can take mine, it's no bother.'

***

There's a definite buzz of anticipation about The Sage, as I approach its main entrance. Before going inside, I peer over the wall at the River Tyne, ebbing gently away towards The North Sea. Even though it's at least ninety minutes before *Das Rheingold* is due to start, once I enter the light and airy concourse, I'm surprised to see so many people, sitting in the warm evening sunshine, enjoying wine and bar food. As I walk across the concourse area, to pick up my tickets at the box office desk, I have to make a detour around several areas which have been enclosed behind portable screens. Risking a quick look around one of these, I see straight away more than a dozen large tables, set with best linen and silver service, for those fortunate enough to have elected to enjoy the pre-performance meal.

As both John Paul and I had to pick up our tickets from the box office, we had arranged to meet there. Just as I pass the souvenir shop and continue along the curved concourse, I catch sight of him, standing on the huge terrace, outside the building. He's on his own and is looking intently out over the river and across towards Newcastle city centre. I'm impressed to see that he has the dress code down perfectly. He's neither in dumbed down jeans and pullover, nor over the top tuxedo, but is smartly dressed in a beige linen suit with a maroon oxford shirt. I smile in satisfaction, as I catch sight of my elegant trouser suit, reflected in the glass wall of the venue, as I approach the door.

'Here you are, and what a delight as well,' beams John Paul, as he rapidly turns away from the river and approaches. He simply offers his outstretched right hand in greeting, rather than attempt to inflict the tiresome and meaningless 'mwa mwa' kiss. I'm still reflecting that the man impresses me more, the longer I spend in his company, when he says,'And what an evening it is. With a bit of imagination, this could be Valhalla and The Rhinemaidens could be singing down there by the river.'

I laugh at the fully intended preposterousness and tease him back,'Now John Paul. I know I said Newcastle is my hometown, but really, there are limits.'

'Nonsense. It's a great city... and I really love your fish and chips. Best I've ever had. Oh, and it's JP, please. A bit American, I guess. But go on,humour me.'

'Of course, JP,' I agree, before asking him the key question which I'm sure will baffle him. 'But, tell me, did you go to Colemans?'

He astonishes me by nodding assuredly and saying, 'I sure did, ma'am. The hotel pointed me to The Metro and I spent a swell morning, walking along the beach there in South Shields. Lunch at Coleman's just rounded things off perfectly. But, say, we'd better get ourselves away to the discussion group. Come on, I already asked where we should to go.'

'I'll just collect my tickets and I'll be right with you,' I say, as I decide that it had, after all, been a good idea to meet John Paul.

Chapter Four

Olivia

JP picks a note out of his pocket and squints at it. I immediately wonder if he normally wears reading glasses. Well, at our age there's nothing wrong with that, I reflect, as I pat my soft shoulder bag to check that I've remembered my own. I've been caught out too many times not being able to read a menu, a timetable or whatever to risk leaving my glasses at home. 'We're aiming for someplace called 'The Squires Lounge and Seminar Room', sounds kinda cool don't you think? A bit aristocratic.'

We walk past the open souvenir shop with its 'Free to Use Cash Machine' placard and curve round into a dead end corridor. At its head is an unremarkable, single, white door, with one of those green, illuminated fire escape signs above it. Large, chrome letters to the side announce that we have found our meeting room. We walk between four small, round tables, each of which is surrounded by three or four padded chairs of bright orange, sky blue or pea green.

JP opens the door and stands back to allow me to enter first. As I pass close by his chest, I get a faint scent of some fresh, citrus cologne which is in stark contrast to the rather stuffy atmosphere which greets us. Even though we are five minutes early, it looks like JP and I will be the last to be admitted to the discussion group. It's a standard, seminar sized room, much like the ones I am used to at the university, with an oblong table, large enough to accommodate about sixteen people. I notice immediately, however, that there are only eight or nine chairs. They surely cannot be expecting many takers, I think. There's a large television, fitted high on the wall to my right, as I enter and a linked beamer, fixed to the centre of the ceiling. The door to the fire escape, which is signposted outside the room, is directly facing me, but I'm dismayed to see that there are no windows in the room. However, one of the long, side walls is entirely covered by a huge mirror. While this undoubtedly makes the room lighter and the size of the group look much bigger, it does nothing to help make it less airless. I find it amusing that the early arrivals have chosen the seats nearest to the door - just like my first year, university students. This means that JP and I have to walk around the table to take up the two places remaining. Again, predictably, these are positioned either side of the man, who I take to be the group leader.

As soon as we are settled, the short, slight and clean shaven man, wearing an 'Opera North' lapel badge on his well worn, creased jacket, coughs quietly and begins. 'Welcome, everybody, to the first of what I hope will be a fascinating and informative discussion group on the key themes in Wagner's Ring Cycle. My name is Gideon and I will be facilitating these sessions. I wonder, perhaps, if we could begin by introducing ourselves, very briefly, and saying what we hope to get out of our meetings.'

I inwardly groan at his use of such a wooden ice breaker and immediately begin to question why I allowed JP to talk me into attending. I'm still mulling this over when, to my relief and surprise, Gideon looks expectantly at an elderly woman, sitting directly opposite him. I wrongly assumed that either JP, or myself, would be the first to undergo this ritual. His eccentric choice of the old dear at least gives me the chance to compose a suitably anodyne self portrait.

Evidently anxious to have been presented with the burden of speaking first, the blue rinsed woman takes a shallow, nervous breath and fusses with her pearl necklace, before beginning. 'My name is Claire and I'm a retired librarian. I'm seventy seven years old and have been a widow for more than ten years.' She pauses at this point,to allow one or two of the group members to express the polite astonishment at her age, which she is transparently hoping for. Gratified, not least by JP's almost over the top, 'Wow! I can't believe it,' she continues with a contented smile. 'I do love Wagner, but, most of all, I do like meeting new and interesting people. And you all look like very interesting people indeed. In fact...'

Understandably fearful of a long winded reminiscence, or some such, Gideon gently intervenes. This evidently pleases the next group member, who, unlike the rest of us, is wearing formal clothes more suited to autumn or winter, than to summer. 'Well, thanks very much for that, Claire,' Gideon says, before looking encouragingly at the dark haired man.

'Thank you, Gideon,' the man begins, a rather cold smile struggling to brighten his extremely pale, saturnine face. 'You may call me Leonard,' he continues bizarrely, 'and I'm a legal professional. But I'm also a very committed and informed amateur scholar of The Ring.' His voice is fluent and unaccented and, interestingly, he doesn't make eye contact with any of the group. This doesn't seem to me to be a product of any nervousness. Rather, it looks very much as if he prefers to enjoy his own performance, reflected in the mirror wall, which is behind me and facing him. He pauses to flick an imaginary speck of dust from his immaculate designer suit, before tearing his gaze away from his own reflection, glancing meaningfully at Gideon and adding, 'I'm here in the hope of sharing some of my interesting and new insights into the maestro's greatest work.'

Gideon looks a little taken aback, but recovers smoothly, saying, 'Well, of course, I'm sure we'll all look forward to that.' Fearing that some of the other group members may be put off by Leonard's arrogant manner, he quickly adds, ' But, let's all remember, the main purpose of being here is to enjoy ourselves.'

An audible murmur of agreement ripples around the table as the group reacts negatively to Leonard's self important contribution. Obviously a little intimidated by Leonard's boastful self portrait, a clumsy looking, overweight, thirty something man, dressed in clean but well worn clothes, blurts out, 'Hi everyone. I'm David. I'm a security guard and, while I'm not that well educated, I've always been fascinated by The Ring. I may not always say the right, or the cleverest thing, so I hope you'll all be very gentle with me.' Gideon, JP, Claire and I smile in sympathy and encouragement and the poor man immediately breaks out into a deep blush of embarrassment.

It occurs to me that, if any of the group members are in danger of nodding off, the next speaker quickly puts paid to that. In a tone which positively insists that she is much more used to issuing instructions than to following them, a matronly,middle aged woman introduces herself as, 'Gillian. Headmistress of a local independent school for girls.' (which she very consciously pronounces 'gels.') With a confident look towards Leonard, which is perhaps aimed at attempting to establish the pair as the 'thinkers' of the group, she adds,'I'm really looking forward to some serious intellectual discussion in the forthcoming meetings.' Leonard doesn't even return her eye contact, still preferring his own reflection. Rebuffed, Gillian abruptly stops speaking. I'm too busy, being fascinated by Leonard's behaviour, to remember that I'm next up. Caught off guard, I play for time, coughing idiotically.

'Ah, well, sorry,' I eventually begin with a smile. 'I'm Olivia and, like most of us, I'm here for some interesting conversation among like minded, Wagner enthusiasts.' Gideon responds with a beaming smile, as if by offering such a short and banal self introduction, I've done exactly what he wanted.

JP is next and I have to admit to myself that I am intrigued as to how he will introduce himself. I've worked with, and met, many Americans at home in Switzerland and at academic conferences around the world. I've even spent a six week exchange at Columbus University in New York. So, I'm very accustomed to the natural ease of manner and oral confidence, which is typical of Americans, at least in comparison to many British people. Nevertheless, I'm very impressed by his skill and humour, in introducing himself simply and self deprecatingly. I surprise myself by recognising that I'm already beginning to view him as a friend.

The incredibly serious looking, young man, sitting on the far side of JP, introduces himself in a stilted, heavily accented English, as Viktor. 'I am student of music from Germany. I have come to witness this very unusual, concert style performance of The Ring. This is what intrigues me.'

'Indeed yes,' adds Gideon, clearly eager to establish potential discussion points. 'I imagine this is something that we will discuss quite frequently, as we move through the performances.' He glances with concern at his watch, as if he is late for a train he simply must catch, before continuing. 'Well, thank you all for those very interesting introductions. Maybe we could start our discussion proper with a quick chat about the contemporary relevance of *Das Rheingold* ? What do we think it has to offer to us, today?'

Having been the first to introduce herself, Claire has been itching to speak again and immediately jumps in. 'I think that's a very important question. In fact, my friends at the retirement home, where I live, think it's simply weird that I'm coming to these performances.'

'I suppose you can understand their point of view,' adds JP, with a smile of encouragement to the old woman. 'I mean, there are gods, dwarves, magic rings, giants and water nymphs in the plot. Not exactly who, or what we'd expect to come across everyday, are they?'

'You're being far too literal and conservative,' replies Leonard dismissively. 'I'd have thought that, as an American, you'd be fully aware of the way in which entertainment such as *The Lord of The Rings* and *Game of Thrones* have become incredibly popular. They don't exactly describe normal life, do they?'

I can sense, rather than see JP's whole body tense at the tone of Leonard's response in which he managed to make JP's nationality sound like the most dire insult. I lean back in my seat, so that I can look at JP, behind Gideon's back. To my concern, a flash of anger, or is more like fury, passes across his face and I attempt to defuse the situation. 'I wonder, too,' I suggest calmly, 'whether a character, who is depicted as a god, giant or dwarf, may still suffer entirely human emotions and display those typical strengths and weaknesses, to which we can all relate.'

'Yes, exactly!' enthuses Viktor in response. 'Like greed and the desire for power..'

'And a preparedness to steal,' adds David, to nods all round the table.

'And what about the dwarf Alberich,' Gillian points out firmly. 'He's not only a thief, but a sexual pervert. The way he treats those Rhinemaidens is nothing short of disgraceful!'

Gideon seems to sense that the discussion could quickly degenerate into people riding their particular hobby horse and he quickly and skillfully interrupts. 'Well, I think we can all agree that *Das Rheingold* explores themes that are highly relevant to human life today. Maybe we could look at how he does this.'

'Great idea, Gideon,' agrees JP and I am relieved that he has recovered his equable tone of voice, after Leonard's slight. The ensuing discussion focuses on the high level of psychological complexity of Wagner's characters and, as an academic psychologist, I judge it both fairer, and better, not to involve myself too much. Rather, I content myself with watching the interaction of the other group members.

David remains, as first impressions suggested, reluctant to volunteer anything. He seems mostly content, simply to nod his head in agreement, or frown with uncertainty. His infrequent, spoken contributions, accompanied by ferocious blushing, occur only when he is specifically invited to speak by Gideon. Over the course of the discussion, I come to see this as something of a pity. The comments he does make are always insightful, well made and gentle. Despite his size and strength, he is clearly in awe of Gillian and Leonard, who vie with one another to establish themselves as the group leader.

Having led many academic seminars, in which the most empty vessels of a group frequently compete to make the most noise, I feel myself sympathising with Gideon. It's always a tricky problem, to restrict the domination of a discussion, while at the same time ensuring an aching silence does not descend. He has a particularly hard time, when the group lurches into a discussion of the controversial topic of Wagner's anti semitism.

Headmistress Gillian argues very strongly that, in a very real sense, Wagner should be regarded as something of a guilty pleasure. 'I mean, one cannot, and should not, ignore his dreadful hostility to Jews and their pretty distasteful depiction in his works. '

Viktor is leaning forward, his body language screaming that he has something to say on this topic. His face red with passion, he finally finds his moment. 'Exactly! Of course, Wagner's beliefs and morality were highly questionable. And I'm talking about a long time before Hitler appropriated his work for the Nazi cause.'

It's obvious to everyone that the young man has simply paused for breath, or to gather his thoughts in what is, after all, not his mother tongue. But Leonard cannot resist another brutal put down. 'Oh come on, please,' he drawls, as if to emphasise his boredom with this theme. 'If you both feel like that, what are you damn well doing here?'

A frisson of shock ripples around the table and, in the absence of any censure from Gideon, it naturally falls to the headmistress to protest. 'Well really!' Gillian bridles, rearing herself up in her seat, like a horse standing on its hind legs. Surprisingly, before she can subject Leonard to one of her severe reprimands, Viktor replies with a harsh laugh.

'That's a good question. And, believe me, I've asked myself a number of times what am I, a Jew whose grandparents died in the camps, doing here? And I answer it, by saying that I love Wagner's music. But the libretto and the characterisation, I do find so offensive that I've never before actually wanted to witness The Ring. However, when I read about Richard Farnes' philosophy, that he wanted to make the orchestra the principal character of The Ring, I decided that I must attend.'

'How strange,' responds Leonard sarcastically, as Gillian remains in danger of spontaneous combustion. 'That was precisely the reason that I considered long and hard whether I should bother attending at all.' Gratified by the sight of Viktor's crestfallen face, Leonard affects a thoroughly unpleasant smirk. 'To anyone with half a brain to think, The Ring without the full blown drama is like Hamlet, without The Prince.'

In the absence of any commanding leadership from the ineffectual Gideon, the group begins to degenerate into a series of separate conversations, over which Gillian persists in trying to retaliate against what we all perceive as outrageous behaviour by Leonard.Recognising that he has lost control completely, Gideon makes great show of studying his watch, before clapping his hands like a primary school teacher, trying to bring a group of unruly infants into order. 'Well, folks,' he lies, with a total lack of shame, 'it appears that our time is just about up. Remember, the next meeting is tomorrow at 2.45, before the performance of *Die Walküre*. Perhaps we could discuss whether or not we think the conductor achieved his goal. See you all then, I hope.'

With that, he grabs his papers and flees, before anyone can instruct him how he should more accurately tell the time. We're all a bit shell shocked and I turn to see JP studying Leonard with an enigmatic expression. I decide to intervene quickly, in order to head off any chance of JP tackling the odiously smug man. I lean across Gideon's empty seat and whisper, 'Come on, I think we both need a drink after all that fuss.'

As we both stand up and Leonard, with an acid smirk, follows Gideon rather stiffly through the door, Gillian is a study in righteous indignation. 'Did you see that?' she splutters to no one in particular. 'What absolutely appalling manners! Why I've a good mind to...'

'I shouldn't bother, if I were you,' David says in gentle consolation. 'People like him are just not worth it. Arrogant bastard, pardon my language, miss. Come on and I'll get us both a nice cup of tea. That'll calm us down.'

I have to smile, as Gillian allows herself to be led meekly out of the room, by someone she initially seemed to treat as her social and intellectual inferior. JP stands aside to let me pass through towards the door and I look across the table to see a still agitated Viktor, half listening, as Claire speaks soothingly to him. As I move out into the corridor, JP is his normal, relaxed self, 'Great idea, Olivia. I could sure do with a stiff one myself.'

Before JP goes to buy two glasses of red wine, I say to him, ' It's a beautiful summer evening. I think we should get a breath of fresh air before the performance, if that's OK with you.' He agrees immediately and disappears into the crush around the bar, while I make my way through the exit, which gives out onto a large terrace, overlooking the River Tyne. Despite the sell out audience, The Sage is extremely well provided with public areas and there's no problem in finding a generous place, between various groups and couples, all drinking their wine in excited anticipation of the first part of The Ring.

'Sure got a bit heated back there, didn't it?' JP says, as he hands me my wine. I wonder, if he's fishing, to find out if I noticed his irritation. So,I reply, 'Yes it did. And you seemed a bit put out with Leonard.'

A brief frown passes across his face, as he acknowledges, 'You're right, Olivia. Can't fool someone like you, huh? Ah well. I guess when people are pretty passionate about something, disagreements are bound to blow up. It's... it's..' he seems to struggle for the right words, before saying simply, Well, I guess it's just that I don't like creeps like Leonard.'

'I don't think anyone does, JP,' I reply supportively. 'But maybe it's best not to let them get under your skin.'

'You're right, Olivia,' he replies with a shrug. 'Point taken. I'll watch myself with him, in future. What did you make of the rest of them?'

'Oh, I don't know,' I laugh, 'A bit like an average undergraduate seminar at university. Though I must say that poor Gideon needs to up his game, if he's to retain control of the group.'

I steal a quick glance at JP, as he stares enigmatically out over the river, towards The Tyne Bridge, before he finally turns to me, smiles and gestures. 'Maybe he needs some advice from a pro like...'

'In his dreams,' I respond immediately. 'Anyway, my seat's up a level from here, so I'd better get a move on.'

'Sure. I guess you'll be heading straight home after the performance..?' he says, disappointment written all over his face. 'So, maybe we could meet for lunch tomorrow?'

We exchange numbers and he smiles, 'I'll give you a ring in the morning and we can sort out our game plan before the next round of the discussion group. If you can bear to go again, that is.'

'Oh, I think we should give it at least one more chance,' I say. 'And, yes, I've a taxi booked already to take me back to my sister's after the performance. So, given there's no interval, I'll wish you much enjoyment and see you tomorrow.'

From my seat in Level 2 of the Sage One auditorium, I can easily make out on the level below JP's silver grey head, as it nods, no doubt in answer to some question from the glamorous looking lady seated next to him. As the lights dim and the first bars, flowing like an orchestral representation of The Rhine, prepare me for the delights to follow, I sit back and surrender myself to Wagner's genius.

It only occurs to me later, as I am waiting for my taxi to ferry me back to Christine's house in Low Fell, that I expected one of the seats next to JP to be vacant. It surely must have been bought for his poor wife. But it was clear that both seats were occupied during the performance. It doesn't take me long to solve the mystery. Pretty obvious really. He must have returned the spare ticket for resale, after her unfortunate demise. I'm just congratulating myself on my powers of deduction, when I see Leonard striding towards me. He's wearing a black overcoat, despite the warmth of the evening, and he doesn't even break step, as I smile and nod in his direction. Of course, it's possible that he didn't notice me. He could hardly have expected to see me and we have only met the one time. My taxi arrives and I catch my last glimpse of his shadowy figure, making its way towards St Mary's Heritage Centre, as I climb into the rear seat.

Chapter Five

4.15am, Wednesday 7th July 2016, Whitburn, South Tyneside.

Sam

At last! I'm exactly where I want to be - stark naked on the luxurious king size bed with PC Alison Creaner smiling down at me. Apart from her smile, her uniform hat and some preposterously high heels, that's all she's wearing. Suddenly, she laughs, takes off her hat and throws it towards my midriff,like a kid trying to win at hoopla at a seaside amusement park. It lands bang on target and spins round in a manner that I find extremely gratifying. She's well impressed too, and, by way of reward, approaches, all smouldering eyes and puckering lips. This is it! She's about to climb on top of me, when I swear I can hear the bloody ringtone of my mobile.

'Shit!' I curse, my erotic dream disappearing as fast as my state of arousal and I flail around, trying to find my mobile. I'm sure that I put the damn thing on my bedside table, by the light. Finally, I lay hands on it and take the call.

For God's sake! It's only that old tosser, Carter, ringing from the station, in his characteristically plodding manner. What the hell does he want? I'm not supposed even to be on standby till Thursday morning. The DCI gave me a day's leave, in recognition of my role in bringing 'The Pelaw Paedophile' to justice. A good job too, given the amount I put away at the team's celebration in town last night. Or should I say, this morning. With a groan, I realise it's only two and a half hours since we staggered out of The Central, after the obligatory 'lock-in.'

'Wakey, wakey, sunshine!' Sergeant Carter says and I can almost see his infuriating smirk. 'We've got a doozy for you here. Your guv says to get yourself down to St Mary's Heritage Centre as quick as you can. And don't forget your Scene of Crime Kit.'

'You got the wrong man, you dozy old sod,' I complain, 'I've just come off seventy two hours straight. The guv said I was off till Thursday.'

'Ah,' the smug pillock replies, 'that was before Lobley and Kent went down with the lurgy. It's no mistake, canny lad. You'd better get down there pronto.'

I must still be well over the limit, so I'll just have to hope that, providing I don't run amok, the traffic plods'll leave me alone. There's not much on the road at this time of day and I make good time from my flat on the coast at Whitburn. As soon as I approach St Mary's Heritage Centre, I can tell it's a bad one. There's police cars scattered all over the turn around at The Sage and up towards the driveway to the Centre itself. The flashing blue lights, combined with the horribly mixed alcohol still sloshing around inside me, makes me feel pretty nauseous. I park up in the first available spot, leap out of the car and vomit profusely onto a stone wall, right by the driveway entrance. Feeling markedly better, I make my way up the cobbled drive, towards the ominous plastic tape which is stretched all around the old St Mary's church building.

'Morning, sarge,' grins one of our uniforms on site. 'I imagine you just got your head down, when the call came through.'

His reference to sleep brings back a vivid image of myself and PC Creaner and I turn to him and grimace, as I slip on my plastic overshoes.'You don't know the half of it, mate.'

Wisely choosing not to ask, he smiles in sympathy and lifts the plastic tape to allow me through. My heart sinks, as I see DI Harrison directing affairs. Shit, I think, if that old moaner's the Senior Investigating Officer, I'm in for a fun time.

'Ah, DS Snow, nice of you to put in an appearance at last.' I don't bother replying and he marches over to me. Ludicrously, given his nickname of 'Halitosis' Harrison, he sniffs loudly and demands, 'Have you been drinking? I'll be watching you very closely, my lad. And, if you so much as pick your nose at the wrong time, the Super'll know.'

Harrison's just a time serving wanker. Mid fifties, with a stupid comb over that makes him look like a frustrated little bank clerk, or even a greasy paedo. He's tried and failed to wangle an enhanced early retirement a few times and now all he wants to do is as little as possible.

'Come on,' he says, 'you should have a look at what we've got here.' He leads the way onto an ancient, curved path with a knee high wall between it and the driveway, The paved path leads us past the large glass entrance doors to The Heritage Centre and around towards the rear of the old church building. Gravestones, many of which tilt drunkenly,and even a kind of mini mausoleum manage to look creepy in the early morning light. I notice that one of the nearer headstones has a skull and crossbones on it. Christ, I think, if what we've got's as Gothic as the setting, it's a good job I've already puked up. Harrison sees me staring at the strange headstone and shouts over his shoulder, 'Plague victim. But don't worry about him. Our business is on the far side of the building. And it's not a pretty sight.'

As we turn the corner, I see that the Crime Scene Manager has taped off the whole area and set screens out in a broad semi circle around this side of the church. It's getting lighter by the minute, but some portable arc lights are still illuminating the crime scene. There's a kind of porch built out of the side of the church which has a very slightly indented door and a sort of small garden, nestling where the cross nave of the church building juts out. I know from past experience that this is a favourite dossing down place for some of the older of Gateshead's homeless. It's very quiet, not far from the town centre and the slightly indented doorway and the two walls of the church can offer some protection against the wind, if not the rain. Not that that would have been an issue, given the current fine conditions. The pathologist has just finished her preliminary examination as we arrive and she stands to permit us to see the sad remains of what used to be a human being.

'Well, gentlemen,' she says, as she squints up at me in the harsh artificial light.'We have the body of a male,I'd guess aged between late forties and sixty, who has suffered fatal trauma as a result of being beaten with a blunt object. I'll be able to tell you more when we get him onto the slab.'

Looking at the bloody, pulpy mess of skin, hair and threadbare clothes, I'm frankly amazed that she can tell us anything at all about the victim. But, characteristically, Harrison is not happy. He makes his prehistoric attitude to female pathologists all too evident with his patronising tone of voice. 'Now, miss, I'm sure you could help us just a little bit more, if you try.'

I can see that she could easily slap the smug bastard's face, or knee him in the groin, or both, so I step in quickly. 'Thanks, doctor,' I say, as I guide her back towards the parked cars. 'Come on,I'll walk you back to your car.'

We're away before Harrison can shut his gaping mouth and she immediately turns to me. 'I don't usually like men leading me by the arm,' she begins, and I fear the submission of an official complaint against me for sexual assault, or some such nonsense. To my relief, her face suddenly breaks into a charming smile and she adds, 'However, on this occasion, I'd like to thank you. You saved your boss some pain and me a possible disciplinary.'

'Oh, never mind him,' I say with a grin, 'he's just a bloody old wo..Er... whinger.'

She laughs and nods, 'And one with hellish bad breath too! OK, now you can ask me your questions.'

I elicit from her that the man was probably killed no more than four hours before discovery and that the weapon was probably some sort of baseball bat , or offensive stick. 'But, judging from the way it looks like some bones have been cracked,' she adds pensively, 'I wonder if maybe something harder, like metal, might have been involved.' With that, and a promise that the post mortem will take place within the next twenty four hours, she climbs into her car and is gone.

On the way back to the murder scene, I meet 'Halitosis' coming back the other way. 'I'm off back to the station,' he says. 'It looks pretty obvious what's happened here. You can wrap it up and report back to me later.... When you're fully sober.'

I stick two fingers up at his retreating back, much to the amusement of one of our experienced WPCs, and turn to catch sight of a pale faced young copper, shrouded in a blanket and sipping from a polystyrene cup. I approach him and ask gently, 'PC Wordsworth? I believe you were first on the scene? Can you tell me what happened?'

The poor sod's hands are still shaking, spilling half of his tea on the ground and most of the rest over his boots, as he sniffs, 'That's right, Sarge. I'd been called out to a false alarm at a shop just near Hill St bus stop.'

I nod in encouragement and he continues, 'I'd just finished checking everything was OK there, when this old tramp comes bustling up to me,screaming about murder and mayhem. Anyway, I calmed him down and he led me here and I.... I found him.'

'That's fine, constable. Could you remember the time?'

'Oh yes, the clock over the river was showing quarter to four when we came up to The Heritage Centre.'

'And the tramp? Is he still here?'

'I think so,' he confirmed, pointing towards a pitiful figure, sitting on the grass, with his head in his hands. 'He's just over there.'

'Did you see anyone else, or notice anything unusual?'

The young man's face screws up in concentration. He clearly feels he owes it to me to give me another possibly vital bit of information. Finally, he shakes his head, 'Sorry, Sarge. I can't think of anything else.'

'That's OK, Wordsworth,' I reassure him. 'You get someone to take you back to the station and I'll have a word with this gentleman.'

'Good morning Mr....' I begin.

39

'Smith' he replies quickly, almost as if it's the first name that popped into his head.

'Ah yes, Mr Smith,' I say, my eyebrows arching, 'Could you tell me what happened?'

He tells me in great detail how he decided to come across the river from the city, in order to doss down for the night. 'It's a pretty good spot,' he explains, 'Not in Winter, mind. When an icy wind can blow up the River Tyne from the North Sea and freeze your very bones. But tonight was fine, warm and dry. Anyway, I knows Geoff, y'see. Geoff, that's the bloke what's been...er... what's died.'

'Geoff,' I repeat. 'What's his surname?'

'No idea, son,' the tramp replies. 'We street folk're not so formal with each other, y'know.' I nod and he carries on. 'Well me and Geoff, we've known one another a long time and he told me that he was going to stay over this side of the river tonight. He reckons that not all audiences at The Sage are as generous as the classical music lot. Those who come to watch stand up comedy, especially the left wing sort, are by far the most stingy, he says. But those who come to the opera, well, he says they're the most generous. He told me to keep this under my hat. He didn't want to alert everybody to the rich pickings to be had here. He said I could come over later on, if I wanted to doss down here. So that's what I did. Now I damned well wish I hadn't.'

'Did you see anyone else, either before you found him, or before the PC found you?'

'No. Saw nothing.'

'And was Geoff dead when you found him?'

'Look, son. I'm no ruddy doctor. I didn't want to get too close to him. All that blood and gore. He certainly looked dead.'

'Did you touch anything? Take anything from the body?'

He looks outraged, but a bit shifty at the same time. 'What the hell do you think I am? I might not be as smart as you, but I have my standards!'

'Ok, Mr Smith. You go off with this nice WPC here. We'd like you to make a statement at the station.' Seeing the near panic in his eyes, I swiftly act to reassure him. 'Don't worry. You're not in any kind of trouble. You'll get a nice warm meal and a bed for the night there, as well.'

I hand him over to the WPC and make my way back to the body.

'Was there anything in his pockets?' I ask the SOCO boys, as they're beginning to pack up their gear and the mortuary crew are itching to move the remains.' A swift shake of the head surprises me. If what the old guy said is true, he should have had quite a bit of cash on him. Could that be the motive?

I take one last look at what was once a human being and indicate that the body can be removed. As the body is carefully placed onto a stretcher, I can't help but notice how tall Geoff was. 'Christ Almighty,' I say to the retreating mortuary crew, 'he must be six foot six, if he's an inch.'

Before going to the station, I instruct the uniforms on site to secure the entire area around the Centre. 'We'll give it a thorough search when it's fully light.' I glance at the sky and say, 'Shouldn't be too long now.'

I don't intend spending so much time at the station. I consider that I've done what was asked of me by the DCI and it's time I was off, back to try to pick up the threads of my dream. Hopefully, just where I left off. Events at the station, however, soon put paid to that splendid idea. I ask the Desk Sergeant, if Smith has made his statement and he smiles broadly, 'He's done more than that, Sam, much more than that.'

Now, I've never particularly liked this officer. He's always seemed a bit of a weasel and a snitch, if you know what I mean. But I try to sound interested, as I say, 'Oh yeh?'

It appears that the poor old bugger confirmed the same statement he made to me and had been asked to empty his pockets, before being shown into a cell for a lie down. 'Well,' the odious sergeant goes on, 'It only turns out that he had over £200 in cash, mainly fivers and pound coins. In two bags, they were. One in each of his overcoat pockets. Both bags and some of the cash was bloodstained. As soon as Inspector Harrison put the statement together with the money, he deduced that this was a simple case of an argument over money that got out of hand.'

I gaze incredulously at him, but he shows no reluctance to deliver the coup de grace, 'The Inspector is charging him with murder, as we speak. Case closed.'

I dash down to The Charge Room, just in time to almost knock 'Halitosis' off his feet as he bustles through the door. 'Watch out, you bloody fool', he shouts. 'You could do somebody an injury, running about like that.'

'Chance'd be a fine thing, you lazy pillock,' I mutter to myself, before saying more audibly. 'I believe you've arrested Mr Smith, the old man who found the body?'

'The shifty old tramp, you mean?' he replies smugly. 'Correct. Case closed, as I just said.'

Before I can express my real doubts about this, a commotion takes place behind us, as two burly police officers drag Smith back towards the cells. The poor bastard looks absolutely terrified and, as soon as he sees me, he shouts, 'I never touched no one, sir. You tell them! All right, I helped myself to the cash, but I was sure that Geoff was already dead and I know he'd have wanted me to have it. He hated all the violent young street people. You know I'm telling the truth, son! You've got to help me!'

His increasingly hysterical voice echoes down the corridor, as he's forced down to the cells. 'Look,' I say to Harrison, blocking his way back to his office, 'don't you think you're being a bit hasty here?'

His face goes a fine shade of puce, as he bellows back at me, 'Hasty, SIR! And get out of my way!' Alarmed by the number of inquisitive eyes homing in on him, he adds in furious whisper, 'And no, I don't. Why look for complications, when there are none to be found? You know the stats on those finding the body being the killer.'

'But sir, 'I say, grimacing as his proximity ensures that he is well and truly living up to his nickname. 'You saw the state of the body. There's more about this than just a barney over a couple of hundred quid. I doubt that old buffer could have done that, even if he'd wanted to.'

'You can have your opinion,' 'Halitosis' challenges me, 'but I will be reporting this as case closed.'

I simply nod and decide that, as far as I'm concerned, it's definitely not all done and dusted.

Chapter Six

Olivia

The weather remains perfect as I hop off the bus at Hill Street, just a five minute walk to The Sage. I'm happy that I decided to wear my grey summer skirt suit. It's fashionably smart and comfortable for such a long performance. I'm also glad that I gave myself sufficient time to enjoy walking to my lunch date with JP at Restaurant Gusto on The Quayside. As I had expected, he rang me mid morning and proposed that we have lunch there at 1pm, which, he pointed out, 'would give us plenty of time to go to the next meeting of our discussion group. Or we could just hang out on the river bank and enjoy the sun.'

Thankfully, my lie in, together with my lunch date, had allowed my sister time for only the most cursory of over breakfast interrogations about my evening's experience. To her irritation, I focused on the excellence of Opera North's production of *Das Rheingold*, when, of course, all she wanted to know about was how I'd got on with JP. I'd limited myself to a bland comment along the lines of, 'Oh, he was charming and we had a pleasant drink before the performance.' I also chose not to tell her about the lunch date with him. Plenty of time to give her the details after the event.

As I cross the road, I turn to my left to see the iconic Tyne Bridge and instantly remember many evenings, clip-clopping across it with equally excited friends, off on a night out in 'The Big Market.' Despite the sunshine, these days the best I can manage in my hometown is a thin linen jacket and I shudder to recall those freezing, snowy nights, when we all traipsed about, without a care in the world, wearing only the skimpiest of dresses.

I had intended to call in at St Mary's Heritage Centre, on my way past The Sage and on towards The Quayside. But as I approach, I'm surprised to find the place cordoned off with blue and white plastic tape, proclaiming the firm order *'Police Line - Do Not Cross.'* I peer up the cobbled driveway to the old church but, while I can see several of their cars parked, I can't see any obvious evidence of police presence.

'Shocking isn't it?' asks a young woman who comes to stand by me. From her appearance and the way she greedily sucks at her cigarette, I imagine she must be a waitress, or perhaps bar staff from The Sage, out for a quick smoking break. I turn to her and say, 'I'm sorry. I've no idea what you're talking about.'

She looks at me with a mixture of suspicion and pity, 'You're joking, right?' She tuts at my definite shake of the head and takes a long drag of her cigarette, in a way that I find most unpleasant. She then blows out smoke while attempting a theatrical shudder, which blatantly contradicts her evident relish in being the one to bring me up to speed. 'I can't believe it. You really don't know?' she asks, but continues without waiting for my answer. Well, apparently some old tramp was only beaten to death. Right there. Right next to The Sage. It's unbelievable.'

'Good Lord, that's dreadful,' I say, in the totally ineffectual way that people like me receive such awful news.

Decidedly unimpressed by the nature of my reaction, she delivers the coup de grace of her account.'Hardly anything recognisable left of him, I was told by one of the coppers. Bashed to a bloody pulp, he said. Makes you think, doesn't it? Men, eh? Minging perverts and thugs, the lot of 'em. I know what I'd do to every last one of 'em. I'd bloody well....'

I've heard quite enough of her distasteful views on this subject and take the opportunity, when someone else approaches and stands by us, to begin to move away. Pathetically, I feel a little embarrassed that I may be leaving her only part way through her ghoulish story, but I don't need to worry. As if a rewind button had been pressed in her head, she immediately homes in on the hapless newcomer, 'Shocking , isn't it?...'

As I skirt the turning circle and walk the few paces to the entrance to The Sage, it briefly occurs to me that I must have been waiting for my taxi not long before such a terrible crime took place, and only a matter of yards away. This thought quickly passes from my mind and I think once more, back to the many nights that I would make my way safely home in the early hours. Admittedly, I'd usually be with at least one friend, but I nevertheless shudder at what might have happened. I'm horrified to find myself thinking like some old person, telling myself that things really are very different today And without doubt,far worse.

My spirits are lifted, however, as I stroll through the bustling and lively concourse areas of The Sage. I'm determined to enjoy the marvellous building to the full. The concourse area is huge, light and airy, the great majority of the outer walls and even some of the triple or quadruple height ceilings are glass panels. People of varied age and appearance are sitting on the numerous dark wood chairs, placed around sturdy square tables of the same material. Most are eating lunch or chatting, over an early afternoon glass of wine. I can hear two or three European languages being spoken and I reflect, more positively this time, on how my hometown has altered during my lifetime. Despite the North East having been one of the so called Brexit capitals of Britain, Tyneside seems to me to be a thoroughly relaxed and cosmopolitan place these days.

I stop to gaze for a few moments out over the river towards Newcastle itself. The far bank of the Tyne is lined by various buildings, some new, some much older. However, while they are almost all several storeys high, they manage to avoid looking like the much more brutal, modern city architecture that I can see in the city centre beyond. It strikes me that The Quayside definitely wouldn't look out of place in a pleasant city in Northern Germany, Holland or Denmark.

I pause for just a few minutes to browse at the souvenir shop and, not for the first time, admire the work of Jim Edwards, a local artist. The colour and joy he brings to his rather naive paintings touches my heart in a way I cannot fully explain. I'm still pondering whether, during my stay,   I should visit his studio and buy one of his pieces, when I glance at my watch and realise that it's nearly five to one and I'm in severe danger of being late. Without delay, I rush out of The Sage and across the terrace, before descending the steps towards the river and The Millennium Eye Bridge. Thanking my lucky stars that it hadn't been raised, I hurry across the river and on towards the restaurant.

JP is already there and has selected a very pleasant table for two, outside in the partial shade. 'Wow! You look sensational,' he says as I offer him my cheek, rather than my hand. 'You don't mind sitting out here, do you, Olivia?' he asks hopefully. 'Only, we're gonna be cooped up in the theatre for quite some time.'

'Of course not, JP,' I reply, 'It'll be perfect out here.' JP looks positively buzzing with energy as he leaps up and helps me into my chair. His eyes are wide and bright, almost as if he's on some kind of drug. 'You look pretty happy with life, JP?' I ask and he sits down with a flourish.

'You can sure say that again, Olivia,' he beams. 'I guess the performance, the weather, the city and, of course, meeting you again. Yes, you could say I'm happy.'

I think about the rather sad reason for making the trip, that he mentioned on the plane from Geneva, and I feel glad that I may have contributed in some small way to his happier mood. We order our food and have just settled ourselves to enjoy a chilled glass of prosecco when JP fixes me with an inquisitive expression. 'You know, Olivia, I don't really know much about you at all, other than you're from here and work at a university. If it's not too much of an intrusion into your privacy, how come you ended up in Switzerland?'

I suppose that I hadn't really prepared myself for such a direct personal question coming so quickly. More than twenty years of living among the Swiss, whose absolute reticence in such situations is legendary, has definitely had its effect on me. I decide to deflect it with a smile, 'Well, JP. It's pretty obvious that you're not a Swiss.'

He looks at me rather strangely, as if he hasn't quite got the joke, before realisation dawns and he laughs. 'Ha! I can't disagree with you there. They're a peculiar lot, in some ways, aren't they? Not at all like we Anglo Saxon types. Direct and open, we are.'

I realise that he isn't going to let me off the hook quite so easily and so I try another tack. 'Oh, my story's not so interesting at all,' I begin modestly. 'But now I come to think about it, it must be well over two decades since I first went to Switzerland.'

'Attracted by the guy who you married?' JP asks, trying to be helpful. Or is he just plain nosey?

'Not at all. I'd actually just graduated from Durham University with a good degree in Psychology.' As I speak, I look away from the river and back towards him and see, or do I imagine, a kind of flinch at the mention of this. I decide not to ask and carry on with my potted autobiography. 'I suppose, at the time, I was full of the kind of youthful ambition that doesn't recognise any boundaries to what is possible. Much to the astonishment of my professors at Durham, I managed to secure a research position under Professor Bonfils, Europe's leading expert in the field of Applied Psychology.'

'Wow, that's quite something,' JP gushes. 'Your mom and dad must have been really proud.'

'Proud, but also a little anxious. You see, the money I received from the Professor's research grant was nowhere near enough to live in what, as you no doubt know, has always been a relatively expensive country. So my parents, God bless them, agreed to subsidise me for two years. Even though they couldn't really afford it. Of course, this was long before the now, everyday notion of 'the bank of mum and dad,' had ever been heard of. As with most well laid plans, life sort of got in the way. So, by the time the initial two years in Lausanne had, thanks to more funding being found, been extended to six, I had completed my doctorate and had also acquired a Swiss husband, by whom I was already pregnant with my son, Sebastian.'

'I bet you were a perfect mother.'

I laugh in self deprecation, 'Well, I don't know about that. But I'm certain that the first five years with my son, living in a gorgeous little garden flat, right next to Lac Léman and loving being a mother, were among the most blissfully happy of my life. I became fluent in French and, as soon as Sebastian was settled in kindergarten, I decided to have a go at resurrecting my academic career.'

'Sounds almost a perfect life plan. So what went wrong?'

I had planned not to get too involved in discussing this aspect of my life. But somehow, and without really saying much at all, JP had got me to open up. Who knows? Perhaps I needed to. 'I suppose, if I was being bitchy, I'd say my husband went wrong. But maybe that's not fair. It takes two to tango after all.' He nods in understanding and tops up my glass.

'But it is true that, initially, when I was struggling to win fixed term, part time contracts, my husband Laurent, was extremely supportive and encouraging. I suppose, while he could see my efforts as just bringing in a bit of 'pin money', he was happy to go along with it. However, as soon as Professor Bonfils invited me to apply for a tenured post at the University of Geneva, where he was then Head of Department, Laurent's attitude changed. He exaggerated even the smallest difficulty, on issues which ranged from childcare to holidays, in order to argue that I should stay with my casual working pattern. Even when Professor Bonfils offered me real flexibility in my commitments on campus, that wasn't enough for Laurent. That's when I decided to accept the Professor's invitation. And that, in turn, effectively signalled the end of my marriage. As soon as Sebastian was ready to fly the nest, I filed for a divorce which, for no good reason other than his own anger that his wife could have the temerity to do such a thing, Laurent has fiercely resisted for three years. But, finally, it's over and I've come back home for a relaxing holiday. So, now you know everything, JP. I bet you wish you'd never asked.'

'Not at all, Olivia,' he replies earnestly, 'sometimes it does us good to unload all that stuff to a comparative stranger.'

While in some senses I agree with him, I'm also rather disturbed by my openness. And I also wonder whether or not this has caused JP to be a touch more reserved. Why on earth did I say so much? Well, there's nothing that can be done about that now.

I turn my attention back to the restaurant. Sitting here, in the dappled sunlight, I must admit that he is a most attractive lunch date. In contrast to many of the other diners, he's dressed stylishly in a pale blue suit which sets off his eyes and hair perfectly. I doubt he has a baggy tracksuit or one size fits all t shirt in his entire wardrobe.

The food and the wine is good and we enjoy ourselves exchanging impressions about last night's performance of *Das Rheingold*. He's particularly impressed by the slide show and text, which enable newcomers to Wagner to follow easily what's happening on stage. 'Normally such things can be so gimmicky. But these worked perfectly.'

I add that I really liked the way that no attempt was made to present an essentially concert performance in full costume, 'That would have been utterly ridiculous and out of place.' Before we know it, it's time to cross The Millennium Bridge and make our way back to The Sage for our pre performance discussion group. 'Let's hope that jerk Leonard manages to fall in the river on his way,' says JP and we both laugh at the thought of it.

Chapter Seven

Sam

After enjoying a much needed few hours of sleep,
unfortunately with no recurrence of the dream about the
delightful PC Creaner, I'm rushing to get to 'The Tilley
Stone' before midday. That's when this particular branch
of Wetherspoons pub stops serving its Large Breakfast
and, right now, I'm in desperate need of its 1629
calories. Every single one of them! It's five to the hour,
when I dash in and place my order. 'Sexy Sandra,' the
regular barmaid, gives me a sideways look, as I astonish
her by ordering a glass of lemonade. 'Long night, last
night, was it, pet?' she asks, using the affectionate term,
even though she must be nearly ten years younger than
my late twenties.

'You could say that, Sandra, darlin,' I reply, though in
truth I'm feeling much better. I grab a copy of 'The
Chronicle' that someone has thoughtfully left on the bar
and make my way to a quiet table. Unsurprisingly, the
local rag's full of the arrest of 'The Pelaw Paedophile,'
and there's even a grainy shot of yours truly in the
lengthy report on page two. I don't imagine the death of
the old homeless man last night will generate such a
media frenzy. All the more so,as 'Halitosis' has already
decided that the poor bastard Smith did him for a couple
of hundred quid. I'm still by no means convinced and,
while I'm waiting for my food, I decide to ring the
mortuary at the Queen Elizabeth Hospital to find out if
there's any news on the post mortem. Luckily, the
pathologist has just completed the procedure and she

passes on the message that she'll be happy to give me a few minutes at about 2 o'clock. Great, I think to myself, as I anticipate tucking into the mountain of sausages, fried eggs, beans, bacon, hash browns and God knows what else besides, that is my favourite breakfast in town.

I decide not to go to the station before meeting the Doc, as I don't want to give Harrison the opportunity to intercept me and order me to go somewhere else. What the old prat doesn't know won't hurt him, until, with luck, I'll be able to kick him in the bollocks with it. But I do call in at the scene of crime on my way to the hospital and find out that, so far, the search party hasn't found any trace of anything that could be the murder weapon.

The car park at the 'QE' is its normal, uncooperative self and I'm glad I gave myself fifteen minutes to find an available spot. I should easily get myself to the Mortuary Office on time. When I arrive, the same doctor as last night is sitting behind a crowded desk, nursing a huge mug of coffee. She gives me a tired smile as I sit down, take out my notebook and ask, 'So, doctor. Have you got anything of interest for me?'

'All the details will be in the written report, which you'll have within forty eight hours. But,' she adds on seeing my face fall, 'how about you ask me some questions and I'll see if I can help you out?'

'That's fine by me, doctor. Thanks. How would you describe the attack on the victim?'

'I wondered if any of your lot would ask that,' the doctor says. 'Before I answer, I'm interested in why you asked that particular question?'

'Well, from what I could see, there didn't seem to be as much blood around the body, as I would have expected from what looked like a ferocious attack.'

The doctor nods in evident appreciation. 'Exactly. I'd say that the attack took place in at least two distinct phases. The first was extremely well targeted, controlled and precise.'

'How do you mean?'

'It's my opinion that the perpetrator deliberately targeted the victim's head while he was asleep and had killed him within a matter of seconds. The skull was shattered clinically and precisely. Death followed very quickly...'

'Hence the lack of blood?'

'Exactly. The more ferocious and uncontrolled part of the attack, during which most of the obvious and hideous damage was done, occurred after death.'

'Why would the killer do that?'

'Ah, now there, sergeant, we're straying into your territory. I couldn't say.'

'And what about the weapon? We've found nothing that looks as if it might be a possibility. Have you had any thoughts on what it might have been?'

'There are many possibilities. I've found traces of wood in some of the most vicious wounds, but, also, smears of what could be metal polish. We won't know for sure, until that's been tested in the lab.'

'So you don't think it was just a random piece of wood that our perp picked up and made use of?'

'Well, of course, I can't be certain. But no, I wouldn't have thought so.'

'You've been very helpful. But may I ask just one final question? Would this crime have required a great deal of strength?'

'I'd say that depends on the weapon used. With something like a baseball bat, capped with metal rings at its head, probably any adult could have done this. The force that can be generated by even a fairly gentle swing is enormous and there's no evidence from an inspection of the victim's hands and arms that he attempted to defend himself at all. He was a tall man, about six six, and while not in the best of health, he was by no means feeble. The poor devil probably never knew what hit him. As I said, knocked unconscious, or worse, with the first blow and killed by the following one or two. The rest was just decoration, or to fulfil some other purpose. It certainly played no part in the death.'

'Well, doctor,' I say and really mean it, 'you've been very helpful. I hope you'll soon be off duty. You look like you could do with some rest.' She sighs and shrugs her shoulders and I leave her to the mountainous pile of papers on her desk.

***

I'm just on my way into the red brick Police Station which is our base in the centre of Newcastle, when I meet a smiling DC Johnson on his way out. 'Hey, Sarge,' he says excitedly. 'Have you heard the news? That old guy DI Harrison arrested last night has only gone and confessed to killing the tramp at The Heritage Centre. The DI's walking about like he's ten feet tall. Amazing, huh?'

Bloody incredible, I think. Especially as it's just utter bollocks. I had serious reservations last night and, after talking to the Doc at the mortuary, I simply cannot see this as a simple killing for cash. I consider going for broke and asking to see DCI Quayle. She's a no-

nonsense, up through the ranks, copper, who,from all accounts, had to fight against all sorts of gender prejudice back in the day. She'd listen. Wouldn't she?

I ring her office to ask if she's available, only to be put straight through. Before I get the chance to say anything, I hear her saying, 'What the hell are you doing here, Snow? I ordered you to take the the day off, after your efforts on the Pelaw case. And I expect my orders to be followed. So you get yourself off home immediately and only come back tomorrow. Whatever it is you want to speak with me about can wait one day.'

She ends the call before I can explain and I recognise there's nothing more I can do. I get in my car and drive home, but for some reason, my appetite for dreams of PC Creaner has deserted me.

Chapter Eight

3.45pm, Wednesday 6th July 2016, The Sage, Gateshead.

Olivia

We aren't the first to arrive at the discussion group and I notice straight away that, again just like a group of first year students in a seminar, the early arrivers have occupied the same seats as they did for the first meeting. JP rolls his eyes when he recognises this and we obediently sit in our assigned places. Once more, we have our backs to the mirror wall and are positioned on either side of Gideon, who is busy writing down a few *aides mémoires*. Idly, I wonder if this room is ever used for ballet exercises.

The mood among the other people present seems upbeat and a lively conversation about the excellence of last night's performance is taking place between Gillian, Viktor and David. The general consensus seems consistent with my lunchtime conversation with JP, in that the conductor's philosophy of making the orchestra the star of the performance is a triumph and that the absence of costumes and props is a positive thing. There's also eager anticipation of *Die Walküre*, the second of the four operas which constitute The Ring Cycle.

My first impression is that it's a far more enjoyable atmosphere than the previous day's meeting and I reflect that I'm probably not the only one who has put this down to the absence of the odious Leonard. I glance at JP who looks at Leonard's empty chair and grins. It's obvious that he's thinking the same as I am; that with luck, the horrid man has indeed fallen in the river. I giggle as JP makes small arm movements to indicate swimming and Gideon looks at me questioningly. 'Sorry,' I mumble, 'just a silly thought.' He nods and returns to his work, content for the time being, to let the conversation meander where it will. I'm struck by how similar he is to an inexperienced tutor, who busies himself with his papers and allows the students to gossip about the previous night's tv, until the precise time for the start of the seminar.

During one particularly dense and complicated observation from Viktor, the music student, I realise that there's another empty seat. I try to remember who it is and then realise that the seventy seven year old Claire has yet to put in an appearance.

Bang on the scheduled start time for the discussion, the door bursts open and, to everyone's palpable disappointment, it is Leonard who strides confidently into the room. JP shrugs and pulls a face at me to indicate his disappointment. Gillian visibly stiffens in her chair, as if ready to do battle and poor David graphically holds his head in his hands. Leonard shows neither interest in, nor concern with these reactions, nor with the almost audible, collective groan that passes around the table. 'Sorry I'm late, Gideon,' he says, making what should be an apology sound like anything but. 'Bloody nightmare finding a place to park. Who'd have thought Wagner would be so popular among the plebs of the North East?' His habitually saturnine features break into a brief, bleak smile, devoid of any warmth or humour and I shudder as I catch sight of his ghoulishly oversized incisor teeth. Almost instantaneously, his hooded eyes and narrow, ungenerous lips restore his default expression, one of supercilious superiority.

Characteristically, Gideon ignores the crass remark and, thankfully, Gillian, for once, chooses not to rise to the provocation. I notice something in JP's eyes, as he stares with undisguised hostility at the new arrival and for a moment I think he's going to take Leonard to task. To my, and, judging by his reaction, to Gideon's surprise, JP says, 'I wonder, Gideon, if you'd mind me suggesting something that I'd sure like us to discuss.'

Gideon mumbles a rapid, 'Of course,' and JP adds quickly, as if afraid the group leader may change his mind. 'You know, I've always thought that a key universal theme in *Die Walküre* is the battle between Love and Law. I wonder what you all make of that idea?'

David, Viktor and Gillian look a little perplexed, as if they cannot quite accept that one of their number, rather than Gideon, the proper group leader, has essentially given initial direction to the group discussion. I can almost hear Gillian's internal voice saying, 'I say, that's not on at all.'

However, it's an uncharacteristically complimentary Leonard who speaks first. 'Thank God for an intelligent comment. I agree one hundred per cent with JP. I think we should definitely address the issue of incest and what Wagner is trying to say about it.'

Viktor and David both look a little embarrassed at the thought of discussing such a difficult theme, especially, I imagine,in a group containing women. Whereas JP looks appalled at the idea that Leonard may be lining himself up as his friend and ally. I sense that Gillian is about to erupt again, so in an effort to head this off, I make an attempt to shift the focus to something perhaps not so challenging. 'That's certainly a thought provoking topic,

JP. And maybe we'll discuss it later. However, perhaps we could warm up by thinking about the way marriage is depicted in the opera.'

Viktor is keen to pursue this and instantly observes, 'Yes, if you consider the marriages of the gods, Wotan and Fricka, and of the humans, Hunding and Sieglinde, they're not exactly loved up, are they?'

All, bar Leonard, smile at Viktor's use of such a modern term and David adds, 'I agree, whereas we can't say the same about Siegmund and Sieglinde, can we?' I feel quite proud of myself for guiding the discussion into areas in which David and Viktor both feel able to contribute. My self satisfaction is short lived, however, as Leonard is not prepared to abandon his preferred discussion topic so easily.

'I think David, almost certainly unintentionally, has made the key point. The only truly loving relationship in *Die Walküre* is that between sister and brother - Sieglinde and Siegmund. Surely, Wagner is...'

'It's perfectly appalling,' interrupts Gillian, much to Leonard's fury. His dark eyes glitter with hostility, but the sturdy headmistress is not about to give way. 'I must admit that I've always tried to draw a psychological veil over that particular aspect of the opera. And I suggest that we, in the interests of good taste, as a group do the same.'

'Ha!' declares Leonard triumphantly. 'Absolutely typical of the small minded, spineless, British middle class. Well, not this time!' There's something aggressive, even violent in his insistence. 'I want you all to think about incest for a minute. Is it so uncommon in mythology? And, after all, that's where Wagner got his inspiration.'

JP surprises me with his knowledge of mythology, as he says, 'Well, I guess you've got Zeus and Hera in Greek mythology and Osiris and Isis in Egyptian. There you have two sets of brother and sister who got married.'

'Exactly!' shouts Leonard, his flushed face testifying to his obvious excitement. 'And these relationships surely are signifiers of what we should understand as the ultimate form of closeness between divine pairs.'

'Maybe that kind of thing is OK for gods,' I interject, much to Leonard's irritation. 'After all, they're not real, are they?' David and Viktor titter at this minor rebuke, while Leonard looks on, pure hatred in his expression. Undeterred, I add, 'For we humans, surely all right thinking people recognise, and accept, that incest is, and should be almost always prohibited.'

'Hear Hear!' says a visibly relieved Gillian. 'It's an irredeemably obscene idea, when applied to people.'

'Oh, for God's sake, do make some effort not to be so utterly narrow minded,' says Leonard sarcastically. 'You're a teacher,' he adds with a smirk, as he deliberately strips Gillian of her headship status. 'You're supposed to be broadening young minds, aren't you? Christ! I wouldn't let you anywhere near a son or daughter of mine.'

'I think you should apologise for that, Leonard,' says Gideon, but without any real conviction.

'Why?' challenges Leonard. 'Wagner didn't think incest was unnatural at all. If it were, he argued, then Nature would not bless such unions with children. No, it is the taboo that we in society impose on incest that is unnatural. Maestro Wagner thought that. And so do I.'

The more I see and hear of Leonard, the more it seems to me that he wants to see himself as an equal of people such as Wagner. It's not a pleasant look at all.

The room descends into a chaos of conversations and shouting when, to everyone's surprise, the door opens and an obviously distressed Claire walks in. Even though I'm one of the furthest from the door, it's me who leaps up and goes to steady her, as she staggers towards her seat. 'Whatever's the matter?' I ask. 'Are you alright? Heavens, dear, you look like you've been crying.'

For a trained psychologist, I frequently say the wrong thing and this gaffe sets Claire off in a series of deep, uncontrollable sobs. Gillian offers her a glass of water and she eventually begins to calm down. 'I've just heard about what happened last night,' she wails. 'Anne,in the cloakroom, told me when I was dropping my coat off there. I've known her for years, you see. Her daughter used to come every week to the library where I worked.'

'What is it that has upset you so?' Gideon prompts gently.

'It's about Geoff,' she says to everyone's utter confusion. 'All right, he might have been homeless, but he was a charming, cultured and harmless man. He was over six feet six , you know. Everyone knew him as Geoff, The Gentle Giant. And someone just beat him to death last night. I gave him a pound, as I was leaving yesterday and now, I'll never see him again.'

So, this was the victim that the young woman had told me about earlier. I suddenly remember seeing Leonard after the performance and, in a moment of devilishness, contemplate asking him if he saw anything suspicious. While I'm wrestling with the imperative to be polite, against my desire to embarrass Leonard, Claire begins to sob again and the group rallies round, offering sympathy and support. It's perfectly obvious that the discussion about incest is far from everyone's mind, but Leonard cannot restrain himself. 'Well, that's very sad, I'm sure we all agree. But we should get back to our discussion. There's a great deal more I want to say.'

That tips my inner argument in favour of asking him about last night, but before I can utter a word, Gideon finds his authoritative voice. 'Unfortunately, you won't be saying it today, Leonard. In such tragic circumstances, I think it would be far more respectful to curtail today's discussion and we will meet again ahead of the performance of *Siegfried* on Friday afternoon.'

Brooking no objection, he gathers his papers and leaves a still distraught Claire to the ministrations of myself and Gillian. A furious Leonard pursues Gideon out of the room, probably to protest about his decision to cut the meeting short. However, we don't hear any voices and by the time the rest of us emerge into the concourse area, there's no sign of either of them.

It's not that I'm an unfeeling human being, but I realise that I simply cannot compete with the extremely maternal disposition of Gillian.That's the difference, I suppose, between spending a working life ministering to the needs and problems of young children and spending it among comparatively independent university students. 'Come on,' JP says to me with a wink, as Claire disappears round a corner, supported by Gillian and David. 'Let's go find my brand new buddy. We can carry on his discussion.'

'Throw the awful creep in the river, more like.'

Despite having had a good two or three glasses of wine over lunch, I agree that I could do with another one and I find a couple of spare seats at a table for four overlooking The Tyne Bridge and the river flowing beneath. The atrium space echoes with the hundreds of conversations taking place and the clatter of cutlery from the screened off areas, set aside for pre performance meals. As he returns with glasses of red wine, JP is not smiling, but he quickly recovers and readily joins in the conversation I have started with the elderly couple, who were already seated at the table.

We all agree that the production is excellent and we exchange pleasantries over our current home cities - theirs being Edinburgh and ours Geneva. The man has just begun to describe a research trip he made to Geneva in the 1980s, in connection with writing a book about John Calvin, when a loud blast of brass cuts through the air. It's the opening bars of 'The Ride of The Valkyries' and is the idiosyncratic way, in which members of the audience are advised to take their seat. We rapidly excuse ourselves and, having wished him an enjoyable time, I arrange to meet JP in the first interval.

I really feel that The Ring gets properly under way with this second of the four operas. Including two intermissions, one of ninety minutes, the whole performance will last almost six hours. As I take my seat, I am pleased to see that I am surrounded by the same people who enjoyed *Das Rheingold* and we all exchange greetings, before the lights dim and the performance begins.

In what seems like the blink of an eye, Act One is over and the audience is filing patiently out of the Sage One auditorium. I spot JP waiting by the coffee stand and he immediately asks if I'd like a cup. He seems rather agitated and I ask if he enjoyed the first act. 'Sure,' he says, 'the standard of performance is still very high.'

I agree, but then suggest that he seems rather distracted. He looks thoughtfully out over the river and I have the feeling that he is choosing his words rather carefully. 'No, it's just that I really like these next two acts. The duets between Brünnhilde and her dad, Wotan, are among the most beautiful in all opera. I suppose I'm just looking forward to them very much.'

'That's good,' I say, touching the sleeve of his jacket, just as the trumpets sound to call us back to our seats. 'You'll have to give me your verdict in the next interval.'

'Oh,' he says absently, 'I forgot to mention. I'm afraid I have to leave the theatre for the next intermission. I had a call from the bank which I must return. There wasn't time in this pause, but with an hour and a half, I'll have plenty of time during the next break. If I don't make it back to see you before Act Three, I'll give you a ring tomorrow.'

Unaccountably, I feel a little disappointed. I suppose it's just that I've come to enjoy spending time with JP. But, of course, we both have our other commitments.

I don't see JP during the long break, but nevertheless spend it enjoyably, eating a light sandwich and cup of tea, in the company of several Wagner enthusiasts. It amazes me how many people travel all over the world, like JP and his wife, to enjoy The Ring of The Nibelungen, especially when all four parts are performed in such a short space of time. I consciously take a back seat and find that the constant flow of memories and experiences, many very amusing, helps the time fly by quickly. In fact, I reach my seat just in time to be introduced to 'The Valkyries' at the start of Act Three.

At the end of the performance, I glance down towards the area in which JP is seated and see him cheering as lustily as anyone in the audience. I smile at the thought that he must, even given his huge experience of The

Ring, have very much enjoyed Opera North's production of one of his favourites.

The taxi driver, on the way home to Low Fell, is utterly horrified when he discovers that today's performance started at 4.30pm. 'But it's nearly half ten now! I'm surprised you can bear to sit in my cab, pet.'

I laugh and reassure him that we had a couple of decent breaks, 'Even so, it's a bit of a marathon, I have to agree. And there's two more, on Friday and Sunday. And they're both longer!'

'Good grief, man,' he says. 'And you call that pleasure? Good luck to you, pet, that's all I can say.'

I sit back and begin to hope that, yes, maybe I will have some good luck come out of attending The Ring.

Chapter Nine

5.30am, Thursday 7th July 2016, Whitburn, South Tyneside.

Sam

My first, semi conscious thought is that this bloody phone ringing in the middle of the night is getting to be a bit of a drag. As I open my eyes fully, I can immediately see a weak sun, sliding into the room at the side of the vertical blinds. I grab the phone and, of course, it's not PC Creaner, inviting me over for a sex romp. It's the bloody station, demanding my presence at another 'incident.'

I've no time to find any clean clothes, let alone have a shower and, inside five minutes I'm stuffing a Mars Bar in my mouth, as I pull the car out of the underground garage and head towards the centre of Gateshead. I'm a Londoner, born and bred, though I've no time for any of that self serving 'Eastenders' bullshit. When I first came to the North East three years ago, I thought it was a total dump, a complete write off. Things have changed a bit since then, however. OK I still think much of the urban areas of Newcastle and Gateshead are a bit of a dump. And as I speed through the almost empty streets, every run down or closed building, every piece of litter or pool of vomit on the pavement kind of reinforces that opinion. But that's not to say I don't like it here. The Geordies make up for anything the area lacks, when compared to London. I know it's a cliché, but they really are the salt of the earth. And I've got a canny flat, overlooking the sea. For Christ's sake, I'm even starting to talk like them now! My ex colleagues in The Met are totally bemused by my staying power up here. 'I'll give you three months, Snowy, and you'll be begging to come back, even as a uniformed plod,' had been the general consensus. But I'm just pig headed enough to prove all those smug bastards wrong and to make a proper go of it here. Once that incompetent DI 'Halitosis' Harrison does the honourable thing and buggers off into the sunset, the Super has already marked my card for a DI post.

The first buses of the day are to be seen as I pass Gateshead Interchange and I whistle softly, as I approach the crime scene. Shit,I think. The traffic types in their jam butty cars aren't going to like this one little bit. No bloody wonder the station wanted me to get a move on and get here fast. The police tape is stopping any traffic from passing down Quaysgate, from its intersection with the A167 over The Tyne Bridge, to its junction with Oakwellgate. I imagine it's a pretty busy area, especially during rush hour and all this tape is bound to cause diversions and problems for traffic wanting to cross the river. Thankfully, I don't have to give a shit about all that and I park up as close as I can get to the tape. I flash my warrant card to the uniform on duty and make my way towards the centre of our attention. It's a boarded up, and obviously unlet property, located under railway arches on Hymers Court. Judging from the faded sign over the front, it used to be some sort of a nightclub called 'Ikon.'

'With a crap name like that, it's no bloody wonder, it closed down,' I say to the Crime Scene Manager, as I don my SOC suit before going in. The whole place seems pretty small for a nightclub, about twenty three yards long and maybe five or six wide. It actually looks more like it was a bar with a bit of dancing. From what I can see, it also looks like any of the fixtures and fittings that could be ripped out have already gone. But it's not what I can see that hits me hardest. It's the smell. It's like I imagine an abattoir would be and I dry heave a couple of times. The walls and ceiling are all painted a nondescript, dark colour which stands in sharp contrast to the far corner, towards which I'm peering. There, bright arc lights shine cruelly down on what is attracting the interest of the SOCO squad. A pale faced young uniform, who I've never seen before, approaches, 'Constable Shearer, sarge,' he says and I raise an eyebrow, before deciding that now's not the time for the inevitable reference. 'OK, PC Shearer,' I say as gently as I can, 'Please tell me everything that happened.'

'Well, sir, I was sent to respond to a phone call, received at the station at 5.10am. The caller was a female and was evidently agitated. When I arrived, she was outside, shaking like a leaf and cradling a young woman in her arms. From her distress and appearance, it was clear that the younger woman been assaulted in some way.'

'What did you do then?'

'I left the two women and came inside. At first it was the smell that hit me. It was, you know...'

'Yes, I know, Shearer. Try not to think about it. What happened next?'

'Well, sergeant, there was no light on in here and it was pitch dark. I searched the place as best I could without moving. I didn't want to tramp all over the place and disturb evidence, you see.'

'Excellent work, officer.'

'And then my flashlight picked him out. I thought at first it was a bundle of wet rags, but when I went carefully over and saw.... '

'It's OK, mate. You just get yourself away back to the station for a good cup of sweet tea. Tell the desk sergeant that Sam Snow says you deserve a shot of dram in it as well.'

The young uniform stumbles off through the door and I say to to the lead SOCO, a middle aged man who's probably seen it all.'That poor young bastard'll never forget tonight, eh?'

He looks at me sideways and says, 'Listen sunshine. Wait till you see the body. I don't think any of us'll forget it in the next few days.'

I get closer and realise he's absolutely right. The body's a young man, early twenties I guess and it looks like he received one fatally deep stab wound to the heart. So far, so everyday. However, his head has been beaten to a pulp and half severed from the torso. There's some blood and it's very sticky underfoot.

'Not a pretty sight, is it?' the SOCO observes casually, 'The doc's been and gone. Said he died within the last five hours or so and that the one stab wound to the heart was fatal. The rest is just post mortem fun and games.'

I nod and ask if we know who he is. 'There's a driving licence bagged up over there. It was in his pocket.' I take a glance at it - it's for a Mykel Stevenson. What does this mean? A foreign connection? Or is it just one of those daft alternative spellings of ordinary names?

I look around at the bleak scene. A kind of washing line has been strung across one corner and some grimy sheets hung up. I go to peer through them and see straight away that this has been done to afford a modicum of privacy. There's an inflatable, king size mattress pushed up against the wall and my first thought is that someone has been dossing down here. As

I look more carefully and note the black satin sheets, the holdall, next to the air bed, which is overflowing with provocative lingerie and the range of boxed sex toys on the floor, the use to which the space has been put becomes crystal clear.

'Looks like some sort of temporary knocking shop,' I suggest to the SOCO.

He nods sadly and asks, 'You didn't see the wee thing they carted off to hospital did you? What kind of a bloody country are we living in?

'Dunno, mate,' I reflect his glum mood, as take one last view at the pitiful sight, 'I just don't know. Is there anything else I should know before I leave you to it?'

He nods and says, 'We found two or three small pieces of metal, very sharp to one side, blood stained and scattered near the body.'

'Do you think they were used in the assault? Or could the killer have dropped them by accident?'

'It's difficult to say to both questions. We'll have to wait till we get the stuff back to the lab, but my gut feeling is no, to both.'

I move over to have a closer look at the bagged objects and ask, 'What on earth could they be?'

'We'll have a better idea when we've had them under the microscope. We might be able to say whether or not they're pieces cut from the same larger piece of metal. If they are, it might suggest they've been taken from something like a large dagger, or even a sword.'

'A sword?' I echo in disbelief. 'Christ Almighty. Sounds like we've got a right nutter on our hands. Right then, I look forward to your reports and thanks.'

The SOCO nods and I exit through the single door which is cut into the metal shutters which, when down as they are now,protect the glass front of the property. The latest recruit to the CID at Newcastle nick, DC Morton, is standing outside, talking to an agitated woman in her late twenties.

'Look, officer,' she is saying firmly, 'I've done my duty by phoning you'se and telling you what I know. Now I've got to get to my job, otherwise the boss'll friggin' fire me.'

I recognise the Scouse accent and approach her with a smile, 'I'm DS Snow and you are..?'

'Morag O'Sullivan.'

'Look Ms O'Sullivan,' I say in my most soothing tone. 'I know it's a right pain, but I'd be very grateful if you would come back to the station with me. We need you to run through everything you heard, saw and did. I promise, it won't take any longer than is absolutely necessary.'

'Shit, sergeant,' she moans. 'Give me a break, won't ya? My boss is a total arsehole and I really need this cleaning job. If I'm very late, I'm toast. Get it?'

'Where is it you work, love?' I ask solicitously.

She looks a little uncertain about the wisdom of answering, but finally shrugs and says, 'I'm contracted by Cassouli's Cleaning Services. It's him what'd roast me if I'm late. I've seen it happen to a few of the other girls.'

'You mean old man Cassouli, the Greek down in Pelaw?' She nods and my face breaks out into a broad smile. 'You don't worry your head about Mr Cassouli, love. As it happens, we're on very good terms and I can promise you, for certain, that I'll square it with him, if you get into trouble.'

After I've found out from Morton that the younger, distressed woman was taken to the QE with unspecified injuries, and given him his instructions to wait until the SOCOs have finished, I invite Ms O'Sullivan to accompany me to the station. She looks dubious, but nevertheless follows me to my car and we drive back to the nick.

As soon as we're settled in an interview room with a nice cuppa and a WPC,I begin the interview.

'For the record, miss, would you mind confirming your name and then explain how you happened to be on Quaysgate so early in the morning?' She's taken off her down jacket and wooly hat and I can really see her for the first time. Her shoulder length, dark hair frames an oval face with regular features. But there's something in the first wrinkles which mark her forehead and the depth of the sockets of her deep blue eyes, which suggests a hard, uncertain and worrisome life. Like many people who just about survive in contemporary Britain, she looks sad and prematurely aged.

'I'm Morag O'Sullivan and I was on Quaysgate, because that's my way to work. I'm an office cleaner and,' as she looks pointedly at her watch, 'I should've been there half an hour or more ago.'

'As I said before, Ms O'Sullivan, I'm sorry to delay you and I'll make this as brief as possible. If necessary, I'll speak with your employer, Mr Cassouli about your assistance in this matter.' This seems to pacify her and she takes her first sip of the tea.

'Is this your normal route to work?'

'Well, it depends where I'm working. I'm contract, see. I go where I'm sent. But I've been based at his place now for over six weeks. It's very handy 'cos I can walk it in twenty minutes from my flat. And it's good money, so I don't want to jeopardise it in any way.'

'Could you tell me exactly what you saw this morning?'

'As I said, I was walking to work and had got part way down Quaysgate, when I saw a young woman slumped outside the empty unit on Hymers Court. She was dressed rather oddly, you know? For that time of morning.'

'How do you mean?'

'Well, she was done up like a cheap tart; micro short skirt, low cut top, high heels, stockings, make up plastered on. At first I thought she'd been on a night out, got pissed and had given up trying to get home. Just crashed and spent the night there, like. But, as I got nearer, I could hear her sobbing and I thought I saw some blood on her head. So I thought she must've been mugged, or even worse. You know, sexually attacked?'

'Did you see anyone else at all, either just before you saw her, or after you'd seen her.'

'No,' she answers emphatically and without the slightest hesitation.

'Did she say anything to you?'

'I'm no expert, but she looked like she was in total shock. I asked if she was OK, but all she could talk about was someone called Micky. She cried her eyes out and kept saying Micky was in the unit and I should try to help him.'

'Now this is very important. Did you go inside the unit?'

She looks mortified and can only reply after wiping tears from her eyes. 'The door was open, but I was terrified. I'd no idea who might still be in there, so I just rang 999. I can't get out of my mind that, if I'd been a bit braver, I might have been able to save somebody. Could I? Did I let someone die, 'cos I was too scared?'

I look at her puffy red rimmed eyes and an image of the part severed head, with its horribly pulped features comes unbidden into my mind. I shake my head firmly and reassure her, 'No, love. No chance. You couldn't have done anything for anyone. You did exactly the right thing.'

Ms O'Sullivan heaves a deep sigh, probably of relief, wipes her eyes and smiles at me, as I ask, 'Did the woman say anything else?'

'Not really. She kept going on about Micky and something about hearing an awful noise. I'm sorry, by then I was really paying attention to keeping my eye out for the ambulance.'

'Of course. Look, we're almost finished. Do you know the woman? Have you seen her before this morning?'

For the first time, the witness seems uncomfortable, shifting around on the wooden chair. 'Well, you know, I don't like to diss anyone...'

'Come on, Morag. If you know something, best to get it out. It'll help us to get the bastard who did this.'

My words seem to persuade her and she starts to gabble, as if, once having decided to tell all, she should get it over as quickly as possible. 'Well, it's like this. I've seen her a few times, when I've been on my way to work. Coming out of that same unit with a young man.'

I lean forward in my chair and ask quickly, 'Always the same man? Can you describe him?'

'Yes, always the same. I'm sorry, all I remember is that he was quite tall, slim, only in his twenties and had long dark hair.'

I thought immediately of the long dark hair on the body and ask, 'Did you speak to them? What did you think they were up to at that time of day?'

I can see the eagerness of my question is interpreted as hostile by her and she goes all defensive, 'No I never spoke to them. And it's actually none of my business what they were doing there. I'm not security or anything. They seemed OK together, no aggression, or violence. I suppose I thought they must be two homeless young people dossing down there. How youngsters manage these days, God alone knows. So, if that's what they were up to, good luck to them, is what I say.'

She's worked herself up into a defiant mood now and I have to try to repair the damage quickly. 'Look, Morag. No one's accusing you of anything. I'm just trying to get as much information as I can. You said you saw them a few times. Would that be every other day? One in three? And over what period?'

She's back with me now and pauses, thinking before answering, 'I really can't say for sure. Probably once or twice a week, something like that. Over the past three weeks or so, I guess. Will she be all right?'

'I don't honestly know, love. I've not seen her yet. But, unless you can think of anything else, I think that's us done now. You've been extremely helpful. Thank you. Just write your address and phone number on this form and I'll get one of the officers to run you to work.'

'Oh, that's not...'

'Don't worry, he'll stop a little way off. No one'll see you getting out of the car. I'll give Mr Cassouli a quick bell and explain the situation. He'll not give you a hard time, I promise.' She looks doubtful and I reassure her further, 'Look. He was very appreciative of my contribution to a recent investigation near his business. He said he owes me a big one.' She seems happy with this explanation and I say, 'Oh and please come back in after you've finished work, so that you can make a formal statement about all this.'

I escort her to the main Reception and organise a car, before going back to the CID room. It's just after 7am now and I know that the duty DI will be coming on shift at 8am. He may well take the case over then, but I decide that, if I get myself off to the QE straight away, I'll get first dibs at the injured woman. I've also got a 10am with DCI Quayle to outline my concerns about the the homeless man's killing and I'll take that opportunity to update her on this new death. So, it looks like I'm in for a busy morning.

Chapter Ten

Sam

As I drive up Sherif Hill towards the hospital, almost all the traffic is going in the opposite direction, towards Gateshead and Newcastle city centres. My hunch that parking will be much easier at this time of the day proves to be accurate and, as soon as I turn into the hospital entrance, I can see several spaces, to the right, in car park 1. The sun's well up and it looks like it'll be another glorious day on Tyneside, as I walk the short distance to the hospital Main Entrance and A&E. At the desk, I'm directed to a small room towards the end of a long corridor. The uniform on duty outside the door acts as the perfect indicator that I've found my goal.

She raises her hand as I make to enter the room and advises, 'The doctor and a nurse went in there a few minutes ago, sarge. I think you'd be better waiting til they come out.'

I nod in acknowledgement, 'Of course. Did you bag up the clothes?'

'All sorted and sent to Forensics half an hour ago.'

'Good work. How's she been. Did you accompany her in the ambulance?'

'Yes, I did. I think she's not too badly hurt, but is in a very disturbed state. I'm not sure they'll even let you interview her.'

Just as she finishes speaking, the door opens and a young doctor emerges. 'Excuse me doctor, I begin. I'm Sergeant Snow of Northumbria Police. I wonder, would it be possible to ask the young lady some questions?'

The doctor sighs and removes her glasses, 'She's had a significant blow to the head and was probably unconscious for a time. I wonder, could your questions wait until later today?'

I try my most winning smile and say, 'Of course, they could. But we are investigating a particularly brutal killing, to which the young lady is our best witness and lead. It would help the investigation enormously, if I could just put a few questions to her. I promise not to put her under stress.'

I can tell from her weary manner that she probably has a dozen more cases to deal with in A&E and she nods her head, saying, 'OK. But the nurse will stay in the room and , if she says so, you must stop the interview immediately.'

'It's a deal, doctor and thank you. But before you go, can you tell me anything about the wound she received?'

'I'd say she was hit by something akin to a short wooden bat or a truncheon. It was enough to knock her out, but not to do any real damage. She'll be fine.'

She starts to move off and I quickly ask, 'Do you have any idea at all, how long she might have been unconscious?'

'I'm afraid that's impossible to say with any degree of certainty. My best guess, and I emphasise that it is a guess, would be no more than a few minutes. Now I really must go.'

'Of course, doctor. Thank you very much for your help.' Before knocking gently and entering the patient's room, I ask the WPC, 'Have we any idea what she's called?'

'She told the nurse that her name's Kylie. But I've no idea about the surname, sorry.'

I'm surprised to see Kylie sitting upright in a chair, rather than lying in bed. Her head is covered in bandages and she is wearing hospital clothes. She looks terrified. I estimate that she's a little above average height, but is thin, rather than slim, and probably in her late teens or early twenties. Despite the premature ageing of her face and skin, she's still a striking young woman and one that would be in heavy demand by punters.

I nod discreetly at the nurse, who stands, leaning against the wall, with her arms folded in what I interpret as a fairly hostile manner. I perch on the edge of the empty bed, so that my head is more or less at the same height as the girl's. 'Hello, Kylie,' I begin softly, 'my name's Sam Snow and I'm a police officer.' At the mention of my job, she visibly flinches and I rush to reassure her.

'Now you're not in any kind of trouble, Kylie. And you're perfectly safe now. I'd just like to ask you some questions, if you feel up to it.' She looks helplessly at the nurse who nods and smiles in encouragement. 'Would that be OK, love?'

She offers an almost imperceptible nod of her head and I breathe a sigh of relief. I'm in! 'Now, Kylie, that's your name isn't it?' She nods in agreement and I continue. 'Can you tell me what happened last night?'

Kylie looks at me, as if I've spoken in a foreign language and then replies with a question of her own. 'Where's Micky? I want to see Micky! He's all right isn't he?'

I reach out and touch her limp hand. She makes no attempt to snatch it away and I look her straight in the eye, 'I think you know what happened to Micky, don't you, love? I'm going to find the person responsible. But I really need your help. Is that OK? Will you help me and help Micky, please?'

A look of unutterable sadness sweeps across her ravaged face and she nods her head again. She then screws up her eyes and starts talking very slowly. 'I was waiting in the bedroom, like I always do, while Micky did the business on the other side of the curtain. They were talking in low voices. But then I heard a funny noise. It sounded like a squelch, or something like that and I heard a soft groan. And then another, louder squelching noise. I didn't hear Micky's voice after that.'

I squeeze her hand and smile, 'You're doing really well, Kylie.'

I'm sure she can't see, or hear me. She's back in the empty unit. 'I just waited on the bed for him to come in. But he didn't. And I couldn't hear anything outside. After a few minutes, I got up off the bed and stuck my head out of the curtain. The next thing I remember is..... The next thing I remember is... Christ help me! The next thing I remember is.....' She then starts to hyperventilate and the nurse immediately steps in. 'I'm sorry, sergeant. You'll have to stop your questioning now. As you can see, Kylie is very distressed.'

I withdraw, while the nurse calms Kylie down. Once she is sitting peacefully again, I whisper to the nurse, 'Look miss, I'm investigating a really horrible murder and Kylie's the only one who can help me. Can I have one more go and if she breaks down again, I'll give it up for now?' I can see that she's struggling to make a decision and I add, 'A couple of minutes. No more. I promise.'

At last she nods and I sit on the bed again. 'OK, Kylie. I wonder if you can tell me why you were in that unit on Hymers Court?' She looks very frightened and I quickly add, 'You're not in trouble at all Kylie. I just really need your help and knowing why you were there would help me loads.'

After staring wildly around the room, like a trapped animal seeking some sort of escape route, her shoulders slump and she starts to sob. 'We're on our own y'see. Me and Micky.'

'Is Micky your boyfriend, Kylie?'

She looks shocked at this suggestion and says, 'No! He's my brother! We never had a dad. And mam threw us out when her latest boyfriend said it was us or him. We both had jobs, me at Poundland and Micky with a window cleaner. But with nowhere to stay, we both lost our jobs.' I nod and offer a sympathetic smile and she responds with the most embarrassed expression. 'I'm not a slag. And Micky's a canny lad. Neither of us would steal. But we had to get our money any way we could. So I, you know, I earned it the only way I could.'

In a funny way, she seems calmer now that she's able to let it all pour out of her. I gently say, 'It's OK, Kylie. I understand. And Micky, did he look after you?'

'He'd never let me be a streetwalker. "No sis of mine's ever gonna have to do that!" he used to say. So he organised that place for me to work. It's a lot safer and

83

he's always there, in case there's you know, any rough stuff.'

She now bursts out with a long keening wail and the nurse looks like she's about to intervene. I quickly ask, 'Did Micky say the client last night was a regular, Kylie? Think, love, it's important.'

Through her tear stained face she manages to say, 'He sorted all the business end out, so I don't know. But I don't think he was, 'cos Micky said he was gonna be the best paid job yet. But I saw him.' My ears prick up in expectation, but she's lost it now, as she howls, 'I saw Micky... I saw what he did to him.. I saw it. I saw it all!'

'Look, officer,' shouts the nurse, as she rushes to console Kylie and to push me away. 'That's enough now! No more. Please leave immediately.'

As I reach the door, I turn back into the room and say, 'I'm so sorry, Kylie. But I promise you that I'll nail the man that did this.' I'm not at all sure that she heard a word I said, but saying it definitely made me feel better.

On the way back to the station, I try to process all I've learned and make plans for the development of the investigation. If only the DCI'll keep Harrison away from this, I'll work every hour God sends to get this bastard.

It's coming up to 8.30am when I get back to the station and I decide to nip to the canteen to get a bit of breakfast, before reporting to the duty DI. Normally, I'd be a 'Full English' man, but somehow, today, my heart's not in it and I astound the canteen staff by asking for a bowl of cereal and a strong coffee.

'Out late again last night, pet? Dicky tummy?' laughs Mavis, one of the older members of staff. Her face changes as soon as she sees my expression, 'Sorry, lovey. You involved in that business down Hymers Court?' I simply nod and she serves my breakfast without another word. We've had two unusually violent and brutal killings within twenty four hours and, in such circumstances, the entire staff feels it personally. It's funny, but we all close ranks and do what we can, until we celebrate as one, when we've successfully made our collar. That's one thing I really like about the job. Almost all of us are in it together, no egos, no grandstanding, just hard bloody work to bring scum to justice.

DI Burden is the duty officer, and I run through everything that's happened. He's a damned good copper and has always been supportive of me, even when others initially thought me an ex-Met, know it all type. Thankfully, I've proved I'm a hardworking team player and am only gently ribbed about my southern accent now. Burden suggests that I report all this and my suggestions for further progress at my meeting with DCI Quayle, 'With luck, Sam, she might give you your head on this one.'

Chapter Eleven

10am, Thursday 7th July 2016, Newcastle City Centre Police Station, Forth Banks.

Sam

I've managed to nip into the Gents to have a quick wash and brush up before my meeting with the DCI. However, I'm dismayed when I look in the mirror and see a scruffy, unshaven, bleary eyed figure looking back at me. I try in vain to straighten my shirt collar under my leather jacket, shrug and head off to the guv's office.

I explained the purpose of the meeting to the DCI's secretary when I rang to arrange it, so I'm not at all surprised to see that   Harrison is already there, when I enter her office. She'd have felt duty bound to give the old wanker a chance to cover his arse, I guess. As I look directly at him, I realise that,even if I'd had hours to pimp myself up, I'd have come nowhere near him. The miserable sod looks like he's been dressed by his mum, even though he's nearly sixty.

'Come in Snow,' says DCI Quayle, in her characteristically businesslike way,and I shuffle further in and sit on the free chair, placed slightly to the left of her large, uncluttered desk. The DCI has a reputation as a coppers' copper, rather than a pen pusher, like so many are who reach her kind of rank. I've not had so many direct dealings with her myself, but colleagues have regaled me with inspiring tales of her earlier career when, as a high flying, career detective, she was something of a maverick and trail blazer for women in the North East. They say she's retained something of her creative approach to police work, even in such an exalted position, so I hope she'll hear me out.

First impression isn't so great though, as she looks carefully at the paper in front of her, removes her reading glasses and fixes me with a hostile stare. 'I've read the report from DI Harrison on the murder at St Mary's Heritage Centre on the early morning of yesterday. I have to say, it seems pretty straightforward. As the report states, we have a signed confession and firm evidence of theft of money from the deceased by the person charged. Can you explain to us, Snow, what exactly is your problem?

I can sense 'Halitosis' smirking at my discomfort and I cough and try to organise my thoughts. 'Well, ma'am, with respect to DI Harrison's report, I do have certain reservations about the suggested solution to this crime.'

'I should bloody well hope you do, sergeant,' Quayle grumbles in her Geordie accent, 'otherwise we're all wasting our time here!'

I swallow hard and go for it. 'First, ma'am, there's the alleged killer. He's just a regular homeless guy. Late fifties, been on the streets for about a decade in Newcastle. Known to be a long standing acquaintance, probably also a friend of the deceased and has never been known to commit a violent act in his life.'

'We can all begin sometime, Snow,' says Harrison dismissively.

'I agree, sir, but with respect, I saw and spoke with Mr Smith at the scene and he showed no signs of having just committed such a violent crime. If he was so full of remorse and wanted to confess, why didn't he do it straight away, when we could both still see the body?'

'Because he knew, as soon as we found the cash on him, he was bang to rights!' answered a gleeful Harrison.

'Second,' I say, undeterred, 'there's the nature of the attack. 'The post mortem report expresses the firm view that this was initially a very skilful, targeted assault. In fact, it states that the first blow probably killed him. If it was an argument over money, as DI Harrison wants us to believe, why did Smith carry on and batter Geoff Grantham's head to a pulp? Surely he'd have taken the cash and scarpered. He'd hardly have wasted time beating the already dead body and then reported it, in the full knowledge that he had the bloodstained money in his pocket, would he?'

We can both see that DCI Quayle is giving this serious thought and Harrison is quick to intervene, addressing his remarks directly to me. 'Well, if no offenders ever made a mistake, our job'd be a hell of lot harder, now wouldn't it? Face it, sergeant, this old tramp's not exactly University Challenge material. He simply lost the plot and made a mistake.'

'OK,' I concede, 'let's accept that Smith and Geoff have an unpremeditated row over money. Let's also suspend disbelief that Smith has the knowledge, and the skill, to apply a quick, single, lethal blow to Geoff. Let's accept that, contrary to all sense, Smith then takes the money and spends a few minutes wasting time and energy, and risking being splattered by blood, in battering Geoff Grantham to a pulp. What kind of weapon did he use? Where is it? Did he simply find it lying there at St Mary's? Or did he carry it with him? If so, bang goes the unpremeditated angle. But all witnesses, who say they saw Smith that night, are clear that he wasn't carrying a stick, or weapon of any kind. The post mortem report also suggests that the weapon was most likely a wooden bat of some kind, perhaps with metal rings near its head.

Traces of wood and metal polish were found in the wounds. It sounds a very nasty, purpose built piece of kit. Now, are we to believe that Smith just happened to find this lying around at precisely the time he decided to kill Grantham? Or did he carry it with him, despite no one ever remembering him carrying such an item?' Feeling rather pleased with myself, I conclude directly to the DCI, 'All in all, ma'am, I submit that we should keep this investigation open.'

'Halitosis' is about to reply, but is stopped and left silent and open mouthed as Quayle gives her verdict. 'I think what you have said has much merit, Snow. However, we can't really get beyond a signed confession. As long as we have that, I can't really justify expending any more scarce resources on this enquiry, especially now that we have another killing to investigate. I'm sorry, sergeant, but there it is.'

Despite a crushing sense of disappointment, I nod my head and stand, ready to leave. Harrison is still seated, as if he intends to wallow in his success in convincing our guv. But Quayle isn't quite finished. 'I'd like to have a private word with you, Snow. DI Harrison, I'm sure you have plenty in your in tray.'

Not even 'Halitosis' could misinterpret such a dismissal and he whimpers like a beaten dog, before scurrying out of the room.

As soon as we are alone, the DCI shakes her head and says with a smile, 'You know, that was very good work there, Snow. You made a pretty convincing case to keep the file on Grantham's killing open. But, and there's always a but, isn't there? I'd find it hard to press for more resources, while allocating staff to continue investigating a crime for which we have a plausible confession.'

There's no point provoking her when she seems to be on my side, so I reply evenly, 'I suppose I can see that, ma'am. But, if Smith were to retract his confession?'

'Then that would be a different kettle of fish. But, at the moment, DI Harrison has my support. Now, tell me about this more recent killing.'

I tell her everything I know about the crime and give her a full account of the interviews with Morag O'Sullivan and Kylie Stevenson.

'So, Kylie was being pimped by her brother, using the empty unit on Hymers Court to keep her off the street? And the brother's the victim?'

'That's about the size of it, ma'am, yes.'

'So, what do you think? A deranged punter? Or is it one or more of the heavyweight pimps wanting to stamp out a bit of private enterprise?'

'Well, ma'am, I don't think we can rule the second idea out totally. But I must admit that the ferocious nature of the killing doesn't suggest the work of a hit man. That would surely look more like a quick, clean execution. There was too much anger, or something even more sinister, at work here. And also, what about the strange pieces of metal, left at the scene of crime? Why would a professional hit man do such a weird thing? Nevertheless, with your permission, I'll talk to the Vice Squad and see if they can shed any light on Mykel Stevenson and how he related to the rest of the sex trade.'

'OK, that'll do for a start.'

'I also think it'd be worth leaning on the owner of the unit and the estate agency which is handling the letting. According to Ms O'Sullivan, Stevenson's arrangement had been going on for some weeks. I believe someone must have known about it. Perhaps they were even taking a cut. Owner and agent are both worth a visit, I think. I'll also take a look at the post mortem and interview the girl again, as soon as she's able. But some help looking for CCTV footage of the area and questioning people around at that time of the morning would be helpful.'

'OK. Good work,' Quayle says with a shake of the head. 'You don't suppose the two killings are related do you? Two inside twenty four hours is a bit unusual for Gateshead.'

'There's nothing at all to suggest any connection at the moment, ma'am. The MO, the victims, the locations, nothing really matches.'

'Just the times,' mused Quayle. 'Anyway, I'd like you to keep going on this one, Snow. I'll speak with Harrison. Obviously, he will have to be the Senior Investigating Officer and you will officially report to him. But I'd like you to keep me up to speed on what's going on.' She accurately recognises this as the immediate cause of a frown spreading across my face.

'But, with respect, ma'am,' I begin to stammer, only to be stopped by the raising of her tiny right hand.

'Now you listen to me, Snow. You've got the makings of a damned good detective and, as you may know, I'd like to see you moving up sooner rather than later. At your age, you've still plenty of time. But, we are where we are. And as long as DI Harrison is here, he will be the SIO and you will report to him. But, I have already told him that he is to give you some scope to stretch your legs on this one. He understands that and, providing you treat him with respect, we can all end up getting what we want.'

'As you say, ma'am,' I say with little enthusiasm.

Her dismissal orders me to 'Get yourself off home for an hour or two to smarten yourself up. I don't want an officer of mine, leading an investigation and looking like you do now. Damn it all, I thought you London boys were supposed to be like the dummies in Next's windows. You look like a bloody scarecrow. Oh, and, don't forget. Let me know where things lead.'

Chapter Twelve

Sam

I know this may sound weird, but the best thing about my flat is the wet room. When I think back to the mid nineties and the constant queues to use the only bathroom in my parents' council flat in Shoreditch, it's no wonder I think like that. God, the way the hot water always ran out before it was my turn. And how, when mum filled the kettle when I was under the shower, the temperature went all to pot. Happy memories - not!

Now, my 'Tropical Rain' shower head and thermostatically controlled valve gives me a heavenly experience every time. I could luxuriate here for ages, but I know I should get back to the station. Reluctantly, I turn off the water and dry myself down, before shaving and dressing in my normal work clothes of black jeans, open necked white shirt and a black leather jacket, just back from the cleaners. I grab myself a couple of slices of jam on toast and switch on the tv, only to see Harrison's smug face. He's giving a press conference and I turn up the sound. '.....the public can rest assured that, thanks to the excellent work of my fellow officers of Northumbria Police, the perpetrator of this brutal and hideous crime is now in custody and awaiting his appearance in court.'

I can't listen to him any more and switch off. I just can't equate Harrison's 'perpetrator of this brutal and hideous crime' with the harmless old bugger I dealt with at the scene of the crime. Anyway, I decide, as I ram the last piece of toast into my mouth and make for the door, I've other fish to fry now.

When I arrive at the station, I find that 'Halitosis' has only gone and organised a team meeting for 4.15pm for everyone on the Hymers Court enquiry. Without even bloody well letting me know. It's clear what the slimy old bastard's game is. He wants me to fall flat on my face, before the investigation's even started. Well, I'll show him. I've a few minutes to prepare, so I make straight for my desk to gather together the most important information from the case and set up what I think should be the further lines of enquiry. At just before quarter past four, Harrison creeps up and says, all friendly like, 'The team's going to be waiting, Sergeant Snow. Are you quite ready?'

It's as obvious as the hooked nose on his pug ugly face, that he's disappointed when I confidently reply, 'Of course, DI Harrison. I'm ahead of you.' I gather up my papers and beat him to the door. I'll be the first to arrive at the Incident Room if it kills me. And I'll enjoy making him follow in my slipstream.

It's a fairly small room, into which the initial team has been invited. There's myself and Harrison, of course, DC Jenkins, Sergeant Walters and PC Armitage of the uniformed branch and a Civilian Investigation Officer, who is going to run the Incident Room and collation of evidence. She's Helen Dutton and I'm delighted she's on board, as I know from past experience that she's a very efficient and helpful team member. In fact, I'm astonished that she's already set up an Incident Board with map, photos and a summary of some key points.

Harrison welcomes the team in his normal droning way, with the information that he will be acting as SIO. There's a certain amount of sideways glances towards me. It's bloody obvious that none of them are any happier than I am that 'Halitosis' is top dog. But there's sod all I can do about it, so I ignore them and keep looking at my papers.

To be fair to Harrison, he points to the Incident Board and thanks Helen Dutton for her work, before asking me to give the team a summary of what we know so far. 'You're the officer who was on the ground, and, initially, I've decided that you'll be taking a central role on this, Sergeant. So I'm sure we'd all be interested in what you have to say about how we should proceed.'

I'm not the only one who raises eyebrows at his pathetic attempt to pretend he had made the decision to give me more responsibility. Everyone knows that we don't get on at all, but I see little point in correcting him. I prefer to suggest the two initial lines of enquiry that I think we should pursue, 'We should work initially on the premise that the crime was either committed by a disgruntled or deranged client, or that it's related in some way to the sex trade in the city.' I'm really happy to see everyone paying close attention and even making notes.

'When's the pm result expected, sarge?' asks DC Jenkins and I answer that it should be later this afternoon, but it's not expected to throw up any surprises. 'However, one odd thing was that small pieces of metal, sharpened on one side, were found near the body.'

'You mean like razor blades, or something?' asks Sergeant Walters with a frown. I explain that SOCO thought they might be parts of a large dagger, or even a sword, but that they didn't seem to be part of the murder weapon. I can see that this unusual feature of the incident has really engaged the group and Harrison has to raise his voice to calm the buzz of conversation.

'Thanks for that, Sergeant,' he says, as if he almost means it, and goes on to assign our tasks. 'Sergeant Walters, I'd like you and your team to work the area near the lock up. Ask everyone you can find, if they saw or heard anything late last night. We don't know when Mykel and Kylie arrived at the unit, so we should cover 11pm-3am. You could also find out if there are any CCTV cameras in the area and get a look at the footage. Hopefully, we'll have more precise times to focus on when we've got the pm results.'

'Sir,' I interrupt, 'Mykel Stevenson's mobile is also missing. It's possible that he used it to make appointments for his sister. So we need to find that, if it's anywhere nearby. The immediate area has already been searched, but we could try broadening that out, if we have the resources.'

Harrison looks towards Sergeant Walters who breathes in through his teeth, as if this is most unlikely. It's all a bluff, as he soon smiles and says, 'Fine, Inspector. We'll do our best.'

Harrison nods in appreciation of the old git actually agreeing to do his job and then tells Helen Dutton that he'd like her to coordinate the Incident Room and to try to find out where Mykel and Kylie were living. 'Sergeant Snow has suggested that it doesn't look like they were dossing down every night in the unit on Hymers Court. So they must have been going somewhere.'

Helen Dutton nods in understanding, before Harrison turns to me. 'I'd be interested in your thoughts on what you and DC Jenkins should do next.'

Whether he's genuinely doing what Quayle has ordered, or whether he's just giving me enough rope, I can't say, but I decide to take him on face value. 'I'd suggest that we follow up with the owner of the unit and the estate agent who handles it. I can't believe that one, or both, didn't know about Mykel's use of it. We could also liaise with Vice, about that angle to the investigation. Also, somebody needs to speak to their mum, when Helen's tracked her down.'

'Very well,' agrees Harrison. 'I'll go and have another chat with Kylie Stevenson, when she's sufficiently recovered and we'll liaise later today about who should tackle the mam. Oh, and I'll handle the press with DCI Quayle.'

Harrison asks if there are any questions and seeing the shaking heads, he concludes the meeting, 'Thanks and let's go and find the bastard that did this!'

The DI is the first out of the room, closely followed by the the uniforms. Helen Dutton is busy fussing with her computer, when Jenkins sidles up to me and whispers, 'Just our luck to get saddled with 'Halitosis'.' This particular DC's been with us for just over a year. She's mid twenties and pretty, with long blonde hair, tied into a neat ponytail. One or two of the matchmakers, who work in the station canteen, are forever reminding me that she's unattached and, for all I know, saying the same thing about me to her. To her credit, she's shown the character required to come, unscathed, through the usual stick some officers like to give to graduate entrants and I'm very happy she's on the team.

'Oh, let's just try to ignore him as much as we can,' I reply. 'After all, he's given us most of the real detective work to do.'

'Like he always does, you mean? While he sits in his office counting the days to his retirement,' Jenkins says with a smirk. Conscious of what Quayle had said earlier, I decide not to rise to this bait, but simply reply, 'Come on, let's see if we can get hold of the pm results.'

As soon as I reach my desk, I open my emails and Jenkins perches on the end of my desk. 'OK, the pm results are here,' and she immediately moves around behind me.

'It's what we thought. Single stab wound penetrated the heart, resulting in immediate death. Further blows post mortem. Estimated time of death 2.00-4.00am.' As I pass down the list of key points, I call out 'Whoa! What's this? The metal pieces are indeed all from one item. Most likely a longer dagger or even a sword. While these were not used in the attack, it's likely that death was also caused by a similar type of weapon.'

'Bloody hell, sarge,' Jenkins blurts out. 'I'd say the odds just swung very much in favour of a nutter.'

'I agree. But, before we dismiss the other line of enquiry, we'd best get ourselves off to speak with Vice. Maybe they can offer something useful.'

If CID's a bit too informal for some of the old codgers in the uniformed service, the Vice Squad is in a different league altogether. Most of them look like users, or pushers themselves. As I suppose they have to. And boy, do they keep odd hours. It's certainly not much of a job for family people. We're lucky, as it's late afternoon now and the head of the unit has just arrived to sort out the distribution of assignments for the coming evening and night. He's not a bad type and is willing to give us a few minutes, before he gets on with his own work.

I explain about Micky and Kylie Stevenson and what we suspect they'd been up to in the empty unit, before asking, 'Has this couple ever come to your attention?'

He must be really on top of his job, 'cos he hardly has to pause to think, before answering confidently. 'Yes. The names ring a bell. But Stevenson isn't a significant player at all. He's not made any attempt to move in on the street patches, which are like gold dust to the regular pimps. So, I'd say their attitude so far has been one of grudging tolerance.'

'We think Stevenson may have made appointments by phone and arranged to meet punters at the empty unit,' Jenkins suggests with a smile.

'Yes, the regular sex trade's less threatened by that kind of operation. Which is why, at the moment I'd say they've not flagged him up as a problem.'

'And if he did become a problem?' I ask quickly. 'What's the most likely action?'

'Hard to say for sure,' he replies candidly, 'after all, they're all different. But I'd say a good beating up would be the most likely first step and, if he really got under their skin, a hitman to remove him with as little fuss as possible.'

'Well, sarge,' says Jenkins, as we make our way back to CID, 'half severing somebody's head and leaving hints of swords doesn't exactly meet the definition of discretion, does it? I think you were right, the Vice angle looks the least favourite at the moment.'

'I agree,' I grumble, 'but I think that makes our investigation a whole lot harder, don't you?'

We return to the Incident Room and Jenkins lodges her notes from the meeting with Vice. Dutton's about to leave for the day and gives us details, both of the estate agent handling the letting of the Unit and of the address of Micky's and Kylie's mum. 'I checked out the owner,' she says as she puts on her jacket. 'He lives most of the time in Gran Canaria. I spoke to him and he hasn't been back in the UK since Christmas.' She looks pointedly at her watch and adds with a smile, 'If you get your skates on, you'll just have time to get over to the estate agency before they close for the night.'

Jenkins and I stare at the closing door and laugh. 'Well,' she says eventually, 'I'd say that's us told what to do.'

The office of Brown's Estate Agency is on Walker Terrace, on the other side of the river from the station. We decide to take a pool car and we arrive just as a mid twenties man and a younger woman are locking up for the night.

'Excuse me, sir, madam,' I say, whilst showing my warrant card. 'Northumbria Police. Would you mind identifying yourselves? And then maybe we could have a little chat?'

The young woman looks shocked as she splutters, 'I'm Charlie Gates. I'm the Receptionist here.' The man tries to bluff it, 'I'm Jerome Hardcastle, Office Manager. Actually, now's rather inconvenient. We're the last here and I have an urgent appointment with a client.'

Evidently DC Jenkins is as unimpressed as I, with the shiny suit and overly waxed hairstyle, because she says firmly, 'Then I would strongly suggest, sir, that you inform your client that you are unavoidably detained. That, and that you open up. I'm sure you'd rather us not have this conversation in public.'

'Do you need me as well?' pleads the young woman and I put her out of her misery. 'I don't think that will be necessary at this stage, miss. You're free to go home.' To my and Jenkins' amusement, she scurries off down the street, as quickly as her painfully high heels will take her.

'Now sir,' Jenkins suggests forcefully, 'If you don't mind.'

He scowls ungraciously, but nevertheless turns back towards the door, unlocks and opens it and, without a word, stalks back inside.

We'd already agreed that DC Jenkins would lead the interview and I sit back in anticipation, as she fixes Hardcastle with a predatory smile. 'Now, sir, if you don't mind, we'd like to ask you some questions about a property which is on your books.'

I could swear that a flash of relief crosses the estate agent's glistening face, before he puts on a confused air. 'Oh, I see. Yes, of course. Anything I can do to assist you.'

Jenkins has also spotted his initial reaction and prods him, 'You seem rather relieved Mr Hardcastle. Were you expecting us to be questioning you about something else?'

He tries, unsuccessfully, to produce a confidently dismissive laugh, 'Not at all, officer. Not at all. It's just not everyday we get the police in here. It's a bit of a shock.'

'Then let's hope our reason for being here doesn't turn out to be a very nasty shock.' The agent shifts uncomfortably on his seat, as DC Jenkins continues. 'It's about one of your to let commercial properties, sir. The one on Hymers Court.'

With those five words his expression changes from mild confusion to real panic, as he stutters, 'The property isn't yet let. It's a failed nightspot. What's the matter? Is there a problem with it? A break in, or something? '

'We don't think so. Does anyone else work here, other than yourself and Ms Gates?'

I'm impressed by the way in which the variation in questioning by DC Jenkins is really unbalancing the witness. 'Err..n... no,' he stutters nervously. 'Well, if you exclude my father, that is. He only comes in once or twice a month. But as far as the day to day business is concerned, it's just me and Charlie.'

'And is business good?'

'What do you think? The Brexit vote has shocked the housing market. It's not quite dead. But it's not bursting with health, either.'

'So, you'd be happy to find a stream of easy income?'

'Who wouldn't? Why do you ask?'

'Is that why you allowed Mykel Stevenson to rent the place off you by the hour, for his sister to use as a place to carry out her work as a prostitute?'

She's caught him with the perfect blow and Hardcastle is reeling on the ropes. 'What? What do you mean? He told me that he just wanted to store a few items there, that's all. For pound notes, you know? The owner lives in the Canary Islands, or somewhere, and couldn't give a toss. So, I thought, until it's let again, why not? But, shit, I'd no idea, officer. You've got to believe me.'

'How long had this arrangement been in existence?'

'Hmm. Let me think. He's paid me twice, so this must be towards the end of the second month. Look, I'll cancel this at once and let him know. I've a bloody good mind to take legal advice. Perhaps I can sue him.'

'I wouldn't think so, mate,' I say. 'The poor bastard's dead. Killed in your let.'

I almost feel sorry for Hardcastle now. He looks like he's about to throw up and rushes out of the office to the back, where we imagine the staff toilet is located. I follow to make sure he's not doing a runner and hear his retching through the door. After five minutes he emerges, looking green and shaky. 'Look,' he begins, as soon as we are all seated again. 'I'll admit I didn't ask too many questions, when Stevenson approached me about the let. It was only a few quid he gave me and I thought, what the hell. It's doing nobody any harm. But murder? For Christ's sake, I'm not involved in anything like that. You have to believe me.'

'It would help if you could tell us where you were last night between midnight and 5am.'

'I was at home, asleep in my flat on the Quayside. And before you ask, I was alone.'

I look at DC Jenkins and she turns to Hardcastle, 'That's rather unfortunate. You'll have to come with us and make a full statement, sir. It will be then up to the CPS to decide whether or not you will face any charges. And in the meantime, do not leave the city. We will almost certainly want to speak with you again.'

'About the death in the unit you mean. But I had nothing to do with that, I swear.'

'Please lock up now, sir and come back to the station with us.'

I'm very impressed by the way Jenkins handled the interview and, as soon as Hardcastle is settled with a uniform and making his statement, I tell her so. 'Would you have said that to a man?' she shoots back at me.

'Of course I bloody well would,' I protest. 'And more than that, I'd have dropped dead with shock if 'Halitosis' had had it in him.'   That breaks the tension and she laughs.

'Now, what do you make of Hardcastle? Involved?' I ask.

'With the murder? No way. He's a suit full of bugger all. On the make and ethically wanting, almost certainly. But involved in prostitution and murder? Especially something like this one? No, sarge, I just can't see it.'

'I agree, but I'm not sure he's told us the whole truth yet. We'll get him back in tomorrow and grill him some more.' Just as I suggest that we go to the canteen and get a cuppa, my phone rings and it's Harrison. The old fart doesn't even try to conceal the noise of the TV in the background. He's obviously knocked off for the day and is at home, but, typically, he lies. 'It's DI Harrison here. I'm too busy to get out to see the dead man's mam. It's got to be done today. So you do it, Snow. With or without Jenkins. Team meeting tomorrow at 9.30am to review where we are.'

'He's got a nerve,' I grumble as I put my mobile back in my jacket pocket. 'Lazy bastard's only plonked in front of Pointless, or some such crap on the telly and tells me he's too busy to go to Stevenson's mum. Christ on a bike, but he makes me sick.'

'Relax sarge,' says Jenkins with a twinkle in her eye. 'I've got the address from Helen. It's only in Deckham. We can get that done and then you can buy me a drink.'

'You're on,' I reply, as I follow her obediently out through the door.

It turns out that Mykel's mum lives in a tiny flat, located over a tattoo parlour on the Old Durham Road. It's in a part of Deckham that's so far been ignored by the gentrifiers and redevelopers. We pick our way carefully round the back, trying to avoid the ubiquitous dog faeces and other rubbish, which almost covers the access. The door looks like a good gust of wind would see it hanging open and, with little enthusiasm, I ring the bell. After a couple of minutes' wait we hear shuffling from behind the door and a loud curse, as someone fiddles with the lock. Jenkins rolls her eyes and smiles as we await our first sight of Mykel's mum. The door finally edges open a crack and a tiny, wasted face peers out at us. The voice, however, is something else entirely; a loud, grating noise that sounds like something hard being scratched along a pane of glass. 'Who the fuck are you? And what the hell do you want?'

I show her my warrant card, 'Police, Mrs Stevenson. We need to have a word.' The manner of her reply convinces me that she is incapable of stringing several words together without at least one expletive. I mean, I know that we police officers can use some pretty fruity language, but this woman is just off the scale.

'Oh, you fuckin' do, do ya?' she answers aggressively. 'Well we'll fuckin' see about that.'

I'm standing there, wondering whether I should just kick the door in and her with it, when Jenkins, bless her cotton socks, steps in with the sweetest smile. 'It's about your son and your daughter, Mrs Stevenson. We've got some very important news.'

'Why didn't that dozy shit you've got with ya say so then?' she grumbles, as she takes off the chain and opens the door. 'Make sure you bloody close it on your way in, shit,' she says, obviously to me. I think ruefully that the putrid smell filling the stairway argues for leaving it wide open.

The place is an absolute hovel, ridiculing the fact that it's located in the fifth richest country in the world. She collapses into a threadbare chair and gestures that we should sit on the tiny sofa. Neither of us are keen, but, given the news we have to impart, standing over the poor old sod is not an option. I say 'old', but, if she had Mykel and Kylie at anything like a normal age, I imagine she can only be somewhere in her forties. Christ, I think, she looks at least sixty.

Before either of us can say anything, Mrs Stevenson says, 'OK. I'm sitting on ma bum now, so let's hear it. Knowing them two, I can't believe it's anything sodding good.' She made it clear that these comments were addressed to Jenkins and I'm happy to leave this to her. Bloody hell, I think, I can't say I blame Mykel and Kylie from bailing out from this old witch.

The DC handles things perfectly, telling her that, tragically, her son is dead and that we suspect foul play. I almost laugh at this... 'suspect foul play,' with the poor devil's head half cut off! Mrs Stevenson shows no emotion, but merely nods, as if in agreement. 'I knew no good'd come of the miserable little bastard. What happened to him?'

'I'm afraid I can't tell you that at this time, Mrs Stevenson. All I can say, is that the circumstances of his death give grounds for suspicion.' There Jenkins goes again and I wonder if she's trying to wind me up and make me laugh, saying such things.

'Did he have any enemies?' the DC asks, pencil poised over her notebook.

'Enemies? Mykel?' Stevenson asks incredulously. 'How long you got, pet? The little bastard only had enemies. He was involved in drugs and worse. That's not like a bleedin' school playground, y'know!'

'Perhaps you could suggest some names,' Jenkins asks without much enthusiasm. I can tell she also thinks its a forlorn hope that the woman will finger anyone.'

'Names?' You can just bugger right off, pet. I ain't no snitch to the police.' She sits resolutely with her arms folded.

'What about your daughter? She's been hurt. Surely you'd like to see her and help us find who did this?'

For the first time since our arrival, Mrs Stevenson loses some of her truculence and becomes a little softer. 'I'm afraid she was lost to me when she went off with that no good shit of a son. I'm sorry, but there it is. Now, if you've quite finished..'

Jenkins asks if she has any idea where Mykel and Kylie have been staying and she simply shakes her head. It looks to both of us as if the old woman wants us out, so that she can dope herself up. That, or judging by the row of large plastic water bottles, full of what looks like cheap sherry, drink herself into oblivion. I leave it to Jenkins to be the first to stand and she hands a card to the woman with the request that she contacts us, if she can think of anything that might help our enquiry.

We both look uneasily at one another as, accompanied by the sound of howls of grief and pain, we make our way back down the stairs.

Neither of us is in the mood for a sociable drink and Jenkins drops me off at the station to collect my own car and get off back home. After being in such a place, all I can think of is getting under my shower and putting it on full blast.

Chapter Thirteen

7.30pm, Thursday July 7th 2016, Low Fell, Gateshead.

Olivia

'Had a nice day, pet?' asks the taxi driver, as soon as I am belted up in the back of the Toyota Hybrid. Now he comes to ask, I realise that, yes, I've had a lovely day, spent mostly in the company of my sister Christine.

As always, when I spend any time in my hometown,at some point we make the trip to the Garden of Remembrance at The Crematorium in Gateshead. Some years ago, we paid for a remembrance plaque to be placed there for my mam and dad, and I always like to go there and leave some flowers that I know mam would've liked. It was such a glorious morning that, afterwards, we took the bus to Gateshead Interchange and then on by Metro to Tynemouth. Having fortified ourselves with a cup of coffee, we walked along the front all the way to Cullercoats, where we enjoyed an excellent Ploughman's Lunch and half of shandy at Browns Salt House, before we headed back home on the Metro and bus. Of course, Christine was very interested in how I was getting on with JP, but there had been many other family and personal issues to take our attention away from that.

'Yes, thanks,' I reply to the driver, 'it's been a wonderful day. And it's not over yet.'

'Aye,' he says with a smile. 'You off to 'Six' for a meal, then? I've never been there myself, mind. It's a bit pricey for the likes of me, y'know. But I've heard that's it's a canny place.'

'I certainly hope so,' I reply. 'I'm meeting three old school friends for a bit of a catch up.'

'Old, pet?' he queries, attempting gallantry. 'Surely you don't mean that?'

We both laugh and he carries on his endless chatter, until we arrive at The Baltic Centre for Contemporary Art.

As the taxi pulls up, I feel a definite surge of pride that Gateshead has made such excellent use of what was, basically, an old flour mill. While some of the exhibitions it hosts might not be to everyone's taste, it nevertheless is a wonderful social resource. I gaze to my right and then to the left, over the river, and am immediately struck again by how successful the reclaiming of the quayside for dwelling spaces has been.

I make my way through the single story entrance into the building proper and the lift which will whisk me to the top floor and 'Six', the Baltic's rooftop restaurant. This is my first time at this particular eatery and I must admit that, initially, I'm very impressed. As I exit the lift, I'm straight into the Reception Area, with the bar and restaurant proper stretching along the length of the building. I ask for the bar lounge and am directed down a short corridor towards the river end of the restaurant. There, leather sofas and low coffee tables invite guests to enjoy a pre dinner drink. I immediately see Laura, perched rather nervously on a leather sofa, which commands a wonderful view upriver towards The Millennium Bridge, The Sage and The Tyne Bridge itself. Laura gets up, smiles and welcomes me into an embrace. 'Olivia! It's great to see you again. And after all these years!' I feel very happy that I told Jayne, another of our band of four old school friends, that I would be in Newcastle, as she had immediately devoted herself to making the arrangements for us all to meet for a meal.

'It must be at least ten years, mustn't it?'

'Nearer fifteen is my guess,' I reply with a shrug. 'But still, Laura, how're you keeping?'

In truth, my old friend looked exactly that - an old friend. The last years had not been overly kind and she had an exhausted look about her.

'Oh, mustn't grumble,' she says with characteristic stoicism. 'I keep plugging along y'know? Like we all do, I imagine. But tell me, have you ever been here before? It looks terribly expensive.'

Eying the half pint of lager she is nursing, I suspect that Laura, as a social worker, married to a teacher and with three kids, has to operate on a fairly tight budget. And typically, Jayne, a successful, child free barrister, had chosen this restaurant, with no thought of cost. Spontaneously I blurt out, 'Oh, I'm not sure. Anyway, Laura, I never treated you for putting me up all those years ago, did I? So, how about this is my treat for you tonight?'

As soon as I've said it, I regret it. What if she's insulted? Humiliated, even? God, Olivia. Sometimes you should just keep quiet.

I'm incredibly relieved, when Laura looks at me and says, 'Oh, Olivia. That really would be very kind of you. I've been so worried about what it all might cost.'

'Then say no more about it. No one needs to know. I'll pay your share and we can say that you're giving me the cash, cos I've no English money. Now, I think I'll get a glass of prosecco, will you join me?'

Laura beams and says, 'Why not? Lager's for everyday. Not for evenings like this!'

I order a bottle of extra dry Prosecco with four glasses, in anticipation of the arrival of the other two friends. While we're waiting for the wine, Laura asks me how I am enjoying the Opera North production of The Ring. I've hardly started with the superlatives when Amy appears. She and her husband, Eric, have worked for years to build up a company specialising in industrial size refrigeration units and, judging by her appearance, business is pretty good.

The waitress brings the bottle and, having filled four glasses, places the bottle in an ice bucket and discreetly removes the lager. Amy looks ready to propose a toast, but over the years in Switzerland, I've got used to taking the first drink only when all guests are present. So I say, 'Let's give Jayne another five minutes. She's only ten minutes late, after all.'

I needn't have bothered, because the final member of our quartet almost immediately appears, takes one look at the Prosecco and imperiously commands the waitress to bring a bottle of Chardonnay. 'Never touch that fizzy stuff,' Jayne says by way of explanation, 'rots your teeth you know.'

The three of us burst out laughing at the inappropriateness of the comment and we all embrace Jayne, before toasting ourselves and our old school. Most of the initial conversation concerns me and my visit back home. It's not long, however, before Jayne pointedly asks, 'What did you Swiss make of the Brexit vote then? More than a bit of a shock, I bet.'

'I'm not sure it was any more of a shock there, than it was here, to be honest,' I reply. 'You know, the Swiss have quite a high regard for Britain. I think they see some shared characteristics, in our sense of independence and not wanting to be dominated by a super huge EU.'

'Really?' says Jayne, as she takes an olive from the complimentary bowl left by the waitress. 'Well I, for one, don't agree with it at all. The triumph of 'The Thickies,' if you ask me.'

Thankfully, the political discussion is cut short when the waitress invites us to table. Jayne looks as if she wants to keep hold of her full glass of wine and the waitress smiles as she assures us that our bottles and glasses will be brought through by the staff.

The restaurant proper is a long, thin rectangular shape, which is great, as both long sides are all glass. Consequently, most of the tables have a window position. Almost all the tables are occupied and the place has a nice, lively feel to it. The decor is very modern, the tables and chairs verging on the functional, perhaps in keeping with the building's historical use. All in all, I must say that I like it. The waitress shows us to a very pleasant circular table, about two thirds of the way along , on the right hand side. But before we can sit down, something's clearly not right. Jayne's face is like thunder, 'What's this?' she barks at the startled waitress. 'I specifically requested a table on the other side of the restaurant. I insist that we are seated there.'

The young woman has probably never encountered a force of nature quite like Jayne in full flow and she stammers in response. 'I'm, I'm, I'm very sorry madam. If you'll just take a seat here for a moment, I'm sure we can sort this out.'

Amy, Laura and myself are perfectly happy with the table and sit, as requested. Jayne, however, refuses point blank and stands truculently, with her arms folded.

'Damn cheek!' she says, sufficiently loud to turn a few heads among the nearby diners. 'They know fine well that I always sit on the river side.'

'Come on, J,' Amy says, in a doomed attempt to avoid a scene. 'This table's fine. Sit down and let's have another toast to old friends.'

'No, I bloody well won't sit down, until that poxy manager comes here, himself, and explains the situation.' Laura looks uncomfortably at me and makes a discreet sign to indicate that she thinks Jayne is already a little drunk. I think, perhaps, she's right and our friend has already had more than a couple of glasses of wine, before she even arrived at 'Six.'

After a few minutes of bustling around in the bar area, the waitress returns with a man who looks barely twenty himself. 'I'm very sorry that you're not happy with your table Ms Kane, but I'm afraid..'

'Afraid?' she roars at him. 'You'll be afraid the next time I speak to the owner of this place! Now, give me the correct table and we'll say no more about it.'

'I'm very sorry, Ms Kane, but as you can see, all the tables on the other side are currently occupied. I'm afraid that there's nothing we can do.'

'Except piss off!' Jayne shouts. 'Right, girls, I'm off out of this crap dump. Come on, we'll find somewhere better.'

Amy, Laura and myself look uneasily at one another, before I say, 'We're perfectly happy here, Jayne. Look, just sit down and let's have a relaxed meal together.'

For one awful moment, she looks so furious that I think she's going to throw her glass of wine, which she is still holding, all over me. However, she knocks it back in one, declares that we were 'always spineless bitches' and marches out of the restaurant.

The 'floorshow' having ended, the rest of the diners turn back to their food and their conversations and Laura and Amy hide behind their menus. I call the manager over and say to him, 'Look, we're sorry about that. If you'd like us to leave...'

He looks at me as if I'm crazy. 'Not at all, madam. We're very sorry that your friend was unhappy with the table. I can assure you that 'Six' is very happy that you are here, as our guests, and we hope very much that you will have much more positive reasons to remember your visit here.'

He's charm personified and makes us feel much more comfortable about staying. Perhaps in order to send a message to the other diners, he insists on coming over personally to take our orders and to advise on a suitable choice of wine.

The waitress comes over, refills our glasses with Prosecco and offers us a beautiful little *amuse bouche*, 'with the compliments of the kitchen.' Amy raises her glass and says, 'Well, here's to our absent friend. May all her bottles of Chardonnay be bottomless.'

We all clink glasses and laugh. 'It's a shame,' says Laura, 'but Jayne's always been a bit hot headed, hasn't she? Remember that time on the school trip to Stratford upon Avon?'

'God, yes!' I agree, as long dormant memories flood back. 'And that poor young English teacher. What was his name now? Parsons?'

'No, he was called Perkins,' corrects Amy and we're off into half an hour of increasingly exaggerated memories of our time together at school.

As the perfectly pleasant evening wears on, I can tell that they're both being almost Swiss, in the way they are discreetly not bringing up my divorce. While we've not met for many years, we have kept in touch at birthdays and Christmases and they both know what has been going on in Geneva. So I decide to break the taboo and say, 'D'you know something? This is my first trip home, as a single woman, for more than twenty years. God! What a thought!'

They both laugh and we turn to a discussion of partners, children, even the price of property. As I suspected, Laura has had the greatest struggle, financially. At one point, Amy shakes her head and says admiringly, 'God, Laura, I don't know why anyone would want to do such an awful job. You get shit when you do your job and intervene and even more shit when you don't. It must drive you crazy.'

Laura nods and says simply, 'Somebody's got to do it, Amy. If I and others like me didn't, who'd look out for the most vulnerable, the weakest and the poorest?' There's not a shred of self righteousness about what she says. It's a simple statement of fact and all the more powerful for that.

'Well, thank goodness there are people like you, Laura,' I say, as I raise my glass of the red that we've moved on to, in toast to her and her many hard working colleagues.

Just then, my phone rings. I see that it's a Swiss number and my first thought is that there might be an issue with Sebastian. 'I'm sorry, 'I say, jumping up from the table, 'I'd better take this.' I can't see how the colour has drained from my face, so I'm a bit surprised at their evident concern. I find a quiet corner, near the lifts, to take the call.

A confused mixture of feelings rushes through me, as I hear JP's warm voice, 'Hi, Olivia. Just ringing to check that everything's OK for tomorrow.' I'm really not very good with phone numbers and berate myself for not recognising his and, as a result, jumping to all kinds of lurid conclusions about who was calling and why. He's evidently confused by my silence and asks with some concern, 'Olivia? Is that you? Is there something wrong?'

'Oh, hi JP,' I finally reply. 'No, I'm fine, thanks. Caught me a little unawares, that's all. Yes, let's meet up just before the group meeting at The Sage. Have you had a good day?'

'Sure have,' he says and I can almost see him smiling. 'I took a car up the coast towards Bamburgh. I never knew it was so beautiful up there. The beaches? Wow. They're like California!'

'If only we had Californian weather,' I add.

'Yeah, well, there is that, I guess. But it was a great day to be alive.'

Something in his voice sounded wistful and I change the subject. 'Did your business matter get itself sorted?'

'What do you mean?' he asks sharply.

'You know? The call you had to make in the interval of *Die Walküre*?'

'Oh, yeah. Sorry. Forgot all about it. Something and nothing in the end. What you up to now?'

'Oh, I'm just out for a meal with some old school friends.'

'Must be fun,' he says and I can once again sense a sort of loneliness about JP. Not surprising, I tell myself, as the poor man has recently lost his wife.

'Yes it is,' I agree, 'but not without its crazy moments.'

'Really?' he asks. 'What do you mean?'

'Oh, I'll explain tomorrow. See you at 2.30. Usual place.'

'You got it. Bye.' and he rings off.

I make my way back to the table and see my friends' anxious faces looking at me. 'Everything all right?' asks a concerned looking Laura.

'Oh, yes,' I reassure them brightly. 'It was just a friend who's also going to The Ring.'

'Anyone we know?' asks Amy in surprise. 'Only I can't really think of anyone I know who'd go to such a thing. Yuk! Now, had it been Robbie Williams..'

'Actually, it's someone I met on the plane coming over from Geneva. A really nice American.'

'Ooooh!' says Amy, rubbing her hands at the the thought of some interesting gossip. 'Tell us more!'

'There's not so much more to tell, really,' I say, as I try to articulate what I actually think about JP. 'He works for a bank in Switzerland. Like me, he's lived in Geneva for ages. And he's typically American, relaxed and charming.'

I can tell from her eager expression that Amy's not going to let this go without a struggle. Laura, who is by nature far more reserved, seems a little embarrassed by this turn in the conversation. Good. When I've had enough of Amy's poking into my private life, I'll enlist Laura to change the subject.

'What's he called? How old is he? Is he good looking?' asks Amy without a second's pause for breath.

'He's maybe a few years older that me and, yes, I suppose most would call him good looking. He's called JP.'

'Oh God!' moans a visibly deflated Amy. 'Why the hell do Yanks always have that stupid thing about initials. It's a real turn off.'

I explain about JP's parents' love of The Beatles and this amuses them both.

'So, you think you'll see him back in Switzerland?' Amy asks. 'You should, you know. He might have other friends who are good company. Especially after you and Laurent, you know...'

'He's just lost his wife to cancer,' I say, in order to throw a bucket of cold water over her matchmaking. 'So I think that might be a bit premature. Anyway, are you two planning any holidays this summer?'

JP isn't mentioned again and the evening breaks up after we've spent sufficient time to finish the wine, enjoy coffee and discuss our travels, planned and experienced. I insist on paying for us all, to which Amy agrees, only if I commit to meeting again the next time I'm back home. We all exchange up to date contact details and finish with a complimentary limoncello from the restaurant manager.

On the way back to Christine's in the taxi, I am left wondering how we, four gawky teenagers, turned into the four very different people we are today. Life, and living it, is the only answer my admittedly alcohol affected brain can come up with.

Chapter Fourteen

8am, Friday 8th July 2016, Newcastle City Centre Police Station, Forth Banks.

Sam

The team is already waiting when Harrison bustles through the door of the dull Incident Room. It's a bright summer morning outside and none of us look overly happy to be in such a poor environment. 'Right, DS Snow. Perhaps you could update us on your interviews last night?'

I explain that DC Jenkins and I visited Brown's Estate Agents, the letting agency for the unit in which Mykel Stevenson was found dead. I then invite her to give an account of the interview.

She completes this task in a quietly efficient way. I register again that she's a very impressive colleague and I reflect that I certainly wouldn't say no to her being my DS, once I get my promotion. 'So,' Harrison says eagerly, during a gap in her presentation, 'this Hardcastle character has no alibi at all for the time of death?'

I can see where 'Halitosis' is hoping to go with this, and I reply quickly, 'That's correct, sir. But we both got the feeling that he was in shock, when we told him about the murder. He readily confessed his role in allowing the property to be used by Stevenson. He did, however, deny that he knew it was for purposes of prostitution and he was definitely horrified at the idea that he might be a suspect in a murder investigation.'

'I agree with DS Snow,' Jenkins adds. 'OK, he certainly seemed a bit of a chancer, running daddy's business, while he's no doubt on the golf course. And we share the conviction that he was aware of what was going on at Hymers Court. But a killer? And killing like that? Somehow neither of us thinks so.'

Harrison is visibly disappointed, but isn't ready to give up on his prime suspect just yet. 'Right, Hutton. You dig around this Hardcastle character as much as you can. I want to know everything about him, especially anything dodgy. Try to get us a few names who we could ask about him. Does he have any enemies? What do other estate agents think of him and his business practices? And is he involved with anyone? When we know more, I'll have him and his receptionist back in for questioning. I'm not convinced he's out of the woods yet.'

Bold as brass, given his swerving of the task last night, Harrison asks me to give an account of the interview with Mrs Stevenson, the mother of Mykel and Kylie. When I've finished, he asks pointedly, 'Do you believe she's had no recent contact with them?'

'I do,' I reply. 'Though I'm not altogether convinced that she doesn't know where they've been dossing down. Maybe we should go back and press her a little more on that.'

Harrison immediately says that he will conduct the interview at the station and tells Sergeant Walters to sort out a car to bring her in.

DC Jenkins is in the middle of outlining our interview with the Vice Squad, when a young PC comes in with a piece of paper for me. I glance at it, but decide not to interrupt her account.

'I definitely think we should keep open the possibility of a connection with organised prostitution,' Harrison declares, even though Jenkins has made it clear that Vice are doubtful of any link. 'So let's keep close to Vice. Make sure we know, if and when they find out anything interesting.' He then turns to Walters and asks, 'Anything from CCTV?'

Walters coughs and explains, 'Well, sir, as you know we are very short staffed. But we've identified five CCTV cameras that should have been working. The tapes should all be in the station by 10.30 and Armitage will give them the once over.'

'Good,' says Harrison to Armitage. 'Make that a priority, son. Could be some vital information on those tapes. Now, anything else?'

'Yes, sir,' I chirp up. 'That was the forensics report on those pieces of metal found at the scene. As expected, no fingerprints and no evidence of them being involved in the assault. But, they definitely come from the same piece of metal.'

Jenkins whistles softly and asks, 'Bloody hell, sergeant. What do they think it was?'

'They can't be 100% certain, but they have confirmed that they're pretty sure they come from a long pointed dagger, or even a sword. Apparently, there's some sort of markings on them. Could be hallmarks. But, at this stage, Forensics doesn't know, if they're significant or not. '

'Right then, that looks to be our best lead so far,' barks Harrison. 'Dutton, you get a list of all outlets, in and around the city, that might supply such items. Snow, Jenkins, you two get yourselves around those places.

Ask if they've sold any long daggers, or swords recently. Show them the pieces and ask if they recognise them.

'But if the killer left the pieces deliberately,' I think aloud, 'isn't it really unlikely that they'll lead anywhere?'

'Possibly,' Harrison says. 'But, you never know. They might have been dropped by accident. Or we might get lucky, in that someone recognises something. It's our only definite lead so far, so let's follow it up.'

***

11am, Friday 8th July 2016, Low Fell, Gateshead.

Olivia

It was only about three quarters of an hour ago that, much to Christine's amusement, I staggered down the stairs, pleading for coffee and paracetamol. Always the caring 'big sis', she contented herself with a shake of the head and a rueful, 'Full on night, was it?'

Now, three cups of coffee and two painkillers later, I'm feeling sufficiently human, that the ringing of my mobile doesn't sound like the top of my head's coming off. Given the time difference with Santa Barbara, I doubt it can be Sebastian, but am nevertheless surprised to hear Laura's voice.

'Hi Olivia. Sorry to bother you, but I just wanted to say that I really enjoyed myself last night. It's been a long time since I had a girls' night out like that. And I especially wanted to thank you again for paying. It was very generous of you.'

'Yes, I enjoyed myself too,' I say, 'and forget about the bill. It was my pleasure entirely.' She's hanging on the other end of the line, not saying anything, but I can tell

123

there's something else. I don't really feel like waiting, till she's ready to speak, so I tell her that I'm just about to sit down to breakfast.

'Oh. Of course,' she says hastily, 'I should've thought. I'm sorry. It's just, I was wondering if there's any chance we could meet today, in town? There's something I'd like to talk with you about.'

I think about the busy day I have in front of me and ask, 'Could we not do it now? Over the phone?'

'Not really. It's not that kind of thing. It's OK if you don't have time.'

I think of all the occasions in the past, when Laura was kind of ignored by myself, Amy and Jayne and a wave of guilt washes over me. 'No, it's fine,' I find myself saying. 'Give me an hour and I'll see you in one of the cafeterias in Fenwicks.

'That's great, Olivia. Thanks a lot. Let's make it Majorca. And this time, it's on me.'

Christine looks at me sideways as I end the call. 'You're as soft as my pocket,' she says, 'always have been.'

When I arrive at Majorca in Fenwicks, it's so crowded that, at first, I can't see Laura anywhere. I'm quarter of an hour late, so I can't believe she's not here. I walk among the tables for the second time, before I spot her. To my surprise, she's not alone. I guess that's why I overlooked her the first time. She's sitting with a young woman who looks the spitting image of herself, when she was in her early twenties. It can only be her daughter and I begin to wonder whether I've been set up in some way.

'Hi, Olivia,' Laura greets me. 'Thanks very much for coming.' On seeing me shoot a questioning glance towards the other woman, she hastily adds, 'Oh. I don't think you'll remember Caroline. She's my eldest.'

'I think the last time I saw Caroline was when she was still in a pram,' I say pleasantly. 'You've certainly changed a lot since then. You're the absolute image of your mam at the same age.'

The young woman laughs, as if it's expected, rather than to express amusement or pleasure. There's something of the hunting dog about her and I begin to feel a little uncomfortable. 'Everybody says that,' she says pleasantly enough. But her eyes are shifty and dart from place to place. 'Would you like a coffee and a sandwich, or something? I'm just going to get us some more tea and a bite to eat.'

We all settle on tea and a cheese sandwich and Caroline leaves to bring the lunches. Laura looks uneasy and finally blurts out, 'I don't suppose you were expecting to see my daughter, were you?'

'Not really. Though it's a nice surprise,' I reply, not entirely truthfully.

Laura leaps on this platitude, 'I'm so glad you think so. 'Cos, to be honest, it's because of Caroline that I wanted to see you.'

'Really? I'm not sure what you mean.'

'Well, she's a reporter with 'The Chronicle' and she's got a chance to fill in for the Crime Correspondent for two weeks. He's on holiday, you see.'

'I still don't quite understand...'

'It's because you're a specialist in Abnormal Psychology. She just wanted to tell you something about the stories she's working on. See if you could suggest anything to help her with her approach. 'Cos, you know, if she can make a good impression with the editor, who knows what good it might do her?'

I frown, as I realise that I was right to have some doubts about coming to the meeting. But I don't suppose there's much I can do about it now. Nevertheless, I try to extricate myself from the situation. 'Oh, look, Laura. I'm really sorry, but, you know? I'm on holiday and, in any case, my field's more Applied Psychology, not Abnormal. Honestly, I really don't see how I could ...'

'Just listen to what she has to say, that's all. It'll only take the time it takes to have our lunch. And after, if you decide there's nothing you can say, then OK, no problem.'

Before I can reply, Caroline returns with a tray full of lunch and I realise that I'm trapped. Sitting across the table from her now, it seems to me that the facial resemblance to her mam is actually not so great. The colouring and general shape of the face is very similar, but there's something around the eyes and mouth that speaks to a much harder and uncompromising character.

'Has mam explained the situation?' Caroline begins in an extremely businesslike manner, as if she were a debt collector negotiating an agreement to pay. I sense Laura flinch at the directness of the approach and I reply equably, 'She has, yes. But I'm not sure how I can ...'

'Oh, I'm sure you'll be very interested, professionally, in what I have to tell you. It's about the murder that took place in Gateshead very early yesterday morning.'

'Surely you mean early on Wednesday morning? The death of the homeless man?' I reply in some confusion.

'No,' she says emphatically, though she's careful to keep her voice down in the still crowded restaurant. 'As I understand it, the police have already arrested someone for that. This was the killing of a young man in an empty commercial unit in Hymers Court.'

'Oh, I see. Well, I'm afraid I know nothing about that.'

'The police have revealed very little so far, but I have a good contact on the force and he's given me the lowdown.'

'Look,' I protest, 'I'm not sure that we should be discussing such things..'

'Oh, come on, Olivia,' she scoffs. 'You know how the world works. Of course the public has a right to know the details.'

It's the kind of self serving argument that I've heard many, many times and it makes me even more doubtful about offering any help to this hard faced, young woman. But before I can object, she has opened a Pandora's Box. 'It's like this. A brother was acting as pimp for his sister and they were using this commercial property, a grotty, closed down nightclub, for her activities. Early yesterday morning, someone knocked the sister out, stabbed the brother with a long dagger, or even a sword. Killed him outright, before half decapitating him.'

'I really don't think you should be...'

'But weirdest of all, was the police found some pieces of metal at the scene. They say they were almost certainly cut from a long dagger or sword. But the pieces came from a different weapon. Not the one that was used in the killing. How bizarre is that?'

She goes on to ask me a succession of questions about the psychology of a brother using a sister in such a way and what such things, deliberately left at the scene of the crime, might mean. I mutter some general banalities, hoping I'm making sense. Because, right now, I can only see and hear Claire, at the last meeting of the discussion group at The Sage, wailing about the killing of Geoff, 'the gentle giant.' I feel like the room is beginning to tilt, like a listing ship.

'Hey! Olivia?' Laura asks with concern. 'Are you alright, pet? Only you've gone a very strange colour. Caroline, go and fetch a glass of water.'

I'm grasping the edge of the table, in an effort to stop myself keeling over and look up to see Caroline's furious face. Evidently, she feels cheated at not getting the scoop that she craves.

'Go and get some water,' Laura repeats to her daughter, who sits, unwilling to move. 'For God's sake get a move on will you? Forget your bloody story for a second and think about somebody else!'

Caroline sullenly gets up and returns with a bottle of mineral water. The first sips start my recovery and, within a couple of minutes, I'm feeling fine. 'Heavens above,' Laura says, grasping my arm on the crowded table, 'you had me worried there, Olivia. But you look much better now. Do you feel OK? What happened?'

Actually, I've a pretty good idea what happened to me. But the last thing I want to do is discuss it in the presence of an unscrupulous reporter. Daughter of a friend or not. 'Oh, you know,' I say with a sheepish smile. 'I did have a bit more wine than normal last night. Maybe all that ghoulish talk made me feel a bit bilious.'

'I'm sorry,' says Caroline begrudgingly. 'But you must see, it's a hell of a story. It's not every day something like this happens in a sleepy dump like Gateshead.'

'Are you absolutely sure of the details?' I ask. 'About the brother and sister and the pieces of metal?'

'Of course I am. My contact is right at the heart of the investigating team led by DI Harrison. Can you give me anything useful for my story?'

She looks so hungry and desperate that I can't just tell her to get lost. Instead, I say, 'I'm sorry, I still don't feel so good. I need some time to recover and then I'll have a think about it. I'll get back to you later today, with whatever thoughts I have. How's that?'

Caroline's clearly able to spot a promise that the maker has no intention of keeping and simply stares at me with a sour expression. Laura, on the other hand, recognises that it was not a good idea to invite me to the lunch and says, 'That's perfect, Olivia. But get yourself back on track first. That's the main thing, isn't it Caroline?'

The young woman merely grunts and places a business card on the table, before standing and saying, 'Well, mam. It's time I was off back to work. Nice to have met you again, Olivia,' adding, in a voice dripping with sarcasm, 'I look forward to your call.'

We both watch her, as she makes her way out of the cafeteria, shoulder bag swinging alarmingly near the heads of the seated people. 'You shouldn't judge her too harshly, Olivia,' Laura says in defence of her daughter. 'The newspaper business, especially in the regional press, is a very difficult work environment for a young graduate in journalism. A lot of the old time servers aren't keen at all and she's had to fight and claw her way to where she is now.'

'I understand,' I say sympathetically, 'I'll do what I can.'

'Get yourself right, before you bother with it, OK?' she orders, before asking, 'now, should I call you a taxi to take you home?'

'No. I'm fine, honest. It was just a temporary thing.' I'm actually very keen for her to go, so that I can try to make some sense of my teeming, lurid thoughts. Not bothering with what I've just been told, I ponder grimly, is no longer an option for me. She also seems eager to be on her way, probably hoping that by the time we meet again, this embarrassment will have been forgotten. She'd be shocked, if I were to tell her that I'd definitely never forget this lunch.

I decide to walk down Grey Street, towards the Quayside. As usual, the base of Grey's Monument is abuzz with young people, taking in the sun and engaging in the everyday activities of chatting, laughing, flirting and joking. It's still lunchtime and the place is full of life. I, in contrast, walk almost zombie like. My mind struggles to process the new information it has and what I should do about it. After a good twenty minutes' walk, I find myself down by the river. Perhaps it's inevitable that I sit down on a wooden bench, facing The Sage.

As I watch the ebb tide slowly flow out towards Tynemouth and The North Sea beyond, I review what it is I know. It seems almost too incredible to be true. But, if I'm right, at least two more people are likely to die, within the next seventy two hours. But, what if I'm wrong? Or I'm not believed? I could make an utter fool of myself. Or be thought of as a cranky, middle aged woman with an overactive imagination. But do I have any right to regard my finer feelings as more weighty than my obligation to tell the police what I suspect? In the end, I decide, as I knew I would, that I have to go and find this DI Harrison and explain to him my theory and my fears.

Reinvigorated by my decisiveness, I march confidently across The Millennium Bridge and up, through The Sage towards the centre of Gateshead and the grim looking police station. The absolute assuredness I felt down by the river has evaporated somewhat, as I approach the bridge which leads to the entrance of the station. Not giving myself the time to reconsider, I push through the door and into Reception. As soon as the elderly desk sergeant raises his eyes from his papers, smiles and says, 'Now then, pet, what can we do for you?' I know it's too late to change my mind.

Chapter Fifteen

12.45pm, Friday July 8th 2016, Newcastle City Centre Police Station, Forth Banks.

Sam

It's not been a very productive morning. Jenkins and I have worn out what must be a month's allowance of shoe leather, pounding the streets of Newcastle and Gateshead. We've been searching for the weird and wonderful shops, where they might know something about the pieces of metal, found near Mykel Stevenson's body. Neither us, in our wildest dreams, thought that such bizarre places existed, let alone did an obviously good trade. But it was all a total waste of time.

As we sat, unenthusiastically toying with our lunch, in the noisy station canteen, our spirits were raised a little by the humorous account offered by a female PC, who'd sat in on 'Halitosis's' futile interview of Mrs Stevenson. From her account, the poor sod would have got off lightly, had he just been called a shit, like me! Armitage, who was also sitting with us, confessed that the CCTV footage was also useless. 'The only ones that might have been valuable were vandalised,' he moaned. In contrast to us, however, he had no problem tucking with relish into his Shepherd's Pie.

And now, to cap it all, I've been summoned to Harrison's office.

'Come in, Snow,' he says, a wide grin on his face and I know immediately that this not going to be welcome news. 'I've an interesting new lead for you to follow. A very intelligent woman has just come in to report a promising theory about the murder. Normally, I'd see her myself, but I just don't have the time and I don't want to keep her waiting. So, she's waiting for you down in Reception. At Gateshead nick.' He sits back with his hands folded across his weedy chest and I feel like punching him.

What a complete waste of my time. Reduced to dealing with the cranks and nutters. Well, I'm not having it, so I protest, 'With all respect, I think my time could be better.....'

He surprises me by the aggression of his response. I didn't realise the old, incompetent git had it in him. 'With all respect, SIR!' he bellows. 'And I'm not in the slightest bit interested in your respects, sergeant. You'll do as you are bloody well told and that's an end to it. As I said, she's waiting at Gateshead station, so you'd best yourself over there *tout de suite*.'

Before I turn to leave, he produces a triumphant smile, 'But I won't be holding my breath to hear what she's got to say. Know what I mean, son?'

I can hardly control my anger as I storm out of his office and barrel straight into Serena Jenkins. 'Oy!' she cries, 'watch where you're going. What's up with you, anyway?'

'Oh,' I hiss, 'that old wanker's gone and given me some crazy fantasist to interview. Apparently she has a, what was it he said now? Oh yes, a 'theory' about the murder.'

Jenkins smiles in sympathy, 'Relax, Sam. You know he's just trying to wind you up.'

'And he's bloody well succeeding,' I concede.

'If it's any consolation, there's nothing better to do. In my opinion, we've hit a brick wall.'

I'm still fuming as I enter the Reception area of Gateshead Police Station. It's a functional, sixties looking building and the Reception looks like some sort of Social Security place. Cheap plastic chairs, smell of disinfectant and a bored looking copper on the desk. Our great new witness is sitting alone on one of the chairs. Dressed as she is in stylish, black jeans, with a short jacket and a plain blouse, she's of an age that, to much younger men like me, is indeterminate. By that, I mean she could be anything between mid to late thirties and early fifties. But she does have lovely flowing red hair and it's two beautiful green eyes that look up and fix me with a confident stare, as I approach. 'Ms Olivia Clavel?' I ask with a smile.

'It's Doctor Clavel actually,' she says, as she rises to meet me.

'Oh, sorry. Doctor Clavel. I'm Detective Sergeant Snow,' I say, as I offer my hand. 'How may I help you?'

'I really hope that it's I who may be able to help you,' she says very correctly and I detect a hint of a foreign accent in there somewhere. French, perhaps? I don't really see the point of buzzing us through the secure door and conducting the interview in the station proper. Rather, I swivel my eyes from the desk officer to one of the two Interview Rooms which run down one side of the Reception. He nods in confirmation that they are free and I say to the woman, 'If you'd like to come with me, we can discuss this in a rather more private place.' She's not a witness as such, neither is she speaking under caution, so I am conducting the interview alone.

Following her into the small, dingy room, I get a very pleasant hint of what I guess is an expensive perfume and I reflect that Dr Clavel certainly doesn't match the normal, loony, time waster we often have to deal with in cases like this.

The room offers only a basic table with four , none too clean plastic chairs. I can't say I blame her for looking rather unhappy at having to sit on one of them and I shrug helplessly. 'Sorry. The accommodation isn't that great, is it?' She simply nods and smiles weakly. As soon as we are seated, and in an effort to break the ice, I say, 'Clavel? That's a French sounding name?'

'I was born in Gateshead, but I've lived in Switzerland for many years,' she cuts in.

'I see. And are you here in the UK on business?'

'Not that it's relevant,' she replies firmly, 'but I'm here to visit family and to attend 'The Ring Cycle' at The Sage.'

I haven't a clue what she's on about and ask her to explain. 'It's Opera North's production of all four of Wagner's 'Ring of the Nibelungen' cycle of operas. It started last Tuesday and will finish on Sunday.'

I'm none the wiser really, but simply nod and ask, 'and you believe you can help us with our enquiries into a recent death in the city?'

'If I'm right,' she says, impressively maintaining her facade of confidence, 'I'll be able to help you with two killings and, hopefully, help you to prevent more.'

Christ on a bike, I think. Despite appearances, it looks like I've got a real crackpot here. She quickly challenges my extremely dubious expression. 'Oh, I realise, sergeant, that you probably think I'm absolutely stark, staring mad. Believe me, initially, I was very sceptical myself. But I've taken a couple of long hours to think about it and now I'm convinced that I'm right.'

I figure that the sooner I get her to outline her bonkers ideas, the sooner I can thank her most sincerely and show her the door. So I say, very seriously and politely, 'Perhaps you could start at the beginning?'

'Well,' she says, 'I suppose the true beginning was on Wednesday afternoon, when Claire burst into our Ring Discussion Group.'

'I'm sorry,' I interrupt, 'who's Claire and what's this group?'

She pins me with a challenging look, 'Are you not going to take notes, sergeant? Surely that's normal procedure?'

I hastily pull my notebook from my jacket pocket and, in an attempt to re establish some of my authority, I say firmly, 'Now, if you'd just answer my questions, I'll decide what's relevant to the enquiry.'

She seems happy with this and begins, 'Claire is a retired Librarian and is a member of Opera North's pre performance discussion group. As am I. It's a group that meets before each performance to discuss themes relevant to the upcoming opera.' I nod to indicate she should go on. 'She came in to Wednesday's meeting very upset, because she had just been told about the murder of the homeless man, earlier that day.'

I sit forward, more interested now, and ask sharply, 'Do you think she knows something about it?'

'Oh no. Nothing like that. It's what she called him that was significant. Geoff the Gentle Giant.'

I'd also heard other homeless people and witnesses call him this, but I can't see it has any relevance. Feeling incredibly frustrated at this waste of my time, I sigh theatrically, put down my pen to indicate my lack of interest and ask, 'And just how is that significant?'

She smiles at me and I have the strangest feeling that this very attractive woman is far from the usual neurotic, attention seeker. 'May I explain that in a minute, please?'

'Of course,' I find myself saying, 'please go on.'

'The next bit is a little bit awkward,' she says, 'because I'll have to tell you things that I'm almost certainly not supposed to know.'

This pricks my interest again and I say, 'Really? You'll have to explain.'

'Well, first I want your assurance that my informant will not get into any trouble. Otherwise, we'll just stop this now.'

'Until I hear what you're going to say, I'm not sure I can give you such an assurance.'

'Very well,' she says, standing. 'On your head be it. With your permission, I'll bid you good day, officer.'

If you'd told me ten minutes ago that this witness would be offering to leave, after so little wasted time, I'd have been euphoric. But, unaccountably, I actually want to hear what she has to say. 'No, wait. Alright. If what you say helps to bring the criminal to justice, we'll not take any action against your informant.'

She smiles, as if she has won some sort of skirmish to establish her credibility and, once again, I register that she's a very interesting woman. 'Well, at lunchtime today, I met the daughter of a friend of mine. She works as a reporter. She told me some details of the killing that happened early yesterday morning.'

My antennae switch immediately to red alert at the mention of a reporter. Nevertheless, I try to keep my voice even, 'Oh, really? And what might those have been?'

'I was told that the man killed was the brother of a young woman who was injured.'

'I think you'll find that this information has already been, or is about to be, in the press,' I say, disappointed that this seems to be going nowhere.

'Really?' she says without batting an eyelid. 'I'm afraid I haven't kept up to date with local news. Anyway, I was also told about something that you found at the scene of the crime.'

Now this had definitely not been revealed to the press. So this woman definitely knows something she shouldn't. Unless, of course, she herself is involved. I quickly dismiss that thought from my mind and ask 'What exactly do you mean we found something?'

'You found some pieces of metal that you think came from a dagger or a sword. Well, I can tell you that they definitely came from a sword.'

This is actually getting quite serious now and I raise my hand, 'Whoa there. Slow down. Let's suppose this information of yours is true, and I'm not, I stress, I'm not saying that it is. How do you know that this was part of a sword?'

'Ah well, now, sergeant,' she says with a beguiling smile, 'to answer that, I'll have to explain my theory about how the killings are linked.'

Now I have never, for one second, believed in the old tramp's confession to the first killing and what this woman said has really shaken me. So I decide to ask DC Jenkins to join us for Dr Clavel's explanation.

✳✳✳

1.45pm, Friday 8th July 2016, Gateshead Police Station.

Olivia

The detective excuses himself, saying that he will return in a couple of minutes and that I should stay where I am. Rather sweetly, he also asks if I would like anything and I ask him for a glass of water. He smiles, causing his piercing blue eyes to twinkle and his whole face to take on a friendly, almost handsome appearance, as he leaves the room.

Maybe it's a sign of my inexorably advancing years, but this policeman really does seem very young. It's not just his narrow jeans, pale shirt and short leather jacket. Nor is it his trendily undercut hair. It's a psychological thing, I suppose. He reminds me of my students back in Geneva. Still, I decide, at least he's not thrown me out on my ear, which shows that he has an open mind to match his boyishly open face.

After waiting for twenty minutes, I'm beginning to think that Sergeant Snow has been distracted by more pressing priorities. The door, however, suddenly bursts open and he follows a statuesque, young woman with long, blond hair tied back in a ponytail, into the room. He's carrying a carafe of water in one hand and three glasses in the other and skilfully kicks the door shut, before sitting on the same side of the table as his colleague. 'This is Detective Constable Serena Jenkins,' he says pleasantly, 'and she will be sitting in on the rest of this interview.'

In one sense, I feel pleased, because this is surely the first sign that the police may take my information seriously. On the other hand, for some reason I feel discomfited by the intrusion of another officer.

'Now, Dr Clavel,' he suggests, 'perhaps you could explain how and why you think that the two recent killings are linked.'

'OK,' I begin, 'If we consider the first killing. This was a homeless man, who was so tall that he was called a 'Gentle Giant,' and who was basically beaten to death. Agreed?'

The female officer looks bored and leaves it to Snow to say, 'Agreed.'

'The murder took place in the hours immediately after the performance of *Das Rheingold*, the first of Wagner's Ring Cycle of operas, which finished shortly before 11pm on Tuesday 5th July. Agreed?'

Snow is shuffling uncomfortably now and replies, 'We estimate that the murder took place in the early hours of Wednesday 6th July. So, yes, agreed. But so far, you're only telling us what is in the public domain.'

'But possibly what you don't know,' I explain, as my heart beats ever faster in anticipation of their response, 'is that a giant is killed in exactly the same way in *Das Rheingold.*' The two police officers exchange troubled glances. 'The giant Fasolt is bludgeoned to death by Fafner.'

'Oh, look, Sergeant Snow,' begins DC Jenkins dubiously, 'with all due respect, this is just...'

I raise my hand to stop her in mid sentence, 'Coincidence? Yes, it could very well be. But before you reach a verdict, please hear me out.'

She sits back into her chair and Snow gazes at the ceiling, as if he's thinking he might have made a terrible mistake in taking me seriously. I don't care. I've come here to say what I have to say and I carry on, undeterred.

'OK, let's turn to the second killing. This was the murder of the young man. He was killed by means of a lethal wound, inflicted by a long dagger, or a sword. His sister was present at the scene of the murder and some pieces of metal that were cut from another sword were found by the body.'

The female detective looks shocked and rounds on me, 'How the hell do you know that?' she demands aggressively. 'There's been a total media block on that information.' She then turns towards Snow and stares at him accusingly.'

The detective sergeant initially looks startled by this and then a hint of anger crosses his face, 'Don't look at me like that. I didn't say anything. Why on earth do you think I asked you to sit in on this? She says she got the information from a reporter.'

'Which reporter?' DC Jenkins demands. 'That's not possible.'

'Oh yes it is,' I say with assurance, 'but how I found out isn't really the point. The point is that this killing took place in the hours immediately after the production of *Die Walküre* at The Sage. And this opera also contains a strikingly similar death.'

Both detectives look sharply at me and I realise that this is where they begin to entertain my theory, or they don't. 'There's a brother and sister in the opera and Siegmund, the brother, is killed by a single sword thrust, when his sword is broken into pieces by the god Wotan. Don't you see? Forget all the stuff about gods.

Essentially, we have a brother and sister, the brother's killed with a sword and pieces of a sword are scattered near the body. Now I call that a bit too much of a coincidence, don't you?'

'So, what exactly are you suggesting here, Dr Clavel?' asks Snow. 'A crazy person who goes about killing people in the manner of Wagner's operas?'

'I'm not sure, but it's certainly a possibility, isn't it?'

'There's one massive thing wrong with your theory, Doctor,' says DC Jenkins in triumph. 'We already have a signed confession for the first killing. And the person in question was in police custody when the second killing took place. Rather blows your fairy story out of the water, wouldn't you say?'

I'm shocked to hear this, but also interested to note that Snow is looking very pensive and saying nothing.

'You say you're a doctor?' Jenkins asks. 'What kind of doctor, may I ask?'

I can see where this might be going and try to answer without sounding overly defensive. 'Actually I'm a professional psychologist.'

Jenkins looks like she's won first prize in The Lottery. 'And what kind of psychologist would you be, doctor?'

'I specialise in Applied Psychology,' I reveal and see her about to speak again. So I quickly assert, 'But I fail to see how that has any relevance, other than, perhaps, to lend my information a greater weight.'

'Depends on how much credence you give to academic theories,' DC Jenkins mutters and I stand up in anger.

'Look,' I protest, 'I've come here, in good faith, to present you with some information and some ideas, which might help you to understand two killings and, perhaps, prevent two more.'

'What do you mean 'prevent two more'?' Jenkins asks sharply. 'Are you saying we have a serial killer on our hands and he'll strike again?'

'Before I knew that you already had a confession for the first murder, I'd have said these crimes were almost certainly committed by the same person. And that this person would probably go on to kill twice more. But now, I have to admit that, maybe, it is all just a bizarre set of coincidence. I'm sorry, officers, it begins to look as if I have, after all, been wasting your time and mine.'

I feel utterly deflated, foolish and humiliated. I was so certain that I was right. But how can I argue with a signed confession?

DS Snow is sitting in silence, staring at a dirty mark on the wall, as if it holds the answers to questions which are obviously swirling around in his head. He seems happy to leave DC Jenkins to conclude the interview immediately, by standing and saying, 'I'm sure I speak for the Northumbria Police, when I say that I accept that you came here in good faith, to offer us the benefit of your thoughts on these recent tragic events. Neither of us believes that you deliberately intended to waste police time. At the same time, however, we both now recognise that there is nothing to be gained from considering your 'theory' further.' I wince as she manages to make the word 'theory' sound absurd, idiotic even.

She then turns to Snow and asks, 'It does, however, leave open the question as to how Dr Clavel knew certain information about the second killing. Perhaps we should interview her about that, sergeant?'

Snow grunts and turns towards us, his face betraying a rapidly churning mind, 'Err, no, that's fine, DC Jenkins. You get on your way back to Newcastle. I'm sorry to have called you in. I'll see to that and then see the lady out. We can call her back in again, if necessary.'

Jenkins doesn't look altogether happy with this, but clearly doesn't want a full scale row in front of me. She stands, shakes my hand and leaves without another word. As soon as we are alone, Snow rubs both hands through his hair, pulling it tight over the back of his head. I can see that he is disturbed and say, 'Look, Sergeant Snow, I'm really very sorry....'

Suddenly, he stares at me and says, 'According to your theory, what would the killer do next? Can you predict who he will kill?'

I'm totally nonplussed and reply softly, 'But I thought the other detective just said you have a signed confession for the first killing?'

'Never mind that. Can you say what he'll do next?'

I'd not expected to be asked this question and, if I'm honest, I'm a still a little thrown, 'Well, er, let me think, the next opera is *Siegfried*. It's on tonight. So, first, if I'm correct, and if the perpetrator maintains his current pattern of behaviour, you'll have another murder, some time early tomorrow morning.'

'But who? Will he have already identified his victim?'

'Again, if I'm correct, I'm certain that he will, yes. Because, if his perverse intention is to mirror deaths in the operas, as closely as possible, he couldn't afford to rely on chance to find the 'right' victim.'

'So, have you any idea who might be in danger?'

I rack my brains, trying to recall the plot of *Siegfried*, especially any significant deaths. 'Let's see. Siegfried kills a giant dragon, so I can't see how that will work. Hang on, he also kills Mime with his sword.'

'Does this Mime have any recognisable characteristics?'

'Yes. In the opera, he's a dwarf.'

'Christ Almighty. That's a fat lot of use. We can't put out a warning to all very short people to stay indoors, can we? Is there nothing else special about him?'

'Not that I can think of. I'm sorry.'

He stands up and smiles. The tiredness and strain on his face are plainly visible. 'Well, Dr Clavel, in the nicest possible way, I sincerely hope you're wrong.'

I grimace back at him, 'Believe me, Sergeant Snow, so do I.'

'Please give me your contact details, in case I need to speak with you again and then I'll show you out.'

'But what about the issue of the journalist?'

'I'll sort that out. I gave you my word and I'll stick to that.'

Once we are back in the Reception Area, I ask him why he didn't just leave it, as his colleague had done. 'I can't really say,' he answers, furiously running his hands through his hair again. 'I think, most likely, it's all a weird coincidence. But you never know. Please don't mention anything of this to anyone else. And I mean anyone else. OK?'

He then says something that surprises me and, actually, causes me to see him in a much more favourable light, 'In the meantime, Dr Clavel, try to put it all out of your mind and enjoy the remaining operas.'

I'm rather touched by his concern and, as I shake his hand, I say, 'Thank you very much, Sergeant Snow. And I can assure you that I know when, and how, to keep my mouth shut.'

Chapter Sixteen

Olivia

'Get me there as quickly as you can, please. I'm dreadfully late,' I plead with the taxi driver, who has just picked me up at Christine's house in Low Fell. 'I should have been at The Sage three quarters of an hour ago.'

'Aye, you young lassies,' the elderly driver gently chides, 'You're always dashing about. And in any case,' he adds, while smiling at me through the rear view mirror, 'a bonny lass like you. He shouldn't complain about a little wait.'

After the conclusion of the meeting with Snow, I took a taxi back to Christine's and, having taken one look at my harassed state, she sat me down to a cup of tea and a stottie cake sarnie, made with ham and pease pudding. 'That's what you need inside you, Olivia. Some proper Northern food. Not all this 'Nouvelle Cuisine' or whatever it's called.'

I laughed and replied, 'God, sis. You're only about twenty five years out of date!'

In truth, I'd barely touched the sandwich at lunchtime, and the Geordie delicacy did taste good so, a quick shower and change later, I was ready for the taxi to take me to The Sage. I'd followed Sergeant Snow's instruction to say nothing about my interview with the police, or about the information I had acquired. I figured that was the least I owed him, after so obviously wasting his time.

Now, sitting in the taxi, I calculate that I'll arrive about half way through the discussion group. I'd wondered whether or not to give it a miss, but had decided that I should get back to normal behaviour, as quickly as possible. And, in any case, I hadn't replied to any of the several voicemails left by JP, after I'd failed to meet him at the agreed time. I didn't want him to think I was just being offhand.

The taxi does a great job getting me there quickly and at 3pm on the dot, I rush through the entrance to The Sage and make for the Squires Seminar Room. I'm still outside the door, but I can already hear raised voices inside. Male, of course. Good Grief! Who'd have thought that opera would generate such strong feelings? Tentatively, I open the door and smile in apology, 'Sorry, I'm late, everyone. Hope I'm not interrupting...'

'Not at all,' gushes Gideon. Evidently, he's happy for anything to create a kind of time out in the argument that had been raging. Silence reigns, as I make my way around the table, to find my usual seat next to Gideon. I catch JP's eye. I'm not quite sure what I see there, but I mouth 'Sorry' and he at least nods in acknowledgement. I feel bad enough about wasting the police's time. If JP takes the hump, I'll be very cheesed off.

'I'm sure we'll all agree that we've given the topic of concert versus full stage productions a decent airing,' says a relieved looking Gideon. 'I think, maybe, we should turn to some of the themes which are seen as key to the opera *Siegfried* itself.' Seeing the many heads nodding in agreement, he asks, 'Now, does anyone have any topic they'd like to discuss?'

Faced with a set of blank faces, he says, 'Well. One thing that has exercised many is the question of the character of Siegfried himself. In particular, is he a hero, a fool or, perhaps a heroic fool? Is there anything there for us?'

'That's a very interesting topic and I'm really glad you've raised it,' says Leonard eagerly. 'I've always found Siegfried by far the most interesting character in the whole cycle.' As I glance towards Leonard, I catch sight of JP. He certainly doesn't look so thrilled with the topic. In fact, he looks thoroughly uncomfortable. Perhaps he thinks it's going to lead to more arguments and the poor man's already had enough of that today.

Unaware and uninterested in the reaction of the other group members, Leonard ploughs his own furrow. 'Of course, we must see Siegfried as a hero. And a good natured, praiseworthy one to boot. Frankly, I can't see how any other interpretation has any credibility whatsoever.' I know it's not a nice thing to say, but I do feel that there's something deeply unpleasant about him, even when, as on this occasion, he is making a fair point.

Leonard's cold smile demonstrates that he's clearly enjoying his challenge to the rest of the group and I wonder who'll pick up the gauntlet and give him the argument, he so obviously craves. To my surprise, it's Viktor, the music student from Germany, who asks pleasantly, 'Really, Leonard? What evidence do you have to support such an assertion?'

Leonard grins to reveal unnaturally pointed teeth. He looks like a predator which has just seen his quarry walk straight into his trap. He steeples his fingers and says in a polite, but at the same time an almost vicious way, 'Well now. What should I say first? Let's begin with his heroic qualities, shall we? For a start, he slays a fierce dragon. He destroys Wotan's spear, thereby ending the god's power, when all others are terrified of it, and of him. And, of course, he walks through and puts out a circle of magic fire and in so doing rescues Brünnhilde from her imprisonment and sleep. Must I give more evidence of his bravery and heroism?'

'It's odd,' begins Viktor with uncharacteristic provocation, 'but I've always seen Siegfried as a musclebound, lumbering, even clownish thug.'

Leonard's previously smiling face rapidly darkens, like a summer sky, when the thunder clouds roll in. 'He's unkempt in appearance, brutish in his manners and easily manipulated by others. In short, he's a thorough oaf.'

Leonard looks as if the criticism has been levelled at himself, personally. Struggling to bring his emotions under control, he smiles crookedly and replies, 'A pretty standard, and in my view, worthless feminist critique, which ignores the positive characteristics of Siegfried.'

'Such as?' an emboldened Gillian demands. It looks like it's 'let's gang up on Leonard' time. However, on this occasion, I fear that they've chosen the wrong ground, on which to fight him.

'I'm really glad you asked that,' Leonard says. 'We could begin by remembering that Siegfried, in common with many mythical heroes, stems from humble origins, yet seems almost predestined to become a world hero. He is not at all ambitious for himself. When it comes to The Ring itself, he has no interest in the power it gives to the person who possesses it.'

'That's true,' interrupts David, almost talking to himself. 'After all, he treats it like a trinket, giving it away as a gift to Brünnhilde.'

'Thank you for that,' hisses an obviously irritated Leonard. The man clearly welcomes no contributions from others, when he is in full flow. 'As I was saying,

Siegfried couldn't care less about the curse on The Ring. He is above such petty human concerns. He also shows no pride, or self regard. He sees his extraordinary feats as perfectly ordinary. He's an utter paragon. How can he be viewed otherwise?'

I decide that I've heard enough of all this and say, 'With regard to the issue of fear and Siegfried's utter lack of it. I suppose this could be regarded as heroic, as Leonard evidently does. It could also be seen as a mark of stupidity. Put bluntly, Siegfried is too stupid to recognise danger, as surely we mortals must. It is not a positive thing to show no fear of something, of which you are ignorant. Were that the case, the infant, which doesn't know the danger of fire, would be heroic, like Siegfried.'

'Exactly!' agrees Viktor quickly. 'Siegfried's 'heroic quality' more accurately reflects his weakness and ignorance, than it does his strength.'

'On the other hand,' I continue, 'what has always struck me about the opera *Siegfried* is how central Nature is to the plot.'

'That's very interesting,' says Gideon, eager to seize on an idea that may lead the discussion into less confrontational waters. 'It certainly could be argued that Nature figures more in *Siegfried* than any of the other parts of 'The Ring'.'

'Yes,' agrees Claire, 'I love the way that most of it is set in dense woodland. It makes me think of happy childhood summer holidays.'

Leonard snorts with derision, but is cut off by Gillian, 'And I've never been that taken with the 'hero' Siegfried. I much prefer him as the young man who learns to speak with the woodbird and who plays in the forest with bears. He even calls one his friend. That's the Siegfried I like. The man who is positively disposed towards nature. Definitely not the thug, waving his sword about.'

Gideon tries to sum up the discussion by saying, 'Perhaps, after all, we should treat Siegfried in the same way that we treat Wagner, his creator. We should rejoice in his positive characteristics and try not to dwell too much on those we might regard as more dubious. Well, thanks very much for attending and I hope to see you all at our last scheduled meeting which, as you all know, is on Sunday afternoon, before the performance of *Götterdämmerung*.'

As the others slowly file out of the room, Leonard still looking far from pleased, I touch JP on the sleeve and indicate that I'd like him to wait for a minute. 'I'm really sorry that I was late, JP', I begin. 'I'm afraid something really urgent came up.' I had toyed with the idea of telling him, both about my theory concerning the killings and my interview with the police. In the end, I felt that, to do so, I would have to explain about the pieces of the sword and this would break my word to Sergeant Snow. So I keep my silence and make up an excuse.

He looks at me with what is, perhaps, a more distant expression than usual, 'Something family related, I guess.'

'That's right. I'm sorry. Anyway, shall we get a quick drink before the performance starts?'

***

4pm, Friday 8th July 2016, Newcastle City Centre Police Station, Forth Banks.

Sam

Jenkins has really, really pissed me off. She only went straight from the interview with Dr Clavel and told Harrison that she was a 'one hundred percent, copper bottomed, fruit cake.' He, of course, lapped it up and he's been making sarcastic comments ever since I got back to the Incident Room. I decide to have it out with her and suggest we go for a quick coffee to plan our late afternoon schedule. We find a table in a quiet corner of the canteen and she sits down facing me. In stark contrast to my grave expression, her eyes are twinkling with amusement. Let's see how long that lasts.

I dive straight in, 'What the hell's that all about, Serena? I thought we were mates, as well as colleagues?'

She sips her coffee and looks at me as if butter wouldn't melt, all wide eyed and innocent. 'What do you mean, sergeant? You surely can't be talking about that middle aged, attention seeking nutcase we wasted our time on?'

'I certainly, bloody well am,' I hiss in reply. 'Let's talk about whether she's a loony in a minute. The first thing in my book is that, if we're going to work together, we stick together. Especially as far as little shits like 'Halitosis' are concerned. You know he bloody well hates me, because Quayle's fingered me to replace him. He wants to pack it in, but he can't stand the thought of someone else, and especially someone like me, taking over. He's just a peevish old git.'

'Oh, come on, Sam,' she says, a bit more defensive and concern wrinkling her immaculately made up face. 'It was just a bit of a joke. Christ knows, we need a laugh, whenever we can get it on cases like this. And that woman was a crackpot.'

The surprise, even astonishment sweeps across her face, as I say, 'Well, I, for one, am not so sure about that.'

'What?' she explodes. 'You can't be serious! Quite apart from her 'theory' being utterly bleeding bonkers. What was it now? Oh yes. All to do with bloody Wagner and his operas, or some such crap? Give me a break! This isn't a film, it's boring, unfashionable Gateshead. Don't glamourise it. Anyway, quite apart from that, in case you've forgotten, we've got a signed confession for the first killing. That's her idea out the window straight away. At least the weirdo had the good grace to accept it.'

I'm shocked by the aggression in Jenkins's voice. What the hell's going on here? As an educated copper, I thought she'd be much more open minded. I decide not to make matters worse by taking her on about that, but choose to reply quietly, 'That's just it, Serena. That's just damned well it. I think Harrison fitted that old guy up for the first one. I was there, don't forget. I spoke to him before anyone else. No way did he do it. You know what 'Halitosis' is like. Not above a bit of leaning on people and it wouldn't have taken much to scare the crap out of that poor old sod.'

To be fair, Jenkins now looks a bit embarrassed, 'Oh, Sam. I'm sorry. But why in God's name didn't you tell me what you were thinking about the first killing? How the hell am I supposed to know? Read your bloody mind?'

'It's OK,' I accept. 'All this shit's as much my fault as yours. I suppose I just lost confidence, after I took my concerns to Quayle and she gave me a flea in my ear. In front of Harrison too. Look, let's just stick together from now on, right?'

She smiles gently and reaches across to touch my hand on the table, 'Of course, Sam. But, honestly, tell me. Do you really believe all that stuff. About giants and swords? It just sounds utterly crazy.'

She leaves her hand on top of mine, creating a new feeling of intimacy between us. I look down at it , then look up at her and shrug, 'I just don't know, Serena. I bloody well wish I did, but I don't. I know all this Wagner stuff sounds preposterous. But I can't get away from the fact that I believe Harrison fitted up the old tramp for the first killing. If I'm right, then Dr Clavel drew our attention to some remarkable coincidences, didn't she? I've checked out online what she said about the operas and she's right. It's definitely made me think.'

'But even if she's right, and I'm not for one second saying I think she is, how exactly does it help us?'

'I'm not sure it does. But we did talk about that after you'd left.' Jenkins narrows her eyes at this information. 'I asked if she had any other thoughts and she said that, if she was right, the killer would strike, during the period between the end of the next performance and tomorrow morning.'

'Hang on, you mean tonight?'

'Yes. She also said that she believes the killer would already have identified his victim. Because, of course, the victim will have to follow the pattern of the opera.'

'What exactly does that mean?'

I shrug and smile helplessly. 'Look, I know this sounds bizarre, but she says that he'll kill someone who is very short, in order to mirror the killing of a character in the opera who's a dwarf.'

Jenkins looks at me with what amounts to pity in her eyes. 'You know, Sam, maybe you should keep that bit to yourself. After all, there's not much we can do to prevent it.'

'I can't do that, Serena. I couldn't live with myself, if Clavel is right. I'm going to speak to Harrison about it. If he won't listen, I'll try to speak to Quayle. Again. I don't care if they both think I've lost the plot. I'm going to insist that a warning is issued to all our beat personnel to be extra vigilant tonight.'

'Christ, Sam. If she's right, I'll be the first to hold up my hands.'

'Believe me, Serena, I don't know whether I want her to be right or not.'

Chapter Seventeen

Olivia

I've never felt anything like this before, when I've been in a theatre, cinema or opera house. My flesh is crawling, my heart is pumping like I'm doing a sprint and my eyes are darting all over the place. It's near the end of Act Two of *Siegfried* and I've just watched Siegfried kill the dwarf Mime with one blow of his sword. When I register what I've seen, my mind begins to race. I think about the dreadful prediction I made and I begin to wonder is *he* here? Did *he* just watch the same scene as I did? Thinking about how magnificent the music and singing are, I'm appalled at the possibility that *he*, at this very moment, is being inspired to carry out his own perverted version later tonight.

All of these thoughts take my mind away from what I think is one of the most beautiful parts of the whole cycle, where the Woodbird talks to Siegfried. The singer playing the part of the bird is located high above the stage on the side balcony. The extra lighting, used to pick her out, casts a glow over a significant part of the audience, sitting, captivated, in the stalls below. The music fades from my conscious mind, as I am unable to banish the thought that, as I look down over the sea of heads, I am actually looking at *his* head. Despite a good few years working in the field of Applied Psychology, I find this the creepiest of feelings. To know that *he's* almost certainly in the same room as me, in all probability eagerly anticipating what *he* is going to do in the early hours of the morning. It's the first time that I've been directly involved in such a situation and I try deploy my rational mind to dismiss, as simply too outlandish, this whole train of thought. I fail, and for one hyper-moment, I actually consider standing up and shouting at the top of my voice. Challenging the bastard to show his evil face.

I sense that the person seated next me is casting quick, nervous glances in my direction. I realise with alarm that my body is as stiff as a board and I force myself to relax. I tell myself that I'm wrong; that the police have the man who committed the first killing; that the pattern I saw was just a fearful coincidence.

But as I walk out of the hall at the end of Act Two, I find myself studying each person, hoping in some way that *he* will give himself away and I won't have to awake tomorrow, fearful that my prediction has come true.

It's a ninety minute interval and I've arranged to meet JP to get something to eat. I certainly feel ready for something to eat, as I've only had the half stottie with Christine, since my breakfast of coffee and paracetamol. It even occurs to me that hunger could be contributing to my febrile state. When I think back to the me, before the meeting with Laura's daughter Caroline, I seem like a different person. The concerns I had then seem paltry, in comparison to the burden I now feel weighing down my spirits. It's truly incredible how something as banal as a meeting for lunch, can change a whole life so quickly and decisively.

I take my time to descend the sweeping staircase which leads to the upper levels of Sage One. I'm one element of a human flow and I cannot prevent myself from looking, more carefully than perhaps I should, at all the male members of the audience. Could I have just brushed shoulders with *him*? Was that *him* who just smiled, as he stopped to let me pass? I try again to pull myself out of this fixation, by berating myself for assuming that the killer is a man. Certainly, Snow gave no indication that the police are working on that assumption. I finally reach ground level and it's with genuine relief that I see JP. He's standing, gazing out of the huge glass wall, towards the skyline of Newcastle, which is bathed in the evening sun, on the far bank of the Tyne. My heart contracts, as I recognise that this is truly a beautiful setting, that the performance is so wonderful, and yet. And yet, here I am, becoming obsessed with something so deranged and evil.

Perhaps JP sees my reflection in the glass, as it approaches him, for he turns when I am just a few feet away. He seems relaxed and happy, though a frown creases his face, as he looks pointedly at me. 'Jeez, Olivia,' he says with concern. 'What's up? Aren't you feeling so good? You look like you've just seen a ghost, or something. Look, if I was a bit sour earlier, I'm sorry.'

I smile wanly at his evident concern, 'Maybe it was a bit warm in there. I'll be fine, once I've had something to eat and a breath of fresh air.'

He seems relieved that he is not the cause of my distress and says breezily, 'Sure thing. Let's see what's on offer.'

He catches me gazing with longing at those patrons who are about to sit down to a silver service meal, at tables covered with fresh white linen. 'I feel the same, Olivia,' he says wistfully. 'I should've reserved places for us there.'

The excited bustle, as people find their correct seats, the happy introductions, as they meet their table partners and, of course, the tinkling of glasses coming together in a series of toasts, fills me with longing to escape into their number. And into their evidently happy lives. But *he* might be there, sitting at one of those tables.

JP gently takes my arm and leads me towards the door. It feels perfectly natural and good. 'Come on,' he says, ' Let's get out of here. You still look like you could use some fresh air.'

Outside, there are three or four stalls, each serving up a type of street food. In truth, there's a disappointing lack of variety. It's mainly burgers, albeit with good beef, filled baked potatoes and, bizarrely, raclette. Neither of us has any intention of coming all the way to Newcastle to eat the traditional Swiss dish, so we both settle on the veggie risotto, on offer inside the concourse. JP immediately offers to bring some, 'You just sit down here and I'll be as quick as I can,' he promises solicitously.

I easily find a seat on the concrete terraces, which face across the large piazza and on towards the river. As soon as I'm seated, I begin to enjoy the cooling breeze, on what is still a fine, dry evening. I reckon I have a few minutes to pull myself together before JP returns, so I try out my trusted, deep breathing exercises. Thankfully, they work and I'm even able to raise a smile as I see him, returning with two portions of risotto and two cups of tea.

'Hey, you look a lot better!' he enthuses. 'Let's hope this stuff doesn't set you back. It doesn't look that great.'

The food actually tastes quite a bit better than it looks and we sit in companionable silence, as we eat as much as we are able. I still can't quite prevent myself studying people, as they innocently pass us. It must be pretty obvious, because eventually JP mentions it. 'You still

160

seem not quite right, Olivia. Kind of on edge and nervous.'

For a brief moment, I contemplate telling him the whole story. But I decide against. I wouldn't want him to think me a complete idiot and, of course, there was my promise to Snow.

'Oh, I don't know,' I say. 'Maybe four of these operas inside a week is proving to be a bit much for me. They are an emotional roller coaster, after all.'

'Yeah,' he says, nodding his head, as he finishes his risotto. 'I know what you mean. And there's those crazy group meetings too.'

'Yes, I must say that I'd have much preferred them without Leonard. He's such a self opinionated prat.'

'I sure wouldn't dream of disagreeing with you there,' JP says. 'But, come on. Time for a glass of wine.'

We find ourselves sitting at a table, for eight, in the bar area and I'm relieved that the last part of the interval goes by without me having to say very much. The other people are more than happy to hold forth, on topics ranging from Wagner to Brexit. I resolve that today is the bad day. Tomorrow, when I wake up to find that nothing has happened, I can just focus on enjoying Sunday's finale, *Götterdämmerung*. JP joins in the good natured, group conversation from time to time and I must say, he looks quite relaxed, as if he is really enjoying himself at this series of performances. When I think about the sad reason for his journey, I feel very happy for him.

The conversation is still full swing when, by playing the now habitual brief variation on one of the opera's leitmotifs, the brass quartet announce the imminent start of Act Three. I quickly wave bye bye to JP and make my way back to my seat.

***

8.30pm, Friday 8th July 2016, Newcastle City Centre Police Station, Forth Banks.

Sam

I can't seem to settle to anything. I feel pretty helpless really. Just waiting for something to happen, rather than getting out there and making it happen. Or, better still, preventing it from happening. The investigation into Mykel Stevenson's murder has made little progress. And, if what Dr Clavel said is right, it bloody well won't. However whacky her ideas were, I actually can't get them out of my mind. And if you once come to believe, as I do, that Harrison got it all wrong with the first killing, the idea that it's all linked to this series of operas, begins to appear more plausible.

I'm sitting alone at a table in the nearly deserted canteen at the station, nursing a tepid and stewed mug of tea. I've got to do something, otherwise I'll go crazy. So I review where we are. Harrison did interview the victim's mother again, but a fat lot of good it did him. I still suspect she's not telling us everything she knows about what her children had been up to. However, the way she'd howled with despair, as Jenkins and I left her grotty flat, persuades me that, despite her rudeness and hostility, she still has some maternal feelings. Maybe we'll eventually break down her reluctance to speak, and that may push the investigation forward.

The estate agent, Hardcastle, and his receptionist have been invited in for questioning tomorrow, by which time we hope that Hutton will have been able to dig some dirt on him. I hope that Harrison will allow me and Jenkins to do that. He's probably the most promising lead we've got and we've got to make sure we get everything out of him that we can. We might also be able to speak with Kylie Stevenson again and with luck, she might even recall some small detail of what happened, that will give us a lead.

The rest of the team have already knocked off, Harrison having told us all to get some rest and be back in early tomorrow. I can feel my pulse speeding up, as I think back to how the bastard never even mentioned what Dr Clavel had said in his final briefing. I'd been to see him and told him what she'd said, but, predictably, he was utterly dismissive of such 'pointless academic theorising.'

'What we want here,' he had advised with a patronising smirk, 'is good, down to earth police work. Not airy fairy rubbish like that. Take it from me, son, she's just a time waster.'

I'm still not so sure and have spent the last half hour debating whether or not to go over his head and present it all to Quayle. Before she left, Jenkins tried as hard as she could to dissuade me, even going so far as to invite me for a meal at her place. I'd have loved to accept, but I still worry that someone else will die tonight. And I want to be able to tell myself tomorrow, that I did everything I could to prevent it.

My decision made, I'm relieved to see that Quayle is still in her office. I have to admire her. She really puts in the hours that she expects of her officers. As I knock and enter, she's sitting behind her huge desk, shuffling files of paper. She obviously has a load of current investigations on her plate, but her desk nevertheless looks pretty damned tidy to me. She looks up and smiles, as I approach the desk. The way she greets me with a cheery, 'Evening, Sam. Thought all your team had been sent home for the night?' suggests that she might have been expecting me. Straight away, I wonder if 'Halitosis' has been in before me, to rubbish what I'm about to say. Sod it, I decide. The DCI's going to hear what I've got to say, whether she likes it, or not.

As soon as I begin my account of the interview with Dr Clavel, I can see that my suspicions about Harrison were correct. Quayle's having absolutely none of it. Of course, she's careful to be very pleasant and, unlike Harrison, superficially sympathetic. But she makes it clear that I should get myself home, have a good sleep and pull myself together.

'Look, ma'am,' I say in a final effort to persuade her, 'I still feel that there are sufficient grounds for doubt over the arrest of Mr Smith for the killing of...'

I get no further as Quayle sits upright in her chair and raises a delicate hand. She may not be physically very big, but by God, she carries some authority. 'Now, you just stop right there, sergeant. We've been over this already. We have a properly obtained confession to that offence. Do you have any concrete evidence that would suggest another perpetrator?'

I look at her uncomfortably. 'Come on! Out with it, pet',   she challenges. 'Let's have it, if there's anything to be had.'

'There's nothing definite. No, ma'am,' I have to admit, miserably.

'And given that Smith was in custody at the time of Mykel Stevenson's death, the two crimes must have been committed by different people. Agreed?' I say nothing.

'Agreed?' she says more forcefully and I know I have to respond.

'On that reasoning, yes. But what about Dr Clavel's theory? Surely that casts a different light on things? We could be dealing with a deranged killer who will strike again tonight. Don't you think....'

She stops me again in mid sentence, this time with an exasperated sigh, 'Look, sergeant. You know I think you've got the makings of a first class detective. But sometimes, you have to see what's in front of your face. I feel like I'm saying this to you every day. But you should get yourself home, have a good glass of red and a long kip and things'll look different in the morning. As to Dr Clavel's theory, the fact that we have a

confession for the first crime really kills that stone dead.'

I have to admit that she's been pretty decent about it and I nod, get up and smile a good night. I do worry, however, that things might indeed look very different for us all, come the morning.

Chapter Eighteen

4.00am, Saturday 9th July 2016, Whitburn, South Tyneside.

Sam

I've been lying awake for the last couple of hours, just willing the phone not to ring. I jump, as my mobile springs to life and its ringtone pierces the air.

'Sergeant Snow?' asks the Desk Sergeant. It's Carter again, but this time there's none of his sarcastic humour. 'I'm sorry to bother you, son, but there's been another one. Three inside a week. Bloody ridiculous. It's damn well not New York here, is it? Anyway, can you get there as soon as possible?'

He gives me the bare details and I shrug myself out of bed and into black jeans, a plain cotton shirt and my faithful leather jacket. A quick cup of coffee and I'm on my way to the appropriately named 'Dead Man's Arch.' Local legend has it, that a train driver, remorseful over his alleged responsibility for an accident, in which there were fatalities, hanged himself from the said Arch.There's even talk of hauntings and hanging bodies being seen there at midnight. All I can think about, as I drive the empty roads towards Gateshead, is the method of death and the height of the victim. The next few minutes will tell me whether Dr Clavel has correctly predicted a murder. If she has, the whole investigation will be blown wide open.

As I drive down Alston Street, it's taped off, twenty yards before it bends around into the singularly inappropriately named Elysium Terrace. It's clear that uniform is out in force, but I seem to be the first CID officer on the scene. Having parked the car and donned shoe covers and a plastic suit, I negotiate the police tape and walk briskly down the paved entrance which curves down to the passage under the railway line. Even on a lovely day, I imagine it would be a bleak place, with it's high stone walls on both sides. Right now, the burning arc lights give it an even harsher aspect. The Scene of Crime Manager and the SOCO crew are busying themselves, around three quarters of the way through the tunnel, where I see a shape slumped against the right hand wall.

I recognise one of our regular pathologists and sidle up to him, 'So, doctor, what's got us both out of bed so early?'

He turns and grins, 'A well directed and fatal stab wound. A long dagger, or even a sword I'd say.'

'So, pretty much like the Stevenson killing?' I murmur.

'Well, I wasn't on duty for that one. But from what I've heard and seen, in the sense that one well directed blow did for him, yes I'd say so.'

'Any first thoughts on timing?'

'Just an educated guess, but I'd say between two and four hours ago.'

'Do you know who found him?'

'I think it was that chap, over there with the WPC. He seems a bit shaken up. I glance over and notice that it's none other than PC Alison Creaner.

'I suppose it'd be too much to hope that there's any I D on him?'

The doctor turns and hands me a small plastic bag, 'Looks like the poor old bastard's bus pass,. And by the

167

way,' he adds mischievously, while glancing towards Creaner, 'get your tongue up off the floor, you randy sod.'

I smirk at the accuracy of his observation, while squinting through the plastic. I can just make out the name Roderick Holden, 'Do we have anything with an address on it?' I ask one of the SOCOs.

'Better than that,' he replies. 'The uniform standing by the far entrance, the one with the glasses, he says he knows him.'

'OK,thanks,' I say, before turning back to the doctor. 'Mind if I take a quick look?'

He's got no idea why I'm so desperate to see the body and merely shrugs, 'Help yourself.'

The old man's wearing a long plastic raincoat, but even so, it's blindingly obvious that he's very, very short. 'Frigging hell!' I say quietly. 'The brown stuff's gonna hit the fan now.'

'What's that?' the doctor asks. 'Have I missed something?'

'No mate,' I reply reassuringly. 'Nothing like that. But that bleeding wanker 'Halitosis' sure as hell has.'

The doctor looks at me quizzically, but I just smile and ask, 'our victim looks pretty short. What'd you estimate him as?'

'Well, I'm no undertaker,' he says, perhaps a little irritated by the question. 'But I'd say he's four foot nine, max. So, yes, pretty short. Why, is that significant in some way?'

I shake my head quickly and mutter, 'Best not to ask, mate. Best not to ask.' He shrugs and says, 'There's one thing that's a bit weird. Something we found in the old chap's right hand. Can't make head nor tail of it really. We left it there for you to have a butcher's before we bag it up.'

I bend over the body and, for the first time, see the face properly. It looks like the faces of so many old men who are still alive - vaguely bewildered. It looks to me, as if he had no idea what hit him. 'He seems a bit confused, rather than in agony, or terror,' I suggest.

'I agree. I imagine it all happened so quickly that he didn't have time to figure out what was going on. The killer approached him from the front and simply skewered the poor devel through the heart. He'd have been gone in seconds.'

I focus my attention on the right hand. It seems to be holding something metallic, a can, perhaps. 'What do you make of it?' I ask the doctor.

'It looks like a small tin of rat poison.'

'Rat poison?' I echo in surprise. 'What the hell would he be doing wandering around with a tin of rat poison in his hand?'

'Well, there you are, you see. He wasn't. The tin was pushed into his hand after death. If he'd been run through like this while holding the tin, it's almost certain he'd have dropped it.'

'So the killer must have put it there deliberately? Some sort of symbolism, or something?'

'Come on, sergeant,' the doctor berates me gently. 'You're the 'tec. Thank God it's your job to figure out what went on and why.'

The police photographer asks me to step away from the body to enable him to complete his array of shots and I move over to the constable, who was pointed out earlier by the SOCO. 'I believe you know the deceased?'

'Aye, that's right, sergeant,' the PC replies in a thick Geordie accent. 'What with him being tiny and everything. In a funny sort of way, he stood out.'

I don't think he's trying to be clever, so I leave the crass remark and simply say, 'Tell me what you know about him.'

'He works in an off licence up on the Saltwell Road. I imagine he'd locked up for the night and was walking home to his flat on Bensham Crescent. His natural way would be through the passage here.'

'Could he have been carrying any takings from there? Could this be a mugging, gone wrong?'

'I can't see it, to be honest, sergeant. I believe the owner of the off licence has a safe on the premises. But you'd have to check that with him.'

'Do you know if he lived alone?'

'Aye, sergeant, I think so. Least ways, I'd never seen him with anyone in particular. Nor have I ever heard anything about a significant other.'

I look up sharply at his use of that absurd term, but again see no indication that he's taking the piss. He gives me the addresses of the victim's workplace and flat and I send him on his way.

'Sergeant?' I turn to see PC Creaner's concerned face looking up at me. 'Maybe you could speak with Mr Bradley. He found the body and he's been waiting some time.'

'Of course, PC Creaner,' I reply, 'I'll be right with him.'

As I approach him, I observe that Bradley seems a bit of a furtive type. Below medium height, thick set, shaven headed and blessed with a face, of which none of the features looks quite the appropriate scale. From his aggressive posture, it looks like he's ready for me.

'Now look here,' he says, all belligerent, ' I didn't expect to be kept waiting for as long as this .'

'I'm very sorry for your inconvenience, sir,' I reply and judge from the way that he's hopping about from foot to foot, that he desperately needs a toilet. 'If you'd briefly tell me what happened, I'm sure you can soon be on your way.'

A relieved expression quickly crosses his face and he begins to gabble, 'It's like I already explained. I was on my way home from a night out. I know a couple of pubs on the other side of the river, where they're happy to have lock ins for the regulars. Well, we were there having a wake for the Toon's relegation from The Premier League, like. So it was later than usual by the time I got here.'

'What time was it and were you alone?'

'It was not long after 3 and yes, my mate left me at Gateshead Interchange. I just live over in Dixon Street. I thought he was a bundle of rags at first. You know how people dump anything, anywhere these days? No bloody consideration.'

I hardly had him down as a fully law abiding citizen himself and stifled a chuckle as he went on, 'I couldn't see any sign of him breathing, so I just phoned 999 right away. The rest, you know.'

'Do you know him?'

'I've seen him around, like, and exchanged a few words in the off licence he works in. But know him? No, didn't even know his name.'

'Did you touch him after you found him?'

'Only on his neck, for a pulse. There wasn't one.'

'Did you see what he was holding in his hand?'

He looks totally baffled, 'Holding in his hand? No. Why? Was it important? Like I said, I thought he looked really bad, so I just felt for a pulse and when I couldn't feel one, I rang 999.'

'Did you see anybody else?'

'No. The last person I saw was my mate at the bus station.'

'Very well. Please give the WPC your address, the name and address of your friend and the pub you were in and arrange to come into the station to make a formal statement. Then,' I add with a sympathetic smirk, 'you can be on your way.'

He looks uncertain, 'Look, about the pub, I don't want to get them in any trouble.'

'Relax Mr Bradley,' I reassure him. 'We're not interested in what went on there. Only that someone can confirm your story.'

Unsavoury type though Bradley may be, my gut reaction is that he's telling the truth. Of course, we'll check his whereabouts on the nights Stevenson and Grantham were killed, but I don't believe he had anything to do with the murders. References to opera seem well beyond his pay grade.

I collect a heavy bunch of keys from one of the SOCOs and set off for Roderick Holden's home on Bensham

Crescent. It turns out that he did live alone and a thoroughly depressing experience it is, going through his few, wretched possessions. There's a couple of photos of what look like family, which I take to the station. They'll be useful for uniform when they return later to interview the neighbours.

It's about 6.30am when I get back to the station and I'm only halfway through the door when I'm told that Quayle wants to see me immediately. I bet she bloody well does.

It's not unusual for the DCI to be in so early, but she nevertheless looks a rather unhealthy grey colour. She's a tough nut, though, and offers no indication that she regrets sending me away the previous evening. 'Come in, Snow,' she commands. 'I want to know everything. Leave nothing out.'

I give her a full report and she contents herself with infrequent nods. As soon as I've finished, she asks, 'And you're sure this Bradley isn't involved? And you've ruled out the robbery angle?'

'We'll speak to Bradley again and check out what he told us, ma'am, but my feeling is that he was just a drunk on his way home. As to the money, I'll get on to the owner of the off licence where Holden worked and find out what they do with the takings. He should be able to tell us if there's anything missing.'

'Very well,' she says, but then surprises me. 'Look, get someone else to do that. I want you to interview Mr Smith, the man who confessed to the first killing.'

I'm determined to enjoy my pound of flesh, so I ask, all innocent, 'If you say so, ma'am. But what about DI Harrison? He'll not like it.'

There's a quick nod. Perhaps even a grudging acknowledgement that she understands exactly what I'm saying and why, before she answers. "I couldn't care a monkey's whether he likes it, or not. 'Cos I'll be in there with you.'

Within an hour, Quayle and myself are sitting in Interview Room 1 with Smith, the homeless man who confessed to killing 'Gentle Giant' Geoff Grantham. He looks far better than the last time I saw him. The warmth, regular food and comfortable (relative to a doorway, that is) bed have clearly had a positive effect on him.

'Now Mr Smith,' I begin gently. 'I'd like to go back over your statement.' He looks at me in genuine confusion, as if he hasn't a clue what I'm talking about. 'About your statement, in which you say that you killed Mr Geoff Grantham sometime during the early morning of Wednesday July 6th.'

He's still looking at me as if I'm talking double Dutch, 'Killed?' he mutters to himself. 'Oh, no, sir. You've got that wrong. I never killed nobody. And who was it, you said I killed?'

Quayle starts to shift her slight body on the chair, but I head off any intervention she might feel like making. 'It was you, Mr Smith, who told us, in this written statement which I have in my hands, that you killed Geoff Grantham.' I push his statement across to him, so that he can check it, before asking, 'This is your statement and your signature, isn't it?'

'Err, I don't know. That is to say, I'm not sure.'

He fumbles with the piece of typewritten paper, squinting at it from all angles. 'You can read, can't you Mr Smith?'

174

He looks at me, shame and anger written all over his face, 'Of course, I bloody well can,' he shouts.

'Then, would you please read the first line for me, sir?' I say as gently as possible

'Err...Hmm...' he hesitates, before saying, 'I can't read it without my glasses. And I don't have them with me.'

I'm certain he's lying, but there's no point in rubbing the old sod's nose in it. So I say, 'It's OK, Mr Smith. What say I read your statement out and you tell me that it's correct? How's that?'

He nods with relief and I read the statement very slowly and very carefully. He looks more and more horrified as I work my way through it and, soon, he begins to shake his head wildly.

I've just got to the the bit where he describes how he beat the lifeless Grantham's face to a pulp, when he shouts out, 'No! No! No! That's all wrong. I never killed nobody. I just found him. He was already dead. I admit I took the money from Geoff, but I swear to God I never hurt him.' He breaks down in heavy sobs and wails, 'Poor Geoff. He was beyond any hurt when I got to him.' He sniffs loudly and then fixes Quayle and me with a surprisingly determined and controlled expression. 'And besides. I'd never have hurt Gentle Geoff. He was my best mate.'

He breaks down again and the DCI intervenes with surprising compassion, 'It's all right Mr Smith. The officer will take you back to your cell for the time being. Thank you very much. You've been very helpful.'

A burly PC helps Smith up and half carries the staggering and wailing old man back to his cell, 'Get him a good sweet cuppa, will you,' Quayle shouts after them.

'Well, sergeant,' Quayle asks, once we're back in her office, 'what do you make of that?'

I have to play this carefully. After all, I did tell her that 'Halitosis' had got it very wrong, by charging Smith and she gave me the bum's rush. 'Well, ma'am,' I begin cautiously, 'I've checked with Forensics and there was no more blood on his clothes, or himself, that would be consistent with him finding the body and stealing the money. And then there's the sheer ferocity of the post mortem attack. Suppose we accept that Smith wanted a bit of Grantham's takings for the night, in exchange for keeping his mouth shut about the rich pickings from the opera crowd. And suppose we accept that there was an argument that escalated. Do we really think it likely that Smith would have beaten his friend beyond recognition, once he was dead? Why would he do that? He'd surely get the cash and scarper as quickly as possible. Why would he report the body? And then, of course, there's the murder weapon. Where is it? It's never been found. Are we to believe that Smith, having killed Grantham, taken the money and then spent time defacing the body, went off, presumably to the river to get rid of the weapon and then went in search of a copper to report it all? With respect, ma'am, it makes no sense.'

Quayle nodded thoughtfully, 'Except in the case of him killing Grantham, doing a runner and remembering about the cash. That would explain the weapon not being found, wouldn't it?'

I have to agree the old girl has a point, but I shoot back. 'But, with respect, if an argument did take place, it was precisely about money. How could he then instantly forget it? And why did he attack Grantham so fiercely after he was dead. No, ma'am, especially after this morning, I really believe that we have three deaths and one killer.'

'Ah!' the DCI says with a shake of her head, 'I wondered when Dr Clavel would intrude into our conversation.'

'She damn well predicted what would happen, ma'am. And we ignored her warning. I'd say that, at the very least, we have to take very seriously what she says and we need to get her advice about whether our killer is finished, or not.'

Quayle nods her head slowly and looks out of her window, over the buildings of Newcastle, covered in bright morning sunshine. I swear these are the longest thirty seconds of my life, but she finally coughs and speaks. 'It so happens that I now share your concerns about the Smith confession. That's not to say that I agree that the murders are linked. I think I'll need a bit more convincing of that. Why not get your opera loving psychologist in and we'll see what she's got to say for herself?'

I had hoped that she might have had more sympathy with the single killer theory, but, for now, I suppose I have to be content with her changing her mind about Smith killing Grantham. Things could all change, however, after she speaks with Olivia Clavel.

Chapter Nineteen

8.00am, Saturday 9th July 2016, Low Fell.
Olivia

The knocking on the door is not loud, but it is insistent and the voice, saying 'Olivia! Olivia! Wake up! There's a call for you,' is suffused with a sense of irritation. As I gradually surface from a deep and troubled sleep, I realise that it's Christine and my first, unkind thought is that she's evidently not used to being dragged out of bed so early on a Saturday morning. As soon as my conscious mind fully takes over, I leap out of bed, hastily grab my dressing gown and fling open the door. Christine is standing there, covering the mouthpiece of the phone, as she holds it in her right hand. 'It's the police, Olivia. They were most insistent that they want to speak with you.'

In my groggy state I can only think that this must be bad news about Sebastian. My stomach sinks about two hundred metres, as I gulp and reach out for the phone with a nod of thanks. I'm still standing on the narrow landing of the conventionally designed 1930s semi that is home to my sister and her husband. It's a comfortable, homely and very familiar place, in which they've brought up their two children and welcomed the same number of grandchildren. Its essential normality stands in stark contrast to my abnormal state of mind, with the result that I shout shrilly, rather than speak, into the phone. 'What is it? Is it to do with my son, Sebastian? Has something happened to him?'

A calm and oddly familiar voice on the other end of the line tries to reassure me, 'Is that Dr Clavel? It's Detective Sergeant Snow here. We spoke yesterday. Is it convenient to talk now?'

My mind doesn't process this information. I simply repeat like an idiot, 'Is it Sebastian? What's happened to him? Is he still alive?'

'Dr Clavel,' the voice says patiently, 'I can assure you that I am not calling about anything to do with your son. It's DS Snow here. It's about what we were discussing yesterday.'

An initial euphoric relief floods through me, as I realise that he is not calling with some dreadful news about my son. It is soon replaced, however, by a clammy sense of dread. I hope to heaven that nothing happened last night, as I croak, 'Oh, yes. Sergeant Snow. I'm sorry. I was still half asleep.' I hastily take the phone back into my bedroom and take care to speak much more softly. 'Of course I remember yesterday. Has something happened? Has he done it again?'

He doesn't answer me directly, but rather says, 'We'd like you to come down to the station, if that's convenient. How would it be, if I send a car for you in forty five minutes? Give you time to sort yourself out and get a bite to eat?' Trying to lighten the mood, he jokes, 'I wouldn't wish our canteen food on my worst enemy.'

I repay him by also not answering, but by reiterating my question. 'Has he done it again? Was I right? I hope to God I wasn't.'

'We'll talk about all that at the station Dr Clavel. Can I send a car for you as I suggested? It's pretty important that I speak with you again, as soon as possible.'

His last sentence confirms to me that the killer has indeed struck again and I hastily reply, 'Of course, Sergeant Snow. I'll be ready in three quarters of an hour.'

Christine has probably been hovering behind her closed bedroom door, because as I go to return the phone I can hear her whispering to Joe. She must have heard my door open, because she immediately pops her head round her door and asks with obvious concern, 'Is everything OK, Olivia? Only you look a bit pale. Come on downstairs and I'll make us a nice cuppa.'

I smile at Christine's natural recourse to the typical English person's default solution to any stressful situation and reply, 'Thanks, Chris. I'll just grab a quick shower first, if that's OK. I've got to go out.'

Already halfway down the stairs, she calls over her shoulder, 'No problem. I'll get the kettle on and sort out the breakfast things.'

As the warm water of the shower pours over my body, its usual de-stressing effect is conspicuous by its absence. My mind is racing and I feel a deep foreboding about what lies ahead. Despite my academic career in the area of Applied Psychology, I have little experience of dealing first hand with the police on an ongoing investigation, let alone acting as some sort of consultant. Rather, I have concentrated my efforts on trying, first to understand the effects of psychological abnormalities and second, to develop behavioural strategies to deal with them. I begin to worry that Sergeant Snow may be putting too much trust in my ability to help them solve this awful case.

Perhaps unconsciously, I find myself dressing in the nearest I have to a police uniform, charcoal jeans, a white shirt and a black, cotton jacket. I run a quick brush through my hair and gallop downstairs to find two worried faces staring at me. They're both still in their dressing gowns and are clearly in need of some reassurance.

'Look,' I begin. 'I'm sorry, but I don't really think I should say what this is all about. Suffice to say that neither I, nor anyone I know, is in any kind of trouble. Or danger. So, please believe me, when I say that you should not worry about this at all. OK?'

Joe seems to take this at face value and says brightly, 'OK. Olivia. Now, who's for cereal?' We all three laugh at his characteristic concern with food, but I can tell that Christine is still unconvinced. We talk about the possibility that we'll have to change our plans to go to the coast at South Shields and the routine nature of the discussion seems to reassure her. At least, that is, until the marked police car arrives to pick me up. Why the hell couldn't he have at least sent an unmarked one? I fume. Anyway, too late to worry about that now and I'm soon on my way to the police station.

I can see Sergeant Snow waiting for me, as I approach the front door. This time we are meeting in Newcastle, though the building looks no more inviting than the one yesterday. I swallow hard, before advancing towards him. He holds out his hand and says, 'Thank you for coming, Dr Clavel. We really appreciate it.'

He shows me quickly through the Reception Area, through a set of swing doors to a broad, institutional set of stairs, which we climb to the top floor. I follow him to the end of a corridor that, even in today's bright sunshine, is dingy and uncared for. He stops before a wide, wooden door, knocks once and enters. He stands by the open door as I pass through, thereby preventing me from reading the nameplate. Was that deliberate? I enter a good sized, regular shaped office with a desk under the window and an oblong table and four chairs to the side of the door. There are several filing cabinets and a display unit with what look like various sporting trophies and police awards on show. There are also one or two photographs of the small, wiry woman sitting behind the desk in the company of celebrities such as Alan Shearer, Kevin Whately and even Prince Andrew. The woman gets quickly to her feet, walks briskly around her desk and offers her hand, 'DCI Quayle. And you must be Dr Clavel. Please, sit down.'

I'm quite impressed that she didn't feel the need to preserve her authority in the situation by remaining behind her desk and forcing me to sit, like a subordinate, in front of her. Perhaps I will get on with this woman.

As soon as we are all seated, Quayle asks if I would like anything to drink and I politely decline. She looks expectantly at Sergeant Snow, who coughs and begins. 'For the benefit of DCI Quayle, I wonder if you'd mind briefly outlining the theory you have concerning the recent killings in Gateshead. The one you explained to me yesterday.'

I'm desperate to find out what's happened, so I explain as quickly as possible about the curious links between the two deaths and Opera North's production of 'The Ring Of The Nibelungen' at The Sage. I conclude that, 'It's not only the timing that is significant. It's also certain characteristics of the persons killed and the method of killing. I thought that it was far too much of a coincidence and I suggested to Sergeant Snow that, if I'm correct, the killer would strike again last night. Or, should I say, this morning.'

'Thank you for explaining that,' says Quayle with little enthusiasm.

It's blindingly obvious that she's already heard all this from Snow and it occurs to me that she wanted to hear me explain it in person, so she can try to get a feel for whether or not I'm a crackpot. Well I'll show her. 'But, forgive me,' I say with a sweet smile, ' I was led to believe by another of your officers that you had already apprehended the perpetrator of the first crime. I'm certain that she told me that you had a legally obtained, full confession.'

The two police officers visibly flinch and I rub it in further. 'So, I imagine that I was totally wrong, when I suggested that a very small man could well be killed last night. Is that the case, officers?'

' I can certainly see why you took Dr Clavel so seriously, Sergeant Snow,' Quayle says, her decisive nod and smile indicating what I take as a growing respect for me. 'What I'm about to say must remain confidential. We have found, err, certain irregularities which suggest to us that the confession, while obtained legally, is not genuine. And a very small man was indeed murdered last night in the manner you suggested.'

'I'm sorry,' I say, 'it was cheap of me to try to score points. I'm here to help you in any way I can. But I'm not sure what further assistance I can offer.'

Quayle raises her immaculately groomed left hand in acknowledgement and adds, 'If your theory is correct, Dr Clavel, how would you have expected the man to die?'

'Well,' I say, playing for thinking time. 'As I explained to Sergeant Snow yesterday, I would have expected the death to be based on that of Mime in the opera *Siegfried*. He was killed by one blow of a sword.'

Quayle and Snow look at one another and the senior officer nods her head. Snow takes her instruction and asks, 'Is there anything else you might have expected. Something noteworthy about the killing, for example?'

I'm not very keen on this kind of 'Twenty Questions' approach, but I accept that, from the police perspective, it probably makes sense. I try to think back to last night's performance and the scene in which Mime is killed by Siegfried. 'Let me think. Siegfried has just killed the dragon and drank some of his blood.' Quayle shifts on her chair, as if she's still very uncomfortable with all this, so I quickly press on. 'This gives him the ability to understand the Woodbird, who tells him that he can now hear what people really mean, rather than what they say.'

'And how might this be relevant?' demands Snow, with what I suspect is a hint of impatience.

'The point is that Mime offers Siegfried a drink, after his fight with the dragon. Because of his new skill, Siegfried doesn't hear what Mime actually says, i.e. that it's a lovely, refreshing drink. He 'hears' what Mime is really thinking, i.e. that it's poisoned and that he just wants to kill Siegfried to steal the dragon's treasure.'

Both police officers sit upright so quickly that their chairs scrape back on the office floor. 'What's that, you say?' blurts out Quayle. 'Tell me again about the poison.'

'As I said,' I repeat, 'Mime pretends to be nice to Siegfried, but has in fact poisoned the drink he offers him. Siegfried has the power to understand the dwarf's true intentions, so kills him.'

'Bloody hell,' murmurs Snow. 'It's unbelievable!'

'What do you mean?' I ask. 'What have I said?'

'A tin of rat poison was found in one of the hands of last night's victim,' explains Quayle with resignation. 'Moreover, we believe that it was forced into his hand by the killer, post mortem. No one knows about this, except ourselves, and the officers who were present at the scene.'

A tense silence descends on the office, while each of us, in our own way, digests this latest information. Finally, it falls to the DCI to break it, with a startling admission. 'Frankly, Dr Clavel,' she says, 'it's absolutely clear to me now that we will get nowhere by treating each case separately. And yours is the only plausible suggestion as to how they may be linked. As someone who, I understand, was born and raised in Gateshead, I'm sure that you'll understand that three murders in just four days is entirely unprecedented here. We need all the help we can get and I'm here to ask you to give any assistance you can to Sergeant Snow, who for the time being, will be in charge of the single investigation into all three cases.'

Chapter Twenty

Sam

Dr Clavel and I leave the DCI to her thoughts and I escort her to a much smaller office. She's certainly nobody's fool. As soon as we enter the room, her eyes are taking in all the old man's personal things; family portraits, children and grandchildren, even a scale model of HMS Victory. I feel a bit uncomfortable, because it's obvious that it's someone else's room. 'Are you office squatting?' she asks me with typical directness. 'I can't believe this is all your stuff.'

I grimace theatrically, before breaking into what I hope she will interpret as a charming smile, 'You're not a psychologist for nothing, are you Doc? As it happens, you're right. The incumbent is not going to be needing this space for a few days, so I've been given permission to use it.' I'm relieved that she has sufficient discretion not to ask any further questions about the displaced person.

As I settle into the room, I'm not even aware that I'm staring at her, until she coughs and my attention is drawn to her green eyes looking quizzically at me. 'Are we ready then?' she asks and I feel a bit of a plonker.

'As the DCI said,' I begin quickly, in a vain attempt to cover my embarrassment, 'We'd be very grateful for your assistance in this enquiry. We now believe that there is a strong argument that you are correct in your view, that the three killings are all the work of one person. Also,

186

that they are, in some way, connected to the performances of the operas at The Sage. I'd like to talk with you in private for a little while and then we'll go and brief the team in the Incident Room. How's that?'

'Oh, look,' she says, for the first time seeming a little flustered. 'I'm not sure that's such a good idea. After all, I carry no authority here. I'm a simple academic. I've no experience of such things.'

'Tell you the truth, Doc,' I say sincerely, 'this is my first multiple murder case. And the first case, of which I've been given charge. So, with a bit of luck, we can help one another out, as we both learn how to navigate new waters.' She still looks unconvinced, so I add, 'And don't forget, without your contribution, we wouldn't even have made the connections between the murders. No, Dr Clavel, honestly, you have every right to have your voice heard and you'll get full support from me. OK? Are you happy to proceed on that basis?'

She nods her head and I begin to read from some notes I made earlier. 'Well, I suggest that the key questions, to which we must try to find answers are: Who is doing this and why? Second, has he finished, or should we expect more? I believe that you can be of great assistance with both.'

She nods thoughtfully and says, 'Yes, I can see that a discussion, both about what kind of person might be doing these dreadful things and what his precise motivation might be, could help you to discover a precise identity. But we'd have to be very lucky. And are we certain that it's a man?'

'Good question,' I reply. 'The pathologists have suggested that the dagger or sword thrusts in killings two and three would require some strength. While not categorically ruling out a woman, they both suggest that a man is far more likely as the killer.'

'So, we operate on that assumption,' she agrees.

'OK,' I continue, 'let's look at what we've got. Our killer must be interested in this series of operas, The Ring, right? That surely must narrow it down a bit.'

She crinkles up her nose in thought and says, 'Well, so far what he's done doesn't require a detailed knowledge of the operas. He could get everything in ten minutes on Wikipedia.'

'Point taken,' I accept. 'But would you say that these operas are important to him?'

'There seems to be some sort of identification taking place. If I were more certain of exactly who, or what, it is that he's identifying with, we might be able to better understand his motives and possibly even predict what he might do next. But I'm afraid that right now, anything would be just guesswork.'

'So, do you think we can assume that he has some definite connection with the performances?' I ask hopefully. 'An audience member, part of the production or service staff delivering them, for example?'

She takes some time before answering, 'It's very strange, but I had the strongest feeling yesterday that he was in the audience watching *Siegfried*. But I have no evidence in support of that. All I can offer you is my gut feeling that he is, in some way, connected, as you suggest.'

'OK,' I say, feeling pleased that we are making some progress. 'Now, would you have anything to say about the kind of person our killer might be?'

She looks at me and shakes her head, sending her wavy red hair swinging across her shoulders, 'Oh, I don't know, Sergeant...'

'It's Sam, please,' I interrupt, 'especially now that we're working together.

She looks a little startled, but quickly recovers and adds, 'OK, Sam. I'm happy to say what I think, but you must understand that it's highly speculative and must not be used as the exclusive focus of your investigation. I'm not trained as a profiler, you know.'

'OK, Doctor err..'

'Olivia,' she quickly offers. 'In that case, I'd say that, if we are going to have a chance of catching this man, we must forget the idea that he's simply crazy. I would say that the man we want is highly intelligent, though he may, or may not be successful in educational or career terms. He's most probably aged from mid thirties to mid fifties and a loner. At least someone who lives by himself.'

'Because,' I offer, 'how else could he manage to wander about the city so late at night, without arousing some suspicion, you mean?'

'I'd say so. Further, despite the bizarre methods of killing and extreme savagery used in the first two cases, I'd say that our man is able to live a perfectly normal life for most of the time. He's definitely not deranged 24/7.'

'A kind of split personality, you mean?'

'Perhaps. That's certainly one possibility. There's no doubt that he's mentally disturbed, but, then again, so are many of us. I'll give that more thought, before I say any more. It's also important to remember that he's been able to plan these killings. He's chosen the victims to match his 'Ring Cycle' narrative. That must have taken time, effort and probably money. These are not random murders. They've been meticulously planned. Indeed, I'd say such orderliness and planning is a real strength of our man.'

'OK, if we accept that reasoning, does it suggest that he's likely to be a local man?' I prompt.

She looks a little bit irritated, as if I've disturbed a vital train of thought, but eventually replies, 'That would be first choice, yes.' After hesitating for a short time, she then adds, 'Or at least someone who has visited here several times in the recent past. Not too long ago, but definitely before this week. He must have been here frequently, in order to make his detailed plans, as regards victims, timing and locations.'

'That's a great insight, Olivia,' I enthuse. 'We can check how long the Stevensons had been using that commercial unit. Our man might well have already visited Kylie there as a punter, to check it out.'

'Can you check visitors to the city who are here now and have been here in the recent past?' she asks hopefully.

'God knows. If we can, I imagine the task would be enormous. But we do have a great IT type on the team. She might be able to suggest something.'

Undoubtedly I'm not as expert as Olivia in accurately reading body language, but even I can see that she's now leaning forward, eager to involve herself fully in the discussion. This is exactly what I wanted, because, while what we've already discussed might prove to be useful, I'm certain that the only way we are going to catch this bastard, is if we can somehow predict, or more likely guess, what he might do next and get there ahead of him. If that's the case, then the next part of our conversation is absolutely crucial.

'That's really helpful, Olivia,' I say, 'I'm sure the team will appreciate you giving them these kinds of avenues to explore. But I want to ask you about the future.'

She suddenly interrupts, 'That's what I was about to say a couple of minutes ago. This man's a careful type, a planner. He needs to feel that he's in control. He must have everything pre planned according to some sort of logic, however skewed.'

I think I see what she's getting at and say, 'So, if we can try to anticipate what he'll do next, we might have a chance of stopping him and catching him?'

'Yes. But that's very difficult and highly speculative.'

'OK,' I accept. 'But let's give it a go. Do you think he's finished now?'

To my surprise, she answers immediately and without any hesitation. 'No. On the contrary, I suspect that he sees these first three killings as merely the build up to a big finish. That will come after the performance of *Götterdämmerung* on Sunday.'

'Four operas equals four killings, you mean? Will he be satisfied then?'

'I think that's probably meant to be his final bow,' she replies more tentatively. 'The epic conclusion to his own performance. But I can't be certain, because I can't read what's going on yet. I can't get his rationale clear in my head. You know, what he's doing and why? However, I do feel it's safe for us to assume that he's planning his most dramatic, most fulfilling and most meaningful act for the night of Sunday to Monday.'

'Act? Performance?' I interrupt doubtfully. 'You make it sound like something positive, something to be proud of, rather than just killing people.'

'Possibly.... Probably,' she stutters. I've never seen her quite so unsure. 'I don't know why I used those words, but they must be suggesting something to me. I just can't quite figure out what it is.'

'OK. It's great that we're forewarned about the fourth killing. Is there anything we can do to prepare for Sunday night? Anything at all?' I plead with her.

'I'm really not sure,' she almost whispers. 'I keep getting flashes of what I think might be insights, but they quickly disappear.'

'Look, it's just you and me here, Olivia,' I say, surprising myself with how much I've come to trust and depend on her. 'Just say what you want, however crazy. It'll go no further, unless you agree. I promise.'

As a professional, I can tell that she's very uneasy about going out on a limb. But I think she must also sense how we two are now bound together by these horrible events, because she takes a deep breath and says, 'OK. I think, maybe our man is now bringing the focus down onto what this whole thing is really all about. I don't understand it yet, but I sense that his next plan involves the opera more directly.'

'The performers, you mean?' I suggest. 'Do you think they might be in danger?'

'Yes. No... oh I don't know,' she vacillates. 'How can I know, Sam? You're asking me unfair questions. Questions, to which I can't possibly have the answers. All I know, is that the successive killings, so far, have mirrored, in significant ways, deaths in the operas.'

'So, we have to figure out which death in the last opera he'll copy?' I prompt.

'Possibly,' she replies. But, to my surprise, it's hardly a confident claim. I thought she was confident, at least about that part of her theory. 'The obvious death in *Götterdämmerung* would be that of Siegfried. But I don't know, it somehow doesn't feel right.'

I try to push her a little further. 'Do you think he might be targeting the singer who plays Siegfried in the opera? That would definitely be a step change in terms of its impact.'

'I don't know, Sam,' she says helplessly. 'It would fit in with the other three victims being male. I have to say that I'm not entirely convinced, but that's all I can come up with for now. What I do know is that, if we can begin to read him more accurately, it will give us our best chance of stopping him.'

I raise my hands in acknowledgement, 'OK, Olivia. I'll not hassle you any further.'

'No, there's something else,' she says decisively. 'The killer has his timetable. He has his plan. He has his victim and he has his method and location. He is also extremely confident, because he is aware that, either we have worked out when the next killing will happen, but we will never correctly guess who and where. Or, he will believe that we haven't yet connected the three murders.'

'Is this important?'

'I think so, yes. Remember that he's left us quite a few clues to what he's up to. The nature of the victims, the method of killing and the pieces of broken sword and poison. Now, why is he doing that? Why is he flagging the operas up so clearly?'

It's incredible how, just talking with Olivia makes me somehow feel I'm getting closer to the killer and I reply, 'He wants us to admire him? To recognise how clever he is and to appreciate what he is doing?'

'Yes, that's entirely possible,' she says. 'So, I'm convinced that we should impose a total ban on anything but the most basic information about these crimes getting to the media. We should not suggest, in any way, that the incidents are being treated as related. That way, he will either have his confidence boosted, that we haven't a clue what he's up to. And this might make him more careless. Or, if he wants us to understand, so that we'll admire him and how clever he is, he'll be frustrated that we're too stupid to follow his clues. In either of these eventualities, he may perhaps reveal more to us. This could be deliberately to show off, or because overconfidence makes him careless. It's not much, but I think it is one thing within our control.'

What she says makes a lot of sense, but I'm still concerned about the performers of Opera North. 'OK, Olivia, but I also think it might be a good idea, if I spoke with someone at The Sage. Just to give them a warning to keep their eyes and ears open and to be extra careful with security. Especially the guy who is singing the role of Siegfried. What do you think?'

She's silent for some time, before finally saying, 'Yes. I think we owe it to them. The only problem would be, if the killer is very close to Opera North or The Sage. That would then alert him to how far we've got.

'Well, that's a risk I think we must run,' I decide. 'But I'd really appreciate it, if you would come with me. You would be far more able to explain the links between the killings and their performances.'

11.30am, Saturday 9th July 2016, Newcastle City Centre Police Station, Forth Banks.

Olivia

Despite all my experience as a university lecturer, I feel a sense of anxiety as I enter the Incident Room, ahead of Sam. Other than watching the odd episode of *Endeavour* or *Vera*, I have little idea of the culture and ways of British police forces. And no experience at all of working directly with the police of any nation. The room is a windowless box and the air smells of stale smoke. It's clear that at least one of the surprisingly small team has clothes which are impregnated with the stuff. The quiet murmur of conversation stills, the instant I appear and Sam winks at me, as he directs me to a seat at the head of an oblong table. I imagine that he intended this gesture to be encouraging. It does, however, reinforce my sense of vulnerability here, as if I am totally dependent on him.

He introduces me to the team and asks them to introduce themselves in turn, before he goes on to explain, concisely and clearly, that he has been put in charge of the entire investigation. This elicits an uneasy staring at the ceiling from the middle aged, uniformed Sergeant Walters. There are clearly internal politics at play here, about which I know nothing. Sam follows this, by explaining what I am doing there and how, in his view, I have already greatly helped the investigation. 'Put bluntly,' he concludes, 'without Dr Clavel's insights and information, we'd still have no idea that we are in pursuit of one killer. We'd still be chasing our own tails, with three separate enquiries. So, please treat Dr Clavel as one of the team. Anything you would say to any one of us, you should say in her presence.'

The woman wearing a badge, identifying her as a 'Civilian Assistant', the young PC and DC Jenkins nod and smile, whereas Sergeant Walters looks on, stony faced. Oh well. Three with me, one against. To be expected, I guess.

'Look, I know it all sounds a bit 'X Files', says Snow, to head off any objections to the linking of all three murders with Wagner's operas. 'Believe me, I had grave doubts and DCI Quayle more or less threw me out, when I first suggested it to her yesterday.'

'Pity she didn't give it fair hearing, I'd say,' says Helen Dutton, squinting out from behind her huge glasses.

'We can all be wise after the event, Helen,' accepts Snow. 'The point is that she's now on board.'

'What about the confession for the first murder?' asks PC Armitage and, for his trouble, receives an angry glare from his sergeant.

'DCI Quayle and I interviewed Mr Smith earlier this morning,' explains Snow. 'He's now no longer considered a suspect in that murder.'

A murmur goes round the group and Snow raps his knuckles on the table to bring some order. He explains that the DCI is aware that the team is light on numbers and has promised reinforcements within twenty four hours. This seems to reassure everyone and there follows a series of short reports, each of which makes clear that forensic examination of the scenes of the murders has, to date, yielded nothing of value.

DC Jenkins then explains that the poison pushed into the last victim's hand is a standard product, available in many shops and outlets locally. 'Helen had the idea of using the batch number on the base of the tin to trace where it was sold,' Jenkins adds. 'It was a long shot, but

196

we've got lucky. It was delivered to the Nun Street branch of Wilko, the household general store. I'm off there later to check out when it was bought and whether they have CCTV of the tills.'

'That's excellent work, Serena and Helen,' says Snow. 'Maybe that's the first big mistake our man has made. Let me know what you find out.'

'Is there anything particular you want me to work on?' asks Helen Dutton and Snow replies immediately.

'Yes, we need to consider the possibility that the killer might not be a local man. The choice of this international event, as the background for the murders, suggests he might just as easily be a visitor to the city.'

'But he must have had knowledge to plan all the murders,' argues DC Jenkins. 'If Dr Clavel's theory is correct, he must have chosen his victims very carefully.'

'Exactly!' agrees Snow. 'And that's where, I wonder, Helen. Is there any way we can check hotels etc for details of who's visiting for the period of the operas, against who has visited in the recent past?'

Helen Dutton looks doubtful, 'We'd have to focus that search quite a bit. I could start with city centre hotels and then broaden the search, if necessary. But it will take time.'

'I know it will, Helen,' sympathises Snow. 'But do your best. Now, we should also get that estate agent, Hardcastle, in and get accurate details of when his sordid little arrangement with Mykel Stevenson began. I suggest, Helen, that you start from that date and look for a man travelling alone. Also, DC Jenkins, maybe you could interview Kylie Stevenson again, about her punters, especially anyone not local. It could be that our man posed as a client to check out the possibilities there.'

The team is beginning to buzz. They accept that their task is like looking for a needle in a haystack, but they are inspired by Snow's leadership, in giving them all positive avenues on which to work.

'OK,' Snow says, concluding the meeting. 'PC Armitage, you keep on looking at the CCTV. I know it's tedious, but you might get lucky. I'm off with Dr Clavel to speak with Opera North about tomorrow night. We've all got work to do and if we do it properly, we'll get this bastard before he can hurt anyone else. Meet again at 6pm here.'

The team, with the exception of DC Jenkins, who looks a touch put out at the news that I am accompanying Snow to the meeting with Opera North, breaks up with a sense of purposefulness and positivity that impresses me greatly.

***

2pm, Saturday 9th July 2016, The Sage, Gateshead.

Sam

Fortunately Jessica Lawler, the Human Relations Manager of Opera North and Josephine Rowe, the Managing Director of The Sage were having lunch together, when I rang to make an appointment to speak with them. Now, having given them an hour to get back to The Sage, Olivia and I are on our way to our meeting with them.

She seems a little surprised at my choice of car, a bright red, Mazda MX-5 and, as we pull out of the station car park, she teases me. 'I've always thought this particular model was known as a 'tart cart.' Seems an odd choice for you.'

'Really?' I reply, as I nose out into the traffic. 'You have me down as some sort of unreconstructed macho man, then? We're in an age of identity fluidity, you know.'

'Of course, you're right. I'm sorry,' she says, all flustered. I leave her to stew for a couple of minutes and then burst out laughing.

'Actually, a good mate of mine, a classic, ditzy blonde, emigrated to the States last year and made me an offer I couldn't refuse on it. Wasn't my choice, but I've kind of got to like it.'

'Touché,' she replies, in good humour, before saying, 'That woman DC back there, Serena... Are you involved with her?'

'Well, that's another very personal question, Dr Clavel,' I say with a smile. 'As it happens, no, we're not. Why do you ask?'

'Oh, probably nothing,' she replies. 'She just seemed a bit put out that I am in on this interview, that's all.'

'Can't blame her really, can you?' I ask rhetorically. She looks genuinely confused and I'm forced to elaborate. 'I mean, what young woman wouldn't be jealous of the company you're keeping?'

She snorts in response and I explain with a laugh, 'Seriously, we've been working these cases together, that's all. It's nothing. She's a great officer.'

As soon as we arrive at The Sage, we're led to a lift which takes us to the top floor. Once there, we follow a staff member who walks swiftly down a short corridor, towards the rear of the building, away from the river. We're shown into a spacious, comfortable office, where two women are waiting for us. Jessica Lawler is a small, gamin type, immaculately dressed, though in a rather too bohemian style for my taste. The other, slightly older and careworn woman looks much more at home and I guess that she is Josephine Rowe, the Managing Director of The Sage. My hunch proves to be correct, as, once the introductions are made, she invites us to take one of the four chairs placed around a circular, conference table.

'I was very surprised to receive your call, Detective Sergeant,' Ms Rowe begins, while casting a curious glance towards Olivia. 'Is there some kind of problem?'

'To be honest, we're not quite sure,' I reply candidly. 'That's why we're here.' I ask them what they know of the three recent killings in Gateshead and they both reply that they know only what they have read or heard in the media. 'Then I must insist that you keep what I am about to say in the strictest of confidence.' The women exchange uneasy glances, as I continue. 'You will certainly not know that it is our belief that the three killings are the work of one person and that this person's actions are linked to the production of 'The Ring of the Nibelungen,' which is currently taking place at The Sage.'

Josephine Rowe's mouth gapes open in silent shock, whereas Jessica Lawler's face drains of all its colour. 'Surely, you cannot be serious?' Ms Lawler asks. 'What you suggest is too outlandish for words.'

'Outlandish, perhaps,' I agree, 'but I'm sure that you will see things differently, when you have heard what Dr Clavel has to say.' I invite Olivia to outline her theory, to which the two other women listen carefully and do not make any attempt to interrupt. Sitting back, watching her explain our current thinking, clearly and cogently, I congratulate myself on the decision to bring Olivia with me.

As soon as she finishes, Ms Rowe says, 'Well, I agree that there are certainly too many coincidences for comfort. But, if what you say is true, then this madman is far from finished. We still, after all, have one opera to perform.'

'Exactly,' I interrupt, 'That's why we are here. To suggest that you take certain precautions tomorrow.'

'What do you mean?' demands Ms Lawler, panic showing itself in her eyes. 'Are you saying that The Sage itself, and presumably the audience, might be in danger? If so, we should consider cancelling the performance.'

'I'm sure that won't be necessary,' I reassure them. 'Everything we know about this man and his previous behaviour, suggests that he will already have identified a carefully chosen target. We believe that no one, other than this individual, will be at risk.'

'But do you have any idea who this target might be, Sergeant Snow?' asks Ms Rowe. 'Surely they must be kept securely away from The Sage, until this is over.'

'I'm afraid that we cannot say for certain who is the next target,' I admit freely. 'But there is a good possibility that it may indeed be one of the performers.'

'Good God!' says a visibly disturbed Ms Rowe. 'Who do you think it is?'

I look to Olivia and, like the reliable colleague she is proving to be, she takes up the discussion. 'The only death in *Götterdämmerung* that makes any sense, in this context, is that of Siegfried. However, I'm struggling to understand how our man might see himself as Siegfried's killer, Hagen. He, after all, is portrayed as a devious and unpleasant character. In my estimation, such a killer as the one we seek, conventionally has a much higher opinion of himself than that. But, I'm sorry to say that, at the moment, that's the best I have to offer.'

The two officials look at one another anxiously, before Ms Rowe speaks. 'We could withdraw Alo Kotkas, who is scheduled to sing Siegfried during tomorrow's performance. But would that make any difference, given that he would have to be replaced by an understudy?'

Olivia answers very quickly, 'I have no reason to suppose that our killer has anything personal against this singer. It is the role that he is playing, which might be putting him in danger. An understudy playing that role would be in equal danger.'

'Then the choice is clear,' declares Ms Rowe. 'Either we cancel the performance, or we speak with Alo. At the very least, we must inform him of the potential risk he would be running, by singing his scheduled part. I propose that we try to speak with him now.'

Ms Rowe takes out her mobile and quickly leaves the room, while the rest of us sit in an uneasy silence. We can hear her through the closed door, as she speaks to someone, presumably Alo Kotkas, before she returns. 'Luckily, he's here at The Sage having a costume refit. He'll be here in five minutes.'

When he appears, I am stunned by the sheer bulk of the man. He's enormous and very powerfully built. For some reason, I'd expected a slender, effeminate man. At Ms Rowe's request, I explain the situation to Mr Kotkas, who, despite being Estonian, evidently understands English perfectly.

When I've finished, he looks me squarely in the eye. 'Detective Sergeant,' he says in a melodious, rich voice. 'As I understand this, I am not at any great risk out on the stage. And afterwards, well, forewarned is forearmed, as you British say. I will not be scared away from performing for my public, by a man who hides in the shadows. I will be ready for him, should he show his face.'

I have to admit that he cuts an impressive figure, perfect for the role of the hero, but I move quickly to reassure him. 'I will ensure that you have protection at all times, both before your appearance and afterwards, until you leave the city.'

'Very well,' he says, 'then I am most happy. With your permission, I will return to the Wardrobe Mistress, with whom I was working.' Before he leaves, I instruct him to say nothing of this to anyone else.

'Is anything planned for after the performance?' asks Olivia, 'a party, or some such?'

'Indeed there is,' replies Ms Rowe. 'This is the final performance of the conductor, who is leaving Opera North. The whole cast and orchestra are taking over the Blackfriars Restaurant in Newcastle city centre for a farewell party.'

'And how will they get there from The Sage?'

'If it's a fine, dry evening, I imagine that many will walk. Other than that, taxis,' explained Ms Lawler.

'That's fine, but please advise Mr Kotkas that we will put on a police car for him.'

I arrange to speak with Ms Lawler before Sunday's performance and we agree that a team of plain-clothes officers will be deployed at The Sage throughout the performance. 'With luck,' I conclude, 'tomorrow's performance and afterwards will go off without a problem.'

I'm unaccountably disappointed when, as we leave The Sage, Olivia says that she must go home to prepare for a dinner date. Somehow, I've come to like her a great deal and really feel envious of her dining partner. But I put on a brave face and say brightly, 'OK. You have my permission to be off duty for the rest of the day. But I'll be in touch before the performance tomorrow.'

She looks at me, as if she's not quite sure whether or not I'm joking. Good. I like to keep my women on their toes.

Chapter Twenty One

Olivia

I feel rather guilty, having left Christine and Joe, without being able to tell them what I've been up to. But Sergeant Snow was pretty adamant about that, 'Tell them anything you like, as long as it's not the truth.' In the end, I promised Christine that I'd explain on Monday what had been going on. It seems strange to think that, whichever way things work out, for me it will almost certainly all be over in less than forty eight hours.

As I sit in the taxi, I'm really looking forward to this evening out with JP. He'd promised yesterday to reserve a table at House of Tides and had confirmed it by SMS message, while I was busy with the police. When I told Christine where I was going, she was incredulous. 'How on earth did he manage to do that? It's the only Michelin starred restaurant in the city and I've been told that you have to wait weeks to get a table, especially on a Saturday evening.'

Even the taxi driver seems impressed, as I tell him where to drop me off. 'Aye. I've heard it's a canny enough place, like,' he advises.'But I prefer me fish'n'chips and a pint, pet.'

I'm glad that I left DS Snow as early as I did, because it gave me the time to get myself properly ready. A long soak in the bath revived my spirits and I feel good now, in my favourite green, summer dress and my hair properly styled. Despite the warmth of the evening, however, I shiver involuntarily, as the taxi moves across the River Tyne and I glance to my right. The Sage is immediately visible, basking innocently in the warm glow, which covers the river bank. The horror, of what something as magnificent as Wagner's Ring Cycle seems to have inspired, leaves me bereft. Now I come to think about it, the sheer effrontery of this unknown killer angers me more than I can say. I'm really not sure that I'll be able, ever again, to enjoy any of this music. And that saddens me immensely.

'Nearly there, pet,' says the driver and I resolve that I must banish such grim thoughts and simply focus on enjoying my evening out with JP. Apart from seeing him at the opera tomorrow, it will almost certainly be the last time that we will meet. Unless, of course, I remind myself, he gets in touch when we are both back in Switzerland. I must admit that I'm not sure what I think about that prospect. I've been rather overwhelmed by my sudden and unexpected involvement with the police. In fact, for the last day or so, I've hardly given JP any thought at all. Maybe that's been a mistake. Now, as I begin to think specifically about him, it seems to me that, on the one hand, he is a charming and cultured companion. There's little doubt that I've very much enjoyed the time spent in his company. However, I'm also keenly aware of his recent bereavement and I'm not at all sure, how ready he is to move on in his private life. The same, I reflect ruefully, could also be said of myself. Maybe this evening will offer some clues and suggest how things might, or might not develop.

House of Tides occupies a large, four storey, stone building, quite close to the riverbank and almost in the shade of The High Level Bridge over the Tyne. It looks like a former merchant's dwelling and the 'house' feel extends to the dining room. My heels click pleasingly, as

I walk across the dark wooden floor to the small window table for two, where JP is already seated. As soon as he hears my approach, over the excited chatter of the many diners and the bustling of the waiting staff, he turns, rises from his seat and approaches.

'Gee, Olivia,' he says, 'you look as pretty as your name,' before leaning in to kiss me gently on the cheek. It's the first time he's attempted any such intimacy and I must admit, it feels quite good. His skin is clean shaven, soft and moisturised and I get just the right suggestion of a light, and doubtless very expensive, cologne.

I allow him to push in my seat and note the experienced way in which he immediately attracts the attention of a waiter. 'I thought maybe we could start with a glass of champagne. I hope it'll help with our study of the menu,' he suggests with a grin. 'It'll sure take more time to read than one in McDonald's.'

I smile and nod in agreement and the waiter disappears. 'My sister was green with envy, when I told her I was coming here,' I say. 'She wanted to know how you managed to get a table on a Saturday evening.'

He looks directly at me and shrugs, 'Oh, I can't claim that it was my natural charm and persuasiveness. The Chef Patron's one of the bank's clients and he was kind enough to squash us in.' The waiter has been very efficient in providing our *apéro* and JP immediately raises his glass to propose a toast. 'To our chance meeting, a great week in Newcastle and, of course, to Opera North's wonderful performances.'

'Hear, hear,' I say, as our glasses clink perfectly and I take a sip of the fine, dry wine. 'Mmmm. Delicious. Just what I needed.'

A frown crosses JP's face, like a cloud scudding across an otherwise bright summer sky. 'Hey! Are you OK?' he asks with concern. 'You have a bad day or something?'

Now I face decision time. Do I tell him about the whole situation with the police, or do I keep silent. I really like JP and instinctively feel that I can trust him. But my sense of duty prevails and I find myself saying, 'Oh, you know JP. Big sis dragged me all around the shops today, 'because things are soooo expensive in Switzerland.' Now, don't misunderstand me, I'm as keen as any woman on buying nice clothes. But, there's a limit. By the time she'd finished with me, I swear, if I'd seen one more rack of women's clothes, I'd have committed to naturism!'

JP's eyebrow arches up sexily and he strokes his chin, musing, 'Well now. You've sure given me some food for thought there, ma'am.'

We both laugh and clink glasses again and he asks if I'm ready to order. We both agree to take the extraordinary looking, tasting menu, figuring that the more examples of a Michelin starred chef's food we can try, the better. A wistful look comes to JP's face as he asks, 'Would you mind if we have the Stag's Leap Cabernet Sauvignon? It's a fine wine from California and a taste of my real home would feel good tonight.'

I'm not sure what he means and say, 'Oh. You looked so happy when I arrived. Have things not gone as you'd hoped this week?' I'm referring of course to his admission on the plane from Geneva that this is the first time that he's done alone, things he used to love doing with his deceased wife.

The smile returns instantly to his face, 'Oh, no. Please don't think that, Olivia. I've had an absolutely unforgettable time here in Newcastle. I can honestly say that the trip couldn't have gone better. Everything's exceeded expectations, from the moment I met you at Geneva Airport.'

I smile and he senses my uncertainty. 'Relax, Olivia,' he says warmly. 'I'm not hitting on you, I promise. Not that I don't find you very attractive. But, you know....' He seems a little lost for words, so I help him out.

'Sounds like you're becoming an honorary Geordie.'

'Damned right, ma'am,' he insists. 'I just love it here. I've had a ball. Met some interesting people and seen and done some truly memorable things. How about you? Have things been good for you?'

Having the question put in such a direct way somewhat throws me off balance. I can't, in all honesty, say that the trip has been without its negative elements. But the fact that JP is totally unaware of the thing which is utterly consuming me now is, in its way, quite refreshing. The police have said nothing to the media about the linking of the murders, so there's no way that he should see any connection with the operas we've been attending. I resolve to enjoy to the full this interlude of normality, before facing what will be tomorrow.

'Yes,' I answer, 'it's been lovely to catch up with family and old friends and,' with my glass raised in his direction, 'to meet new ones. And, of course, there's been the opera.'

'Yes,' he says quietly, almost as if he'd rather keep these thoughts to himself. 'The opera. Indeed. I had worries about whether I was doing the right thing, you know? After what happened.' We are between courses and his hands are palms down on the small table. Without consciously thinking about it, I reach out easily and cover his right hand with my left. He looks up and I think I can see real pain in his eyes. He looks at my hand on his and smiles, before saying, 'but it's all turning out for the best. I really feel much better about all that. Ready to go on with things, if that makes sense?'

I gently withdraw my hand and sigh, 'Of course it does, JP. I'm so glad that you've enjoyed yourself. It's good to recognise that life must go on.' I sense a deepening intimacy between us, but it's broken by the arrival of the waiter with another of our tasting dishes. It's Lindisfarne Oyster, Cucumber, Ginger and Caviar and, as soon as the plates are set before us, he looks at me and softly whistles. 'Wow! Would you just look at that. I've never seen such beautiful food before.'

Over the remaining courses, we never quite rediscover the closeness which had been developing earlier. We enjoy discussing our views of the three productions we have seen so far and JP impresses me very much with his appreciation of the music. 'You know,' he says at one point, 'I can admit now that I wasn't sure about the concert style of production. But the conductor's absolutely right, it literally brings the orchestra on stage and makes it every bit as important as the key characters.' He even goes all misty eyed as he begins to talk about Brünnhilde, 'I can't tell you how much I love Kirsty Cole Harding. It's great to enjoy such perfection from one of my fellow Americans. I think she'll give a performance to die for tomorrow in *Götterdämmerung*.'

Inevitably, we turn to our pre performance discussion group and what we've made of the various personalities, or lack of them. While I am more critical of Gideon's ineffectual leadership of the group discussions, JP is far more negative about Leonard. 'I mean, where does that guy get off, being so superior?' he asks, as he rolls the last of the excellent Cabernet around his glass. 'I guess he's educated and so on, but he's so arrogant. He clearly sees himself as some kind of super brain.'

He'd not said anything like this to me before and I have to admit that the strength of his opinion makes me reconsider my thoughts about Leonard. I had thought him just a self absorbed, arrogant man, but what JP says makes me wonder if there's an even more unpleasant side to him. The last thing I want, however, is for the evening to wind down as a bitching session, so I say simply, 'I don't know, JP. There are a lot of little people, mostly men, who big themselves up in the same way that Leonard does. He's a bit pathetic, if you ask me, but that's all.'

JP looks at me, as if he he's unsure whether he should say anything else on the subject, before evidently deciding against. 'So, Olivia. How long will you be here in the UK, before you fly back to Switzerland?'

I haven't booked my return with Easyjet yet and haven't really given it much thought, so I reply vaguely. 'Oh, I've no fixed plans yet. That's the beauty of being an academic in the summer. I don't need to be back on campus until late September.'

'Wow! You guys really have it tough,' though his smile indicates that he's just being gently sarcastic. 'I won't be sticking around much after tomorrow.'

'We each have one another's numbers, so we can keep in touch after you go home,' I say, as he raises his hand to ask for the bill.

He waits outside in the surprisingly balmy air and we agree to meet, as usual, shortly before the last of our group discussions. 'I've really enjoyed myself this evening,' he says, as my taxi pulls up. 'Thanks for everything.'

'I enjoyed it as well,' I say honestly and, just before I climb into the car, he leans in to give me another, slightly less chaste kiss.

Chapter Twenty Two

1am, Sunday 10th July 2016.

I feel completely safe and out of the reach of those little people who may wish to stop me from finishing what I have started. I have distracted myself these past minutes by watching the treacly looking water of the river ebb towards Tynemouth and the dark, dangerous waters of The North Sea beyond. But now, I turn back into the room. The green light on the stereo system blinks furiously as it greedily accepts the pristine compact disc with which I feed it. In moments, the ethereal music begins to swell and my breathing calms as I sit, relaxed, on the deep, red leather sofa. I contemplate how surprisingly easy it has all been.

This afternoon, The Sage looked quite different, because no performance was scheduled to take place. I'd purposefully chosen to go there after 3.30pm, between the busy lunch period and the time when the post shopping crowd calls in for a beer or a glass of wine. Everything looked completely normal, which confirmed to me that the police have no idea what's going on. It really gives me a buzz to think that no one has yet connected the deaths, nor come close to understanding how magnificently it will all end. I could have spent all afternoon thinking about what's to come, but I reminded myself that there is so little time and so much to do.

I recall glancing idly across from my seat overlooking the Tyne. Immediately I was able to pick out the older, thick set man and the three younger,

*fitter looking men, all dressed in the same uniform
They were sitting almost close enough for me to
eavesdrop on their banal conversation, should I have
wished. Needless to say, I didn't. The drivel of such
limited creatures didn't interest me in the slightest.
Rather, I smiled contentedly at my accurate
assumption that, at that time, they would be enjoying
their mid afternoon cup of tea.*

*Sitting here, now, as I re run the events of this
afternoon, I feel that it's almost like I'm watching a
film of myself. In my mind, I can see myself, discreetly
glancing around and verifying that I am attracting no
attention, before I slip quietly down the stairs into the
lower floor area of The Sage. There's not a lot of
natural light down there and I rush along the corridor
until right at the end, I find my goal. The lock is pitiful
for such a place and, hardly a great picker myself, I
am inside within twenty seconds. I nod my head at my
own ability to predict exactly what the layout and
contents would be. Within a further two minutes I
have found what I need.*

*After carefully making sure that I have left no trace,
I relock the room and, like a ghost emerging from its
tomb, I slide unnoticed into the happy people in the
concourse.*

*I smile as I remember deciding to treat myself to a
celebratory coffee and even to find the time to join in
the excited chatter of the people around my table.*

*Would they have talked to me so readily, I wonder,
if they had had the first inkling of what I'd already
done and what I have planned to do in the next twenty
four hours? Of course they wouldn't. They'd have been
horrified, terrified, outraged - any damn thing you
choose, they'd be it. Because they're insignificant,*

profoundly ordinary people, who could never dream of aspiring to what I will achieve.

In a way, I feel sorry that the whole performance will soon be reaching its finale. I have felt more alive these past few days than for the previous several months. But I know the crescendo that I will achieve with my final acts will be a fitting conclusion to everything.

I'm almost overcome with desire as I sit staring at my favourite framed photograph.'It's almost time to begin my final journey to you, my love,' I say to the always smiling face. 'Be patient for just a few more hours, my darling. We will soon be together forever.'

Chapter Twenty Three

*12.30pm, Sunday 10th July 2016, Newcastle
City Centre Police Station, Forth Banks.*

Sam

I don't need to be a great reader of body language and
facial expressions to tell that the DCI is well pissed off at
having to be here. My guess is that at this time of the
week, she's normally gearing up at the nineteenth hole
of the fancy golf club, at which she, and all the important
movers and shakers, exchange gossip and make deals.
Commitment to the job is one thing. Losing a Sunday,
and one with such gorgeous weather, is something else
entirely. She sits, glowering, on one of the desks in the
larger Incident Room, to which they've moved this
enquiry, since the team was expanded.

I ask her to outline the current state of play with the
press and she's immediately on her feet, as if she wants
to get her contribution over and be off back to her club.
'This enquiry is still being spun to the press as three
separate investigations. We've managed to keep a lid on
the fact that we're actively looking for just one killer and
that's the way we want it to stay. They've bought totally
that the killing of Grantham was an argument over
money, that of Stevenson vice related and that of Holden
a mugging gone pear shaped. Three killings in so short a
time is very unusual here, but as long as they're not
linked, it's being seen as just a freak of timing. Nothing
to get into a panic about. So, if any of you lot have ideas
about how to earn that bit of extra spending money for
your holiday by blabbing to the press, I have only one

thing to say. Don't even think of doing it, or I really will have them on a plate.'

She nods to me and hastily leaves the room. I turn to DC Jenkins, 'How'd it go at Wilko, Serena?'

She's obviously still irritated about yesterday and looks daggers at me, before replying unenthusiastically, 'Dead end. The check out staff don't remember anything about who might have bought the poison and the CCTV had already been wiped.'

'Too bad,' I say. 'And Forensics have produced nothing of use from any of the scenes.'

'We haven't managed to track down any witnesses to any of the attacks,' adds Sergeant Walters glumly. 'And CCTV of the areas has yielded nothing.'

'How's it going with tracking visitors, Helen?' I ask hopefully. But she just grimaces.

'The estate agent, Hardcastle, confirmed that the arrangement with Mykel Stevenson, concerning the commercial property, had lasted two months. I've begun comparing lists of current hotel registrations with those going back over two months, but it's back breaking work. Even limiting the population to solitary male visitors, it's going to take a long time. You'd be surprised how many small hotels still use a handwritten register system. And, of course, there are countless bed and breakfasts and even platforms like airbnb.'

The room groans in sympathy and I try to sound positive, 'Thanks very much for all your work on this, Helen. I'm sure it'll prove valuable to the investigation.'

The DCI's instruction that we are looking for just one killer seems to have surprised many of the new recruits to the team. So I give a quick outline of our current thinking on how the killings are linked. I then brief them on the more important matter, of what we believe may take place during the upcoming night, after the final performance of the opera. This causes a bit of a stir among some of the officers and I have to demand their attention. 'It's important that we're on our mettle tonight. Our man's been very, very careful so far and he hasn't given much for forensics to go on at all. It could well be that tonight is our best chance of feeling his collar. So, pay close attention to what I'm about to say.'

I comply with Dr Clavel's request that I don't highlight her role in the development of our thinking, as I explain that there are strong reasons to believe that tonight, our killer may try to bow out with something extraordinary. 'We think that he's going to try to top everything he's done so far. That suggests that he intends to come much closer to the performances themselves, perhaps by targeting one of the performers.' There's not a sound now, as I add, 'The best guess we have, based upon his previous behaviour, is that Alo Kotkas, one of the singers with Opera North, will be his target.'

I point to the large plan of The Sage which Helen has attached to one of the notice boards and run through the disposition of each member of the team for this afternoon and evening. I pay particular attention to the two officers who have been selected to act as protection for Mr Kotkas. 'I don't want you to let him out of your sight, from the moment he leaves the stage at the end of the performance, until he's tucked up in his hotel room. So, you stay with him during the party at Blackfriars Restaurant. The rest of the team will keep an general eye open at The Sage. Then, after the performance, you're to keep a close watch over the other cast members on their journey between The Sage and the restaurant and then back to their hotels. OK, everything clear?'

A chorus of 'Yes, sergeant,' eventually dies down and I say, 'Right. Get yourselves a drink and a bite to eat. The performance starts at 3.30, so we should start arriving at The Sage, discreetly, in ones and twos, from about 2.30 onwards. Good luck.'

Chapter Twenty Four

1.45pm, Sunday 10th July 2016, The Sage, Gateshead.

Olivia

Gideon looks much happier than I have seen him since the start of the first meeting of the discussion group. Perhaps it's the realisation that he's about to lead the last session of what has been a difficult mix of people. In any case, JP and I met fifteen minutes ago and promptly decided to maintain our one hundred per cent attendance record. Viktor is busy chatting amiably with Claire and David is listening carefully, as Gillian holds forth. Unsurprisingly, Leonard sits in silence, smirking as he examines his immaculate fingernails, before adjusting the visibility of his gold cufflinks.

Gideon begins with a general enquiry, 'OK, folks. We've now experienced three of the four operas. How's it been for you?' As no one seems willing to start the discussion, he asks Viktor directly, 'Viktor? You said that you were intrigued by the concert style performances. Have they met your expectations?'

The young German coughs nervously, before catching sight of Claire's encouraging smile and replying, 'Oh yes. Yes, Gideon. Without doubt. The orchestra for me has been the star of the show.'

'No. No. No. And once again no,' interrupts Leonard, in his characteristically dismissive way. 'Young man, I realise you have limited experience. But have you not ears to hear?' He seems gratified by the almost palpable way Gillian and Claire bridle, as they wonder how best to protect Viktor from such condescension. 'It should be obvious to anyone, with even half an appreciation of Wagner, that some marvellous performances, especially Brünnhilde, have been struggling against an over powerful orchestra. At times, I've actually felt like approaching the conductor and asking him to give the wonderful Ms Harding a chance to be heard.'

'I don't quite know where you've been sitting, Leonard,' says JP in his charming, unpretentiously American manner. 'Way up in 'The Gods,' maybe. But from where I'm sitting, I can hear the singers just fine.' At that precise moment, I could go straight over to him and plant a big kiss on him. But, as I look around the table, it's obvious I'd have to get in the queue behind Claire, Gillian, perhaps even Gideon.

'Couldn't agree with you more,' says David. 'In fact, for me, too, the orchestra has stood out magnificently.'

Leonard's normally pale and unhealthy looking face has gone an extremely dark shade of puce and I fear he may suffer some sort of seizure, so I say quickly. 'Let's not forget that it's entirely right that we all have different opinions about the detail. But I'm equally certain that we should all be able to agree that it has been a worthwhile experiment.'

Murmurs of agreement circulate round the table and a surprisingly determined David adds, 'I agree, Olivia. And we should also remember that Scottish Opera's full production of The Ring Cycle back in the noughties more or less bankrupted it.'

'An excellent point, David,' says Gideon. 'I think I can speak for all of us, when I say that none of us would wish Opera North to be put into financial peril by one production.'

Leonard excepted, David has managed to create such a positive feeling in the group that Gideon, recognising his opportunity, risks suggesting a final discussion topic. 'I wonder whether you'd be interested in discussing one theme of *Götterdämmerung,* which could also apply to the whole Ring Cycle?'

'Sure, Gideon,' answers JP on behalf of the whole group. 'Let's have it.'

'Well,' says the group leader, steepling his fingers and gazing around the table. 'Why do the gods have to be totally destroyed at the end of the opera? The Rhinemaidens get the Ring back, after all. Why does it have to end in such a cataclysmic way?'

It's actually a really interesting question and one that seems to stump the group, as no one rushes to offer an opinion. In the end, I feel that I must set the ball rolling. 'I wonder whether the extent to which Wotan is prepared to do terrible things, in order to try to protect his own authority and position, means that he has to be punished?'

'That's exactly what I was just thinking!' exclaims Gillian. 'Just think of his decision, in effect to order the death of his own kin, Siegfried. That is surely sufficient for him to be treated as he is.'

I sense, rather than see, JP suddenly stirring on the other side of Gideon. I look at him, expecting him to say something, but he remains silent. My attention is drawn back to the discussion, as Viktor adds passionately, 'And think how he selfishly takes the branch from The World Ash Tree. Remember, that causes it to dry up as the source of wisdom and knowledge. OK, he lost an eye doing that, but it's hardly the action of the top god, is it? Shows his egocentrism and lack of any consideration for anyone, other than himself. Or anything else, other than his power. I'd say that he got what he deserved. Absolutely.'

Leonard looks around the room with something close to disgust on his face, 'I think you're missing the point here. Doesn't Wotan fundamentally lose the will to live, when he realises that the children he hoped would survive him, and maintain the gods in Valhalla, are themselves all dead?'

'You mean, he just gives up at the end?' asks David. 'He's actually glad that Valhalla, and with it all his power, is destroyed?'

'That's right,' says Leonard, as if to a particularly unintelligent child. 'Surely we can all see that when he feels compelled, effectively to order the killing of his son Siegmund by Hunding, he loses the will to rule, even to live. The fact is that he doesn't want it, not that he doesn't deserve it. It's his choice. And, while I don't expect everyone here to agree or even to understand, it's a brave choice. A wonderful choice.'

Leonard's argument is certainly interesting, strong even. But it's the way he outlines, then defends it, which is so unpleasant.

Looking disdainfully at Viktor and Gillian he says, 'Your verdict on Wotan is all too typical of the mediocre world, in which I am forced to live. A world, in which insignificant people can and do rejoice in the bringing down of the great. That's something that I, personally, will always struggle to prevent in any way I can.'

I'm not quite sure what Leonard means by this. Does he mean that he regrets the loss of belief and respect in contemporary society? If so, I imagine many may agree with him. Or, does he mean that he sees himself as one of the superior humans, who must fight to prevent themselves being dragged down by the inferior masses? Or, is he at the same point in his own life, as his view of Wotan? Does he desire an end, albeit a dramatic one, to what he sees as his futile, earthly existence? I'm aware of an idea, so sinister and terrifying, beginning to form in my mind. A hint of a dark figure moving through shadows suggests itself, but I can't quite define it. Too quickly, I am distracted by Claire, who has been silent throughout this exchange. She is staring at the table, with what look like tears in her eyes. 'Oh, Gideon. I'd always thought that, tragic though it is, the eternal togetherness of Siegfried and Brünnhilde testifies to the power and ultimate redemptive quality of love. Are you telling me that that's not so?'

'That's an excellent question, for each of us to take into our own experience of what many call Wagner's masterpiece,' Gideon replies. 'We should each make up our own mind.' Drawing the discussion unmistakably to an end, he smiles, 'Thank you all very much for a most stimulating and enjoyable series of meetings.'

Predictably, Leonard is the only group member not to burst into spontaneous applause. He simply stands, looks down his nose at each of us in turn and stalks from the room. 'What an absolutely appalling man,' declares Gillian, to unanimous agreement. 'I hope I never have the misfortune to see him again.'

We all congregate at one of the concourse bars, where JP, seemingly recovered from his withdrawn approach to much of the last meeting, is back to his personable best. He is generous enough to buy everyone a drink and David accompanies him to the bar, in order to help with the glasses. The rest of us take seats around a small, circular table which, fortunately for us, has just been vacated.

'You know, dear,' Claire says to Gillian, when we are all seated, 'if you'll permit me to say. Age has taught me that big headed men like Leonard are neither unique, nor special. You should not give them the power to irritate you.'

Gillian only has time to agree, before the men return with the drinks and we all toast the present members of our group.

The sound of the brass quartet summons us to enter Sage One and, having arranged to meet JP in the first, longer interval, I set off to my seat. I'm suddenly shocked to come face to face with Sergeant Snow, who is making his way down the stairs, as I am mounting them. I realise, with a sense of dread, that, while I have managed to escape the terrible world of serial killers and police investigations for an hour or two, I'm about to be be plunged straight back into it.

**

I feel a certain melancholy that my self imposed challenges are almost at an end. Despite the warm afternoon sunshine streaming into the concourse areas of The Sage, inside, I feel that winter and a final ending are almost upon me. If I am honest, I have felt this way for several months, since that dismal December day when the floor of my life was ripped away. But I feel a sense of pride in the way that I have refashioned myself and given new purpose to what might have been a sad decline. Of course, the people surrounding me now would never understand that. They have not developed the sense of vision and clarity, of which I have proved myself capable.

Everything is in place to ensure a successful end to my work. Not even the sight of several people, who I take to be plain clothes police officers, milling around in their ludicrously transparent way, can divert me from my chosen path. For a moment, I wonder why they are here. Have they finally connected the deaths? I shake my head in wonderment at their stupidity. I certainly left sufficient clues for any intelligent and cultured person to correctly interpret. But it doesn't matter at all. They can have no conception of what I have planned for the finale of my own 'Ring Cycle.'

Indeed, I feel no sense of remorse about the three necessary deaths. They were largely worthless lives, which, by their small part in my drama, at least achieved something notable in their ending. Neither do I hesitate to carry out my plan for the fourth death. I'm am certain that, when all is finally revealed and explained, it will be embraced with love and joy.

I am at peace with myself, as I make my way through the excited crowd to take my place, near my now familiar neighbours in the auditorium. The orchestra is, of course, already on the stage, warming up and tuning their instruments and an anticipatory buzz rises from the rapidly increasing audience. At last the conductor appears, to warm applause from those around me. The lights dim and the first bars of the wonderful music embrace me and I prepare myself to be enthralled for the last time in this world. I smile at the thought that no one in the surrounding seats has any notion that, very soon, I will be able to enjoy an infinity of ecstasy.

***

Sam

The audience is now safely seated inside the Sage One hall and I can just about hear the orchestra and the singers through the sound insulated walls. Bloody hell, I think to myself. People actually pay to listen to this stuff? Shaking my head, as I muse on the bizarre taste of some of my fellow human beings, I make for the entrance at the opposite end of the concourse. This is the location which I selected for our team meeting. DC Jenkins and a male DC have been assigned to remain in the area between the dressing rooms and the stage. I didn't want to take the risk that our man might surprise us all, by acting before the end of the performance. He's never done it before, but that doesn't mean that he won't start now.

Most of the rest of the team are there already, some lounging outside in the glorious afternoon sunshine, taking the chance to get a nicotine fix. I suggest to the rest that we also get ourselves a breath of fresh air and we stand to the right of the entrance, overlooking the river. One by one, the team report that everything seems perfectly normal and we rehearse our responsibilities for the remaining interval and the period immediately after the performance.

Suddenly PC Armitage pipes up, 'It's a very peculiar feeling, Sergeant. To think that we're standing here and this bastard is, in all likelihood, sitting calmly in the audience, back there. Wish we could just round up all the men and grill the lot of 'em. We'd soon find him.'

Several of the older officers smirk at his youthful exuberance. I was in the same place as him not so long ago, so I offer him some support. 'I understand your sentiments, Armitage. But don't forget, whatever the clowns at the BBC and The Guardian might think, we don't operate in a police state.'

I decide to head off and find Serena, both to make sure everything's OK and to check if she still has a cob on with me.

***

Olivia

I feel quite sentimental as I stand, waiting for JP to bring the drinks. I'm at the railing, overlooking the Tyne, in more or less the same spot as we had our first pre opera drink, before the performance of *Das Rheingold*. God, I reflect, that seems like half a lifetime ago. I'm astonished, when I calculate that it's actually fewer than five days. While I don't regret taking my ideas to the police, especially if it assists in some way to apprehend this monster, before he can do any more harm, I am sorry that it has prevented me from spending more time with JP. My mantra of recent years has always been 'it's too soon to risk any sort of involvement with anyone else. But I have to say that, in his case, I could easily see myself making an exception.

Good God, woman, I chide myself. Just listen to yourself. What on earth makes you think that he'd be interested in you? And yet, there's something in his attentiveness, something in his enthusiasm to meet frequently that suggests that maybe he does, or at least could have some interest in me. On the other hand, I have to admit that he's not shown any sign that he's been disappointed in the shortness of the time we've spent together. Certainly, I had imagined that we might well have spent at least one of the free days together. But JP is obviously a self reliant man and can occupy himself without my help.

As he approaches, smiling, with two glasses of chilled, sparkling wine in his hands, I find myself saying, 'It seems kind of strange that this is the last time we'll be doing this.'

He clinks our glasses in a toast and laughs, 'how will the bar cope with the fall in its takings, you mean?'

I tap him playfully on the sleeve and add, 'don't be so glib. I'm actually very sorry that I never got the chance to show you round my hometown. You seemed quite keen on the idea, on the plane from Geneva.'

He looks genuinely sad, 'Yeah. You're right, Olivia. Time does seem to just run away with us. What can I say? I've been a lot busier, found a lot of great things to do and experience here. But, I'm really sorry if you think...'

'Oh, no, JP,' I hasten to make clear, frantic that I don't burst out in a lurid blush. 'I suppose I was just thinking aloud. Put it down to an 'end of term' like feeling. Four operas, and really long ones at that, in just over 120 hours. It's a very, very special experience.'

He gazes out enigmatically over the sun dappled water of the river. We can see the many bars and cafés on the Newcastle side, full of happy people, dressed in summer clothes, having a good time. He gestures towards them, 'Not exactly the idea of Newcastle that I had in mind before I arrived.'

'The Tyneside Riviera, you mean?'

'No joke, Olivia. I love this city. I feel, in a very important way, that it's been good for me. It's helped me to face my life again. I'll always be grateful for that.' It's clear that he's talking about the loss of his wife and I decide not to comment.

As usual, neither of us really feels like trying the food on offer from the various stalls outside and so we venture back into The Sage. In what seems like five minutes, the upcoming end of the interval is signalled by the four trumpeters, issuing their now habitual call to the audience. A spontaneous round of applause bursts out, when they have finished and they make their way back to join the rest of their colleagues on stage.

I sense that it's now, or never. So I say, 'Well, JP. Have a safe flight back to Switzerland and, don't forget, you have my number. It'd be good to hear from you.' I lean in and give him a peck on the cheek and he looks at me with the most inscrutable of expressions, before saying, 'You got it,' and making his way back through the crowd.

There's a nice, congenial atmosphere, as I make my way slowly, and for the last time, to my seat. People are smiling and nodding at one another, as if we are all members of a special group of people, which has experienced something incredible and highly unusual. I suddenly have the urge to see, for the final time, JP sitting in his seat, ready for the performance. But the lights go down so quickly that I am unable to locate his position in time.

Act Three of *Götterdämmerung*, the final part of the whole fifteen hours of The Ring Cycle, is up there with the most dramatic and moving episodes in opera. Feeling a little emotional, as I was when I sat down, I fear that the whole thing may simply overcome me. I think back how, over the past years of bickering, disagreement and, ultimately, irretrievable breakdown of a relationship, I have tended to keep my emotions locked safely away. I didn't want to be hurt so badly again, I suppose. Now, however, sitting in this darkened venue in my hometown, luxuriating in the magnificent music and peerless singing, I feel again fully at one with my whole self. I know that emotion, which has always been a very important part of who I am, can return to its key position in my character and disposition.

With my newly acquired self understanding, I'm thoroughly enjoying the performance, until we reach Siegfried's treacherous murder. Unbidden, something starts to niggle away in my mind. As the Funeral March booms out over the audience, my thoughts become more anxious. Thoughts tumble through my conscious mind. True, Siegfried is killed. But, really, the other deaths that were copied by the killer are of an entirely different order. They were much less significant characters, for a start. And it's not Siegfried's *death* that is a highlight. It's his *funeral*. Surely, the killer doesn't intend to copy this, by sacrificing Alo Kotkas in a fire? No, that really doesn't make sense. Two of the killings have mirrored Siegfried's own actions, so to stage manage that same character's death seems unlikely. Kotkas would then be the hero, not the killer.

Just as Brünnhilde, having ordered a funeral pyre to be created for Siegfried, rides her horse into the flames to join her dead lover, it suddenly hits me. Siegfried isn't the *victim*. He's the *perpetrator*. He's the *hero*. But, in that case, who is the victim? Very quickly, a real sense of dread envelopes me, as I realise that it must be Brünnhilde. And if I'm right, the police are guarding the wrong performer.

In panic, I decide that I've got to warn Sam as soon as possible. Ignoring the outraged reaction of my neighbours in the audience, I more or less push my way past them. At last, I reach the passage and scurry off toward the exit door. I can't see where I am putting my feet and as I approach the door, I stumble badly, and am extremely grateful for the presence of a young usher, who manages to catch me and prevent a serious fall.

'Whoa, miss,' he whispers and I can just make out a friendly grin. 'It's not that bad, is it?'

'Oh no. No. You don't understand. I must get out of here and find Sergeant Snow as quickly as possible.' A concerned look replaces his smile. He obviously thinks I'm crazy and I don't help matters by hissing, 'It's a matter of life and death.'

The usher opens the door quickly and, I feel certain, heaves a huge sigh of relief as I barrel out into the concourse, thereby ceasing to be his problem. Frantically, I look for a policeman that I recognise, but I can't see anyone. I rush down the stairs and, paralysed with uncertainty, decide to go right, towards the box office. I'm running around the edge of the gift shop when I hit a woman head on, pushing her into a stand of postcards, which topples over, causing her to fall to the ground. 'I'm really terribly sorry,' I say, as I reach down to help her to her feet. With a sinking feeling, I recognise DC Jenkins, struggling to retain her dignity as she tries to disentangle herself from the collapsed display stand. Her eyes flash with understandable anger, as she recognises me. 'You! You stupid fool. What the hell do you think you're doing? I should arrest you for assault, dashing about like that.'

I try to look contrite as I babble, 'I know, officer. And I'm very sorry. But, you see, it's absolutely vital that I speak with Sergeant Snow immediately.'

'Oh really?' she replies slowly. 'And why, exactly might that be, Doctor Clavel?' The way she almost sneers as she drawls my title makes it crystal clear that she values it not one jot. I'd love to return her antagonism with interest, but bite my tongue and try to explain. 'We've got it all wrong. The target isn't Siegfried, the *killer* is Siegfried.'

Even as I say this, I realise that I'm talking gibberish, and, understandably, she looks dubious. 'What? Are you saying that Alo Kotkas is our killer?'

I don't get to finish my sentence, before she puts both hands in front of her chest and says savagely, 'I've no time for your bullshit theories. Just leave us to get on with the real job of policing and finding this bastard.' She turns away abruptly and walks straight into Sergeant Snow who looks from one to the other of us, a sly smile creeping around his mouth.

'Now, now, ladies. What's going on here? We're all on the same team, you know?' He looks pleased with himself and it's evident that he feels he has the situation completely under control. Well, I'll soon disabuse the poor devil of that idea.

DC Jenkins and myself both start to answer at the same time, but are both silenced by the noise coming from the auditorium. The performance must have finished and the Bravos, Hurrahs and wild cheering surges over us, as the exit doors are opened and a few people rush out. Perhaps they have a train to catch, I ponder pointlessly, before Snow pulls us both to one side, away from the trickle of people making their way from the auditorium. 'Look, let's get over here,' he says. 'And then, please tell me what's going on.'

Jenkins goes first, dripping with sarcasm, 'Well, apart from assaulting me, Dr Clavel has suddenly developed a new theory about our man, sir. Apparently, we should be arresting Alo Kotkas rather than protecting him.'

Snow's face darkens and he turns to me. 'Is this true, Olivia.' Jenkins flinches at his familiar use of my first name, but I take no pleasure in that. There's no time to lose and I have to explain.

'Of course it isn't. I believe that our killer is incrementally modelling himself on Siegfried.'

'What do you mean? He isn't after Kotkas?'

'I don't think so. He's *becoming* Siegfried.'

'So who the hell is he after? Were we wrong to think it's a performer?'

'No. I think we're still right. Only we have the wrong performer. I think he's after Brünnhilde. If he sees himself as Siegfried, then his final act will certainly be to unite himself with his love, Brünnhilde.'

To my surprise, Snow looks relieved, calm even. 'That's OK then. We've got officers all over the dressing room area and, judging from the racket coming from the hall, the performers are all still out there, taking their bows. Come on, let's get round backstage and you can tell me how you came to this conclusion.' We both set off, but DC Jenkins remains rooted to the spot, looking furious. Snow stops briefly, turns around and says tersely, 'Come on, Jenkins , we haven't got all day.'

Chapter Twenty Five

I allow myself a small smile of self congratulation which I can see in the rear view mirror of the luxurious saloon. Beyond the reflection of my face, I can see the image of my love, Kirsty Cole Harding, shifting uncomfortably on the deep leather rear seat. Her eyes dart like a nervous animal out of the heavily tinted rear windows. She's still in her stage costume and I chuckle at the idea that, had this not been a concert performance, her gorgeous hair might have been squashed and hidden under a helmet, replete with horns. As it is, she is wearing a black evening gown and her long, blonde, wavy locks flow seductively over her exposed right shoulder.

'Where are we going?' she asks in her natural, charming, North American accent, thereby interrupting my reverie. 'How long before we get there? Do you know how my daughter is?' I recognise the increasing uncertainty in her voice, as she fires successive questions at me.

'We'll soon be there. Five minutes at most, The traffic is pretty light,' I reply reassuringly. 'As to your daughter, I'm afraid they didn't tell me anything. All I do is drive, y'see.' This seems to pacify her, at least for now and she worries away at what I think must be some sort of mark on the skirt of her dress. Don't worry about that, I think, soon neither of us will have further need of such earthly things.

As I move the car easily through the thin city traffic, I ponder on just how easy it was to succeed in luring Ms Harding from The Sage. A luxury hire car, a chauffeur's uniform from a theatrical costumier and a charming manner resulted in no one seeming suspicious at all. The theatre staff were just worried for Kirsty Cole and the 'bad news, but nothing to be too scared about,' that I brought via her hotel from her home in the USA. As for the police, they seemed very much to have their attention on another member of the opera company. Fools! They couldn't even work it out, even when I'd left such obvious clues.

An unwanted thought suddenly insinuates itself into my mind. Such obvious clues. Why did I have that thought? Could it be that I actually wanted them to catch me and to stop me? This leads to an even more unpalatable thought. Is there a part of me that actually hates what I'm doing? Are there two versions of me: the one from before and the one of now? Does this mean I'm going just a bit crazy? The cold determination that I have honed over the past months soon reasserts itself, as I gaze with half an eye on my prize, now nervously pulling at her long, lustrous hair. No. My purpose is clear and the means of achieving it are now all in my grasp. I just have to lay low for a few hours, take my prize where no one will expect and fulfil our joint destiny. Tomorrow and for many years after, my name will be inextricably linked with that of Kirsty Cole Harding and our wonderful end.

By the time my passenger is starting to become really suspicious, it's too late. The electric remote works perfectly and I ease the car into the large lock up, checking both ways that no one is about to notice. The huge doors close automatically and I casually climb out of the driver's seat. Now, I have all the time in the world. The really risky part of the plan is over. From now on, it'll be as easy as pie.

As I expected, Kirsty Cole looks terrified. Well, I think confidently, as soon as she understands what I have in store for the two of us, she'll embrace her fate with open arms. After all, who wouldn't?

Chapter Twenty Six

Just Before 10pm, Sunday 10th July 2016, The Sage, Gateshead.

Sam

God knows what those two were up to before I arrived. What with Jenkins half on the deck and an upturned display unit spilling its wares all over the place. Certainly Olivia looked shocked and distressed and Jenkins's tight jeans looked to have a tear around one knee.

Were they fighting? What the hell about?

I've no time nor interest in that now though. What Olivia said sends a massive pulse of uncertainty through my whole being. Christ! Have we got it wrong, as she implied? Is the killer going to outsmart us? Will we ever get the bastard? I try to sound confident, as I urge them to follow me backstage. Jenkins is obviously struggling in her ankle boots, perhaps she's twisted her ankle in the skirmish. But I've no time to waste hanging about, so I almost jog on ahead.

I soon see the smiling face of PC Armitage, looking relaxed and rather self important in his civvies. 'Hi Guv,' he says, using the language he's no doubt picked up from watching too many police shows on tv. 'Mr Kotkas has just come off stage and is being escorted to his dressing room. It looks like our man hasn't made his move yet.'

'I hope to God that you're right, Armitage,' I say and his face immediately falls, as he notes my expression and tone of voice. 'Please tell me that you know where the performer playing Brünnhilde is. It's absolutely vital.'

Armitage quickly takes a piece of paper from the inside pocket of his leather jacket and studies it carefully, obviously not wanting to make a mistake. 'Let's see,' he says slowly. 'That would be Ms Kirsty Cole Harding. Hang on, I'll ask around.'

I don't wait for this junior plod to work his way quietly around the crowded backstage area, instead I push past him, shouting, 'Ms Kirsty Cole Harding! Police! Has anyone seen Ms Kirsty Cole Harding! I need to know her whereabouts immediately.'

A wall of worried faces turns to face me, before Alo Kotkas says, 'No. She didn't come back to take her bow at the end of the performance. We all thought it was strange, but somebody said something about an emergency.'

'Emergency,' I shout, 'what kind of emergency? What do you mean?'

He looks at me helplessly, before suggesting, 'You need to speak to The Stage Manager. He should know.'

Shit! I spin round and see a middle aged man, wearing a badge, which identifies him as the Stage Manager. 'Is there a problem?' he asks calmly.

'Can you tell me where Kirsty Cole Harding is?' I demand, trying to keep the growing concern from my voice. 'It's extremely important.'

He looks confused, before he replies enigmatically, 'Well, in a way, yes.'

I'm in absolutely no mood for such games and tower over his barely five foot frame, 'What the hell is that supposed to mean? Do you know where she is, or not?'

He purses his lips in an almost comically stereotypical way, before replying, 'Well. if you'd just let me explain.' He points to a burly, vacant looking man, squashed into an ill fitting uniform. 'This is Gavin,' the Stage Manager goes on. 'He's one of The Sage's own security personnel and I think he can put your mind at rest.'

'OK, Gavin,' I say as calmly as possible, 'let's have it.'

Gavin clears his throat noisily before saying, 'It's like this. Just before Ms Harding came off the stage, a driver from her hotel appeared.'

'Just a minute,' I interrupt, 'was this just now with the rest of the cast?'

Gavin looks at me vacantly and it's left to the Stage Manager to explain. 'No. That would have been before the end of the performance. Her character isn't on stage at the very end.'

I see,' I say, without really seeing anything. 'So, Gavin, you were saying something about a driver. What exactly do you mean by a driver?'

'Well a chauffeur, like,' he replies, struggling to get his thick Geordie accent around the French word. 'He was all togged up. Like you'd expect him to be. Y'know.'

'And what happened next?'

'Well, like I says, this uniformed driver appeared, said he was from Ms Harding's hotel. Said there'd been an important phone call from the States - she's a Yank, you know, Ms Harding. Lovely woman, she is. Always got a ready smile and friendly word, unlike some of the prima....'

'Yes, yes,' I cut him off. 'Just get on with it and tell me what happened.'

'Well. It seems the call was about her bairn, you know? Back in the States, like. So, as soon as she comes off the stage, she tears off with him in his car to the hotel, to get the details and ring back home, I suppose. Didn't even stop to get changed out of her stage costume. Mind you, she looked a million dollars in that frock, you know,' he adds with a lascivious wink, before I interrupt again.

'I'm not interested in your pathetic fantasies. What the hell were you doing, letting her go off with an unknown man? What, in the name of God, do you think all we police are here for? The bloody music? Didn't it occur to you that this seemed odd?'

Gavin is having none of this and immediately retaliates. 'Why on earth should that occur to me? According to two of your lads, who I was chatting with over a fag outside, you were only concerned about Mr Kotkas. Nobody mentioned anything about Ms Harding. Just because you lot don't know your arse from your elbow, don't take it out on me!'

I realise dejectedly that he's right. This leaves me with a horribly sinking feeling about this development. 'OK, point taken. I don't suppose you remember the car registration number?'

Gavin has also calmed down a bit and thinks before replying. 'No, why should I take note of it? But I do remember it was a really nice black Merc. Just the sort of high end car that comes here for important types, like. But there's CCTV around the stage door. You could have a look at that.'

'Good idea,' I compliment him, before turning to the Stage Manager. 'Where can I get a phone number for Ms Harding's hotel. We should ring them first and hope to hell that we're panicking over nothing.'

Before he leads me to his office, I call Jenkins and Armitage over. 'Get the team speaking to as many people as possible, who might have seen something. We're interested in Ms Harding, the chauffeur and his black Mercedes car. Also, one of you call in to the station. Get them to put out an alert for a black Mercedes car with two people. Tell them that the car should not be approached, but rather they should track it as inconspicuously as possible.' I turn back to the Stage Manager, 'Is the audience leaving now? Can we stop them?'

'Absolutely impossible,' says a female voice from behind me and I turn to see Josephine Rowe's firm expression. 'Just come with me for a second,' the Managing Director of The Sage says, before leading me down a short corridor and out through a fire door. I can immediately see hundreds of happy concert goers, thronging the concourse area and streaming down the stairs from the higher levels of the auditorium. 'As you can no doubt see,' she continues, 'any attempt to stop people leaving could cause panic and even injury.'

It's very unlikely that anyone in the audience could offer anything of value to the investigation, so I nod my head and we both return backstage. The Stage Manager leads Ms Rowe and myself to his office, turning and saying, 'I'm sure I have her hotel number somewhere. You do think she's all right, don't you?' The general, post performance euphoria among the cast and backstage staff has rapidly shifted to an atmosphere of deep worry, tinged with real fear. One of the older performers even touches me on the sleeve and asks authoritatively, 'What's this I hear about Kirsty Cole? All rubbish, I trust?'

I'm pleased to see that Jenkins has taken a couple officers to the Stage Door area, while Armitage and the remaining officers have already started to conduct brief interviews. I notice Olivia Clavel, deep in conversation with a younger cast member. I feel that I have to reply and take a deep breath, 'At the moment, sir, we are checking on Ms Harding's whereabouts. As soon as I can confirm her location, rest assured that you will all be informed.' I then shout, as loud as I can, 'In the meantime, I would be grateful, if you would all please stay here and wait to be interviewed by one of my officers. Thank you .'

We leave the buzz of concerned voices behind us and enter the small, incredibly neat office of the Stage Manager. Within a couple of minutes I'm through to the Jesmond Dene House Hotel, only to be met with confusion. 'No, sergeant. No car has been despatched from here to The Sage for Ms Harding. No telephone call has been received for her from the USA. I've been on duty since 4pm, but I'll check our phone logs.'

The Acting Manager couldn't have been more helpful, but, as I wait for her to return to the phone, I know we've cocked up royally. Christ! I don't want to think what the bloody papers'll make of this, when they get hold of it.

I thank the Duty Manager and ask her to be ready to speak to one of my officers who I'll send to take statements. I know it's pointless, but it has to be done. By now, a good proportion of the audience has left The Sage and the backstage area is gradually becoming quieter, as more of the cast have answered the questions and gone to their various dressing rooms. Opera North's HR Manager, Jessica Lawler is standing fidgeting, obviously waiting for me as I emerge from the office. 'For God's sake, tell me it's not true!' she cries and I'm lost for the words to reply. Not tolerating my silence for more than thirty seconds, she screams through a weirdly distorted mouth, 'But you were so sure! You knew Mr Kotkas was the target. You never mentioned Kirsty at all! You, you, bastard...' With this, she suddenly makes a moves towards me and, despite her small stature begins hitting me repeatedly on the chest. A DC makes to restrain her, but her blows are feeble and I indicate that he should stay back. It doesn't take long for her outburst to subside into wailing sobs and she buries her head into my shoulder.

'It's OK, Ms Lawler,' I say, with as much conviction as I can muster. 'I understand. But we'll find Ms Harding. I give you my word, we'll find her.'

'But when?' she mutters into my shoulder, almost to herself.

I manage to pass Ms Lawler over to one of her female colleagues and summon the Stage Manager, 'Where can I get hold of the CCTV footage, especially from the area by the Stage Door?'

Normally, the viewing of CCTV footage is one of the least desirable jobs in any police investigation, involving, as it almost always does, hour after hour of trying to concentrate on often grainy and boring images of the same thing. I've known several enquiries, where the vital moment was missed, simply because of the attention destroying tedium of the task. This time, I reflect grimly, it's very different. We more or less know the crucial time that the singer was abducted. It should be easy to locate that and then work back to the arrival of the car. With luck we'll get the car's registration number and, if we are really fortunate, a usable image of our man.

I sit next to DS Jenkins, who I've recalled from the Stage Door area, in the tiny, security office at The Sage. We're sitting so close together that I can feel her pressing against me from my ankle to my shoulder and the scent of her perfume fills my nostrils. But we have a job to do and we finally manage to get the footage from one of the relevant cameras. This is positioned high on the wall, pointing down towards a narrow, bridge like passage which leads directly to The Stage Door. 'We should get a good look at our man when he approaches,' says Jenkins. 'There's nowhere for him to hide there.'

There's a surprising amount of coming and going but, given that the conditions were pretty much twilight, the light could have been a lot better. It doesn't take us long to spot our man, dressed in chauffeur's uniform, striding confidently towards the door.

'There he is! Shit! That peaked cap's pulled down pretty bloody low. Can't see a thing,' moans Jenkins, for both of us.

'And just our frigging luck!' I add. 'He's only wearing bloody gloves. Can you Adam and Eve it? On a night as warm as this?' She looks at me with a wry smile, at my lapse into Cockney Rhyming Slang and I brush it away with a wave of the hand. In truth, all we can see, is that he's above average height and medium to slim build. Facial features: negative. Hair colour: negative. Possible fingerprints: bloody well negative.

We watch, beguiled by the thought that this is the bastard that we're after, as he waits patiently, having seemingly given a message to someone at the door. I send Jenkins to speak with one of the DCs, 'Tell them to find whoever he gave the message to. They may remember something.'

'Yes, sarge.'

She's quickly back and snuggled against me again. 'We'll run this, until he disappears with Ms Harding,' I say. 'With luck, he might take his cap off, when he speaks with her. He could then show a bit more of himself. Then we'll try the other door camera and finally look for one that might have caught the car. If we can get the number, assuming it's a hire car, we might get onto him that way'.

After six or seven minutes, he appears again on our screen. But, given the angle of the elevated camera, towards the 'bridge' access, we can't see any of the interaction, just our man, still capped, leading Ms Harding away from the Stage Door. 'Shit!' I groan, 'I feared as much. Come on Serena, lets log on to another camera. We have the times now.'

The Security Technician is a typically nerdy, somewhat scruffy type with long, greasy hair and a rather uncomfortable expression on his face. He mutters shiftily that the second camera is positioned, at about eye level, a couple of metres from the Stage Door itself. 'Great,' I say. 'We should surely nail him now. However low he pulls down his cap, we should be able to get a good view of his face.' As soon as I see the footage, I understand why the technician looked as worried as he did. To describe the images as grainy would be a huge understatement. They flickered, disappeared frequently and, when a picture was visible, it offered precious little detail.

'What the hell's up with the picture?' I bellow at him accusingly. 'Surely, you can do better than that? It's absolutely, bleeding useless.'

'Talk to the General Manager, if you've got a complaint,' he retaliates. 'I've been telling her for weeks that that camera's up the spout. But she won't listen.'

It's incredibly infuriating to sit, watching a stream that should be very helpful to the enquiry, only to see shadowy shapes and outlines flicker and jerk around the screen. We watch through all the relevant footage, gaining nothing of real value. In fact, from what we can see and guess, all we deduce is that he looks pretty relaxed, keeping his back to the cameras as much as possible.

'Cocky bastard, isn't he?' I ask Jenkins, as I stop the replay machine with an irritated jab on a button. 'Get the tape, or the stick, or whatever the hell it is out,' I order the technician, 'so we can send it to our labs. Maybe they can retrieve something from this bloody mess.'

The next half hour is spent on a fruitless review of the other cameras around the back of The Sage. It's a narrow, congested area between The Sage and a multi story car park, then a terrace of small, arched workshops, beneath what looks like an old railway line. Some of the units are unoccupied and stare out, like blackened, rotten teeth, whereas the doors of others are daubed with graffiti. The area is full of waiting vehicles. Apparently it's often like this whenever a performance is about to end. We get an odd glimpse of what is probably our man's Mercedes, parked in a disabled bay, but not a sniff of the registration number. Shit!

'Looks like we'll have to broaden our search to street CCTV,' I say to Jenkins, without much enthusiasm. She looks at me sideways, before replying. 'That's going to take a few hours to sort out. I think we both know it'll probably be too late by then.'

The news from the person who took the message to Ms Harding is also not encouraging. Apparently, the chauffeur only said, 'For Ms Harding' and his accent was thick, Eastern European sounding. 'I'll bet next month's salary that he's disguised his voice,' says Jenkins softly. 'It's crap. We've got nothing, have we?'

I run my hand through my hair in frustration and, I suppose, just for something to do. 'I know, Serena. I bloody well know,' I say in a defeated tone. 'Look, let's think. There's still the street CCTV. What's available and when can we have it? We know the time we're after and, who knows? We might catch a break. Anyway, come on, let's go and see if the other interviews have yielded anything useful.'

What an almighty cock up! My big chance to lead a high profile case and I've screwed it up big time. I'll be lucky if I'm not pounding the beat with a tall hat on, this time next week.

The interviews with performers and staff are almost complete, but a series of glum shakes of the head confirms what had already seemed inevitable. We have no useful information and the bastard has got away scot free.

As I walk dejectedly back into the now semi deserted concourse of The Sage, I see Olivia. Christ, I think, she looks even worse than me.

***

Olivia

I think I must still be in a state of shock. I don't even notice DS Snow coming towards me, until he says, 'How're you bearing up?' I can scarcely look at him. I feel I've let him down so terribly and his concern for me is just too much for me to take.

'Look, Sam,' I begin, trying to stop the tears from filling my eyes. 'I'm so very sorry. I should have..'

He interrupts me by raising both his hands, palms facing me, 'Now look,Olivia. I don't want to hear any more of that kind of nonsense. Nothing in this is remotely your fault. So you can just put such thoughts from your mind.'

I catch sight of DC Jenkins's unsympathetic expression, as she stands beside him. I bet you wouldn't agree, would you, love? But Snow hasn't finished yet, 'Christ! If it hadn't have been for your insights, we'd have still been chasing two or three killers. And we'd have had no notion of the importance of these bloody operas to what was going on.'

It calms me somewhat to recognise that, actually, he's right. I smile in gratitude and ask, 'I don't suppose there's any news?'

'Afraid not,' he says forlornly, but adds, perhaps in an effort to rally himself, 'However, we do have other possibilities to look at. We're not about to give up on catching this bastard, before he can do any harm to Ms Harding. I'm just going to round up my team now and then we'll head back to the station.Can you wait here until I get back?'

I nod my head dumbly and he quickly disappears towards the same seminar room, in which our pre opera meetings had taken place. He shouts to DC Jenkins, 'Get everyone together in 'The Squires Seminar Room.' He might have a head start on us, but we'll get him, you mark my words.'

Looking out through the glorious, glass form of The Sage, towards the twinkling lights of the city, on the far bank of the Tyne, I'm shocked at how normal it all looks. The more I think about it, the more I feel certain that I'm ignoring something that I already know. Something that will help to solve this awful series of crimes.

It's not far short of midnight by the time Snow returns, his face set in a grimly determined expression. 'Right,' he says with at least an attempt at a smile, 'We're clearing off back to the station. All the other performers are accounted for and the Security here want to lock up for the night. We'll send in Forensics tomorrow morning, or should that be later this morning?' he asks wryly, while looking at his watch. 'But that'll be a waste of time. He was wearing gloves throughout.'

'Is there any chance that CCTV on the surrounding streets will pick up the car and give us some idea of the direction he went in?'

'It's our best hope, Olivia,' he replies, shaking his head. 'But it's a pretty long shot. I'd better go face the music with DCI Quayle. Harrison'll be rubbing his hands with glee when he finds out what's gone down here. Anyway, I've imposed too much on you for one day, Olivia. I'll give you a lift back to your sister's. Low Fell, isn't it?'

'You'll do no such thing!' I say firmly. 'It was my theorising and input that helped get us here. Like it or not, Sergeant Snow, I'm with you on this until the end.'

He looks directly at me for a full thirty seconds, his deep blue eyes locking onto mine. It's an experience that I find oddly disconcerting. Finally, he smiles, nods and puts his arm around my shoulder, in what is purely a gesture of friendship. 'Then, come on Doc. Let's get this over with.'

Chapter Twenty Seven

12.30am, Monday 11th July 2016, Newcastle City Centre Police Station, Forth Banks.

Sam

Quayle is surprisingly sympathetic, as I explain the current state of the enquiry. Her eyes are hooded and tired, but there's not one hair out of place. I have to admire someone, who must have been summoned from her bed, and yet can look as immaculate as she does,

'Do we have anything yet from CCTV?' she asks hopefully.

'Not yet, ma'am. It'll take about an hour, before we can start looking at the relevant cameras. Our traffic people are advising which would be the best ones to start with. If we can trace the direction he went in, we can perhaps narrow the search down.'

She nods her head, before saying, 'But it's all likely to be too little, too late for Ms Harding. Wouldn't you say, sergeant?'

The way she emphasises the last word suggests to me that my chances of any sort of promotion are disappearing fast. Or, more probably, have already vanished.

'I'm not sure, ma'am,' I reply, obviously piquing her interest. 'I've discussed this with Dr Clavel and she...'

'Ah! Yes, Doctor Clavel,' she says, with a wintry smile. 'Remind me, sergeant. Would that be the same Dr Clavel, who seemed so certain that another performer,' here she shuffles a few pieces of paper on her desk, until she finds what she's looking for. 'Ah yes. A Mr Kotkas, the person playing Siegfried, was it? He was the one at risk.'

I'm not having that. I don't care if it blows my chances with her, but I'm not standing by, while Quayle rubbishes Olivia. 'With respect, ma'am, that is far from fair. Dr Clavel made it absolutely clear that she was far from certain that Mr Kotkas was the intended target. When pushed by me, she may have accepted that, as the only concrete possibility we could come up with, but she was by no means 100% sure that we were correct. Any mistakes are clearly mine.'

'Well, I certainly agree with that last sentence, Snow,' she hisses and I can see that my first impression of how well she's taking this, is way off. 'I don't ever want to see, or hear from that woman again. And as for you.'

At this moment DI 'Halitosis' Harrison knocks and enters the room. To describe him as the cat who got the cream would be a massive understatement. The cat which has just won a lifetime supply of cream, mice, 'kit-e-kat,' you bloody name it. That's what the incompetent old tosser looks like.

'Ah DI Harrison, perfect timing, as usual. As from this moment, Sergeant Snow, you are off this case and DI Harrison will be leading the enquiry. I suggest that you take yourself off home and leave this to the grown ups'

I've done my bit for Olivia, now, it's for me. I'm determined not to take that kind of shit from anyone and immediately hit back, 'Again with respect, ma'am, I think you're forgetting that it is through my and Dr Clavel's work that this investigation has progressed at all. Before that..'

'Enough!' Quayle screeches, as she slaps her right hand down on her desk, causing a half full cup of coffee to splash over her papers. Always a stickler for a neat desk, she seems totally unconcerned by the mess and says, ominously quietly, 'My decision is final. I will hear no more from you, Snow. I suggest that, if you want to avoid serious repercussions, you make yourself scarce. As of this moment.'

She turns to Harrison, smiles and beckons him to sit down. Pointedly ignoring me, she says, 'Now, Inspector. Where are we with this investigation?'

I can see no point in remaining and, still furious at the unfairness of it all, I leave her office. I don't care what the old bag thinks, I grant myself what is, arguably, the most immature of satisfactions. I slam the door gratifyingly hard on my way out.

I stomp down the stairs of the redbrick building and pause at the floor, where CID is located. Through the window in the fire door, I can see Jenkins and the rest of the team, huddled around a table. They've clearly been told something's afoot, but I decide to save their faces and mine and carry on down to the ground floor Reception, where Olivia is waiting. She gives a small start, as she sees me appear and rises to her feet. 'Does the DCI want to see me, Sergeant. I'm perfectly willing to take the flak for this.'

'That won't be necessary, Olivia,' I say with a shrug. 'I've been taken off the case and told to go home. Harrison is back in charge.'

If it were possible, I'd say she's even more furious than I am. At least, she certainly looks it. 'That's a bloody disgrace!' I can tell she's really worked up, because I'm sure that's the first time I've heard her say anything worse than 'drat' or 'bother.' 'I'll go up there myself and tell that stupid, short sighted, old cow you call a DCI, just what I think of her and her decision. It's, it's just...'

'Inevitable, I'm afraid,' I say with a rueful smile. 'The force will need someone to blame for this cock up. And I'm it.'

'But it wasn't a cock up,' she insists. 'Surely that's the point. Human behaviour isn't so easy to predict and we got it almost right. Besides, I've been thinking, Sam. And I know it's sounds crazy, but I really think I may know the killer.'

I look at her with a wistful smile, 'Nice try, Olivia. I appreciate it. I really do. But it's too late. It's over for me.'

'No, really,' she persists. 'There's this creepy chap in our pre opera discussion group. He ticks all the psychological boxes. I've even remembered seeing him, just after the first opera, while I was waiting for my taxi. He was sloping off, alone, towards the place where the first body was found. Now, if we could just...'

'No, Olivia,' I say firmly. 'It's up to Harrison now. Look, I'm officially off duty and, I don't know about you, but I don't feel quite like going home just yet. What say we find a late night watering hole to drown our sorrows?'

She looks sad at my unwillingness to give any more thought to the case. But I really don't want to be alone, so I add quickly, trying on my best, boyish charm, ' Come on, Olivia. Just the one. It'd mean a lot to me.'

'OK,' she relents and five minutes later we're in my Mazda, careering down Neville Street, which leads us to the 'nightlife' part of the city centre. Neville Street becomes Collingwood Street and I immediately swerve the car into a parking spot on the right, just as it's being vacated by a clubber.

'The night's still young,' I joke, 'He's not got much stamina, has he?' Olivia takes in a sudden, deep breath, as if she's shocked and I turn to smile at her. She's gazing across the street at the frontage of the grand building, 'House of Smith',shining out in white block capitals over the window awnings.

'What on earth's that place?' she says uncertainly. 'It looks like a rather upmarket, traditional shop.'

'That, love' I say with a laugh, 'is where we are both going. Come on.'

I usher her out of the car, lock up and escort her across the road. There's quite a queue of would-be patrons waiting outside, but I'm well known to the doormen. 'Good evening, sir,' says the nearest one, with a broad smile. 'Just yourself and the lady tonight is it , sir?' he asks and I nod my head. He immediately allows us to pass through, much to the obvious irritation of some of the queuers.

We're quickly led through the dense crowd to a small booth, with a rectangular table and a curved padded sofa. The hostess discreetly removes the small 'Reserved' sign from the table and asks what we'd like to drink.

'It's OK, love,' I answer, 'I'll get the drinks from the bar myself. You've been very helpful. ' As I add my thanks, I slip a twenty pound note into her hand.

I sit down, part way around the table from Olivia. As I look at her, I begin to feel more relaxed and say, 'OK, doc, what's it to be?'

***

Olivia

I'm still furious about the DCI's decision and bemused by Sam having given up so easily on the case. I suppose I just don't understand the humiliation of being removed from the leading role in the enquiry. Sitting here, waiting for him to return from the bar, I'm beginning to think that it wasn't such a good idea to come here. I look around the nightclub and take in its appearance. Behind our seating is a tall column, with vintage brick exposed. On both sides are huge mirrors, with tied back curtains. I have to admit that the purple and white up and down lighting certainly helps to create an atmosphere, even if it's not really to my taste. In another part of the club, it's obvious that dancing is going on. I can hear the deep bass thud of the insistent music which, thankfully, is not oppressively loud. A far cry from *Götterdämmerung,* I muse and chuckle at my own joke.

'What's so funny?' Sam asks, with an inquisitive smile, as he approaches with two lurid looking cocktails. 'Don't you like it? Oh, and by the way, you should smile more often. It really transforms your face.'

I ignore the compliment and say simply, 'It's fine, sergea..'

'Call me Sam, please,' Olivia. 'As I said, I'm off duty now. We're just a couple of mates, having a drink and shooting the breeze together. Yes?'

'OK, Sam' I say, 'But what's this? I thought I asked for mineral water.'

'Must have misheard,' he replies with a cheeky grin. 'Anyway, here's to us!' He raises his glass and we clink, before he takes a long slurp of his drink and I take a

256

tentative sip of mine. The liquor immediately warms up my throat and I say, 'Good God ! What's this?'

'Dunno,' he says disarmingly. I asked for two of the barman's specials and that's what we've got. So, just drink up and enjoy.'

He picks up the card which is standing on the table. 'We might be able to get some food here, if you like. Do you fancy anything?'

For some reason, the thought of eating makes me think about Kirsty Cole Harding and I put my hand to my mouth, fearing that I will retch. 'I'm sorry, Sam. The very idea of food just now...'

'It's OK. I know what you mean, Olivia,' he replies sadly. 'But, you know, we just have to accept that it's out of our hands now.'

'Come on, Sam,' I urge him. 'This isn't like you. Are you just going to give up on Kirsty? We both know that Harrison's clueless and that by the time conventional coppering grinds its procedures out, she'll be dead. We're her best chance of getting out of this alive. No question.'

'I certainly agree with what you said about Harrison, but I don't see we're any further forward than him.'

Things have been whirling around in my head, ever since I realised that Brünnhilde was the target and I decide to come clean with him, however chaotic and disjointed my thoughts may seem. 'Well, as I said, I think it's really possible that our killer is this man Leonard, from my discussion group. He's got the right profile, personality traits and behaviour patterns. And some of the things he's said. I really think it could be him.'

'But how does that help us? Do you know his full name, or his address?'

'No,' I say miserably. 'I only know him as Leonard and the way he first introduced himself makes me think that it may not even be his real name.'

'Then, there's really nothing we can do. Especially at gone 1am and me off the case. Admit it, Olivia. It's finished for us.'

'No it's not,' I insist. 'Let's go back to what we were saying yesterday.'

'We said a lot, Olivia.'

'OK, point taken. But remember we were saying that the only way we can catch him, is by trying to work out what he's going to do next and intercepting him. Well, essentially, that's still true. In some ways, we're no worse off than we were before he took Kirsty.'

'How do you mean?' Sam asks and I'm gratified to see a flicker of interest cross his face. 'You think that he's going to kill someone else, other than Kirsty? How does that help her?'

'No, I don't mean that. Think about it, Sam. We know he's obsessed with Siegfried and The Ring Cycle. I'm not sure why yet, but he's definitely obsessed. I really think that he sees himself as Siegfried and now he's got his Brünnhilde, I think he intends that they both die.'

'Whoa, doc. Hold up there,' Sam says, all interest in his 'special' cocktail now evaporated. 'There's been absolutely nothing in his behaviour, or the nature of the crimes to suggest he's suicidal.'

'No, Sam. Not suicidal. Think about it. Richard Wagner, the composer of The Ring has determined that

Siegfried's got to die. So, it's not suicide. He's just fulfilling the plot.'

'But why would he do that?'

'I'm really not sure. But I believe that both he and Kirsty will die tonight, unless we can stop him.'

'But how does that get us any nearer to finding Kirsty?' Sam says, while hitting the table in frustration. 'What difference does it make, whether he dies or not? It doesn't help.'

'But I think it does, Sam. I really don't think that our man - Siegfried - is going to die with his Brünnhilde, without making something of a statement. He sees himself as a hero, don't forget.'

'So, this will all happen somewhere special? Not in some crappy, little room somewhere?'

'That's right.'

'But he'd be taking a great and unnecessary risk, wouldn't he? I mean, we know the car he's driving. He's going to figure that we've got an alert out for him.'

'Unless...' I add, ready to surprise him.

'The bastard had another car all lined up,' he says to complete what I imagined was a most perceptive thought. 'So, you think he's taken her to somewhere temporary, where they'll stay, until the heat dies down. And he always intended to go somewhere else for the final act? In which case, he'll certainly have got himself another car.'

I'm getting really excited now. I feel we're really making progress and nod my head vigorously. 'Just think of the planning and preparation he's put into this. Nothing has been extemporised. He's made his plan for each of the killings and executed it, to the letter. You think there's any chance, he won't have chosen a suitable place to hide out and the means to leave it relatively safely? He must have been obsessed with this, the final act, for months. It's really what it's all about for him.'

Sam listens and nods his head slowly in return. It looks like he's beginning to buy into what I'm saying. But, as if to put a dampener on my rising level of excitement, he almost whispers, 'But where, Olivia? Where's he going to take her? By car, it could be anywhere, within a hundred mile radius of here. And there's plenty of lonely spots in that size of area.'

'That's what we need to try to tease out now, Sam. Not sit here drinking cocktails and feeling sorry for ourselves.' I remember that it was I , who set him off on the wrong track earlier, so I screw up my face and say decisively, 'Actually. It's what I need to tease out.' Suddenly, I get a flash of insight. I look quickly at his troubled face and say, 'But he won't go somewhere lonely will he, Sam? This is his big finale. He'll want to sign off with something noticeable and memorable.'

Over the next few minutes, he throws ideas at me, but none of them make sense. Finally, he looks at his watch and says, 'It's 2.30am. This place'll be closing in half an hour and we may already be too late.' His face is a picture of despair, as he groans, 'Let's face it, Olivia. We're right back at square one.'

'Wait!' I say urgently. 'What did you just say, Sam? Whatever it was, it caused a connection for me. Another light came on.'

He looks confused, 'Err. I can't remember. I was talking about being too late..'

'No, that wasn't it. You said something else.'

'Only that we're back at square one.'

'That's it, Sam. I think I know where he's going to take Kirsty. Come on. Let's get a move on before we're too late.'

Chapter Twenty Eight

2.45am, Monday 11th July 2016, Newcastle upon Tyne.

Sam

I've never seen Olivia so determined and forceful. She more or less drags me out of the 'House of Smith', much to the amusement of the staff who know me. 'Go to it, Sam!' one of the doormen says, grinning lasciviously, as I stumble in Olivia's wake, her hand dragging me along with surprising strength. 'Looks like you've well pulled there, matey.' I smile helplessly back at him, but once we're out of the crowded club and in the relative cool of the city centre street, I re-assert myself and pull Olivia back towards me.

'Just hang on a second, Olivia,' I insist. 'What exactly do you mean that you "think you know where he's going to take Kirsty?"'

'I'll explain in the car,' she pleads. 'We've not got very much time at all. Come on, let's go!'

'But I'm off the case now,' I say. Even as I say the words, I know I don't believe them in the slightest. She suddenly stops, looks at me with a knowing expression and says, 'That's not you speaking, Sam. You've got more about you than to give up, because of some piddling little technical issue of protocol. Especially not when a woman's life's at risk.'

She's right, of course. Although, if the truth's to be told, this 'piddling little technical issue' could cost me my career, if it all goes pear shaped. I shrug helplessly and open the car, into which she jumps at great speed. 'Now you can show me what these fancy wheels can do,' she says, her face alive with the possibility of us making good our earlier mistakes. 'And don't spare the horses!'

When she tells me where to go, I'm highly sceptical. Surely it would be too much of a risk? But the more I listen to her rationale, the more I'm convinced and focus my efforts on getting there as quickly as possible.

'Aren't we going the wrong way?' Olivia protests, as I roar through a red light and pass the dark bulk of the Cathedral Church of St Nicholas on our right hand side.

'Believe me, this is the quickest way,' I reply.

She looks even more dubious as, for a short time, we are driving towards the North Tyne coast. However, before she objects again, we've shot around a large traffic island and are heading back to The Tyne Bridge. I'm grateful for the lack of traffic at this hour and am oblivious to the frequent flashes of speed and other traffic cameras, which seem to be applauding our rapid progress to our destination.

Olivia looks to her left and shivers perceptibly, as we speed across The Tyne Bridge. The dark mass of The Sage sits, its large glass shell reflecting the moon, which periodically peers out from behind high clouds. I drive up to The Sage, but am disappointed to see no car parked anywhere near the entrance. 'Shit!' I curse and can almost feel Olivia's anxiety that she may, once again, have got things terribly wrong.

'Maybe he approached from the other side,' I say, now more in hope than expectation. I drive towards the dead end, to the side of The Sage with the Stage Door. I'm driving more slowly now. I don't want to alert any ears that may yet be listening out for the police. We crawl down the narrow roadway, straining to see any sign of movement. Then, finally, we both see it! A silver saloon, parked sideways across three or four parking bays, parallel to the road.

'Clever,' I mutter. 'He's trying to hide it, behind these walls. You'd have to come more or less all the way down here to see it.'

Olivia gasps in alarm and covers her mouth with her hand, as she begins to comprehend that her hunch was correct . And what that implies. We'll have to confront the killer to stop him carrying out his final atrocity. 'Can you not call for backup, Sam?' she asks desperately. 'Isn't that what you're supposed to do?'

I look at her and shake my head, 'Not yet. They'd not listen anyway. Let's make sure the bastard's in here, before we call for the cavalry.'

She looks worried, but I'm really pumped up. 'You wait here, while I have a look at the car,' I instruct her, firmly.

The bonnet's still quite warm, so he's probably not been here that long. Otherwise, the car has nothing to tell us.

'It looks like he's not long arrived,' I say softly. 'So there's a chance that we may be in time. Come on, let's go around to the main entrance. See if we can see, or hear anything.' As we pad quickly around the curve of the building, I'm struck by how peaceful the location is. I can't hear, or see anything out of the ordinary. The main door is locked, of course, and there's no sign of any forced entry. I curse in frustration, but am brought back into focus by Olivia's rapid intake of breath.

'There!' she whispers excitedly. 'I saw a couple of quick flashes of light. At least, I think I did.'

'A torch, you think?' I prompt. 'He wouldn't be so crazy as to put on the lights, so he may well need to use a torch.'

'Could be,' she says without conviction. 'Maybe we'll see it again.'

We both stare through the glass wall of The Sage. After a couple of minutes, we both see faint flashes of light from inside. 'There it is again,' I say excitedly. 'It looks like the bastard's in Sage One. Just like you said in the car. Back to square one!'

I grin at her in congratulation, but she just says, 'Can we call for help now, please.'

She doesn't understand that I want to end this myself, so I ignore her and, instead, start to look for a way into the building. I hastily backtrack towards the parked cars. These rear doors may well be the most amenable to a spot of breaking and entering. Just by the bridge leading to the Stage Door, a set of steps goes one floor underground. I rush back to my car to retrieve a torch and a crowbar from the boot. Olivia's eyes widen in surprise and I grin at her, 'Not what you imagine your average Mazda sports car driver carries around in the boot, huh?'

'But...but what are you going to do?'

'Get in, as quickly and quietly as I can,' I answer over my shoulder, as I make my way swiftly down the stone steps. I imagine the door leads to some sort of service level, below Sage One and the concourse area. I really hope or man's focusing on himself and what he's doing. That way, I may get in unnoticed.

It takes a couple of minutes and a bit of work, but eventually the slim end of my crowbar starts to gain purchase on the door. 'I hope he didn't think to set the burglar alarm,' I say to an ashen faced Olivia, as I finally prise open the door. The whole thing might have taken longer than I'd have preferred, but we're now inside The Sage, having created surprisingly little noise.

Initially, we try to make our way down what seems to be a wide corridor, without using the torch. But it's absolutely pitch black and I've no idea where we're going. 'Hang on,' hisses Olivia. 'I think I've got something that may help.' She fishes around in her shoulder bag for a minute or so, before producing a very large pair of sunglasses. I quickly break off the plastic sides and then split the two lenses apart. One lens easily covers the torch and does a good job at reducing the light.

I smile at her and whisper urgently, 'Thanks, Olivia! That's much, much better. Now, it looks like they're in Sage One.'

'I think he'll be on the stage, Sam,' she says firmly. 'It's the only place that will satisfy him. It has to be there.'

'OK,' I reply. 'Then let's make our way up to that level. We could slip inside and see what's going on.'

She nods her head in agreement and we make our way, much more easily by torchlight, down the corridor. She's bloody game, that's for sure, I'm well impressed by her courage. We soon find a flight of stairs, leading up to ground level. I douse the torch and creep up the stairs, by the little light which comes into The Sage from the city, across the river. We emerge quietly into the main concourse area. The whole place seems ghostly in the intermittent moonlight, a far cry from the excited bustle of just a few hours ago. We decide that, initially, we should take a look at what's going on in Sage One by creeping into the side circle. That way, we can get a good view, but, unless he's staring right at the door, it's unlikely he'll see it open, as it doesn't directly face the lighter area on the river side of the building.

We slip inside and crawl down to the front row, where neither of us can believe our eyes, or our nostrils.

***

Olivia

It's an astonishing sight, to be sure. But what really shocks me is the strong smell of petrol.

'Christ Almighty!' Sam whispers, 'can you smell it? If we don't stop him, the whole damn place is going to go up like a bloody Roman Candle. I know you said he'd want to make a statement, but so help me God, I never expected anything like this.'

Dozens of candles have been lit all around the stage. By their flickering light, we can see that, in the centre of that part of the stage which had accommodated the orchestra, a pile of wood and other flammable materials has been built. Kirsty Cole Harding is sitting on a chair to the side. Judging by her erect posture, I imagine that her hands and feet have been bound to the chair and her silence suggests that her mouth has been gagged. A dark figure is hastily moving between us and what is, I'm certain, intended to be their funeral pyre. He's emptying the contents of a jerry can onto the wood and other material, causing the smell of petrol to become even stronger.

'It's at times like this that I wish we coppers were allowed to carry guns,' Sam hissed. 'I could just shoot the bastard dead. Game over.'

Despite my lifelong belief that it's a hallmark of the essential civility of British society, that our police officers do not routinely carry firearms, at this moment, I can surely see Sam's point. He indicates that we should retreat from the auditorium, while the killer's face is turned away from us.

Once we are safely out in the concourse, he says, 'OK. This is what we're going to do.'

Chapter Twenty Nine

3.20am, Monday 11th July 2016, The Sage, Gateshead.

Olivia

I still think that we should phone for help, but Sam's having none of it. 'Look, for a start, I'm off the case, in case you'd forgotten. And, just suppose Harrison is prepared to listen to me, what do you think that nutter in there would do, as soon as he hears all the heavy brigade bashing down the door? Have you smelled the petrol? No, the best bet of saving her is to keep things nice and quiet and take advantage of our element of surprise.'

Reluctantly, I agree to this and he explains what he's going to do. He plans to go to the far side of the auditorium and enter Sage One by the stalls level door, nearest the stage. 'What I want you to do, is to go back inside here, give me three minutes exactly and then attract his attention. You don't need to stand up. Stay hidden behind the balcony and shout out something. Ask him what the hell he's doing, or something. Hopefully that'll get im to look in this direction and I can get in to tackle him, while his back's turned. Simple. Can you do that?'

'What if he sees you? I don't like it.'

'That's why it's vital you give me the best chance to catch him from behind. Try to keep him talking. Anything to draw his attention this way. OK? Come on, Olivia. You can do this. Right, you slip back inside, and give me three minutes from now!'

He gives me one last smile and thumbs up and he's gone, stealthily slipping down the stairs and moving around to the other side of the auditorium. I suddenly feel terribly alone and frightened. When I get back in position, I'm shocked to see that the killer is no longer visible on the stage.If he's not there when Sam comes through the door in three minutes, he might walk into a trap. Relax, I tell myself. There's plenty of time. Kirsty's still in there and he's probably too far to this side of the stage for me to be able to see him. The seconds tick by and there's still no sign, until at last he appears, carrying more material to throw on the pyre.

He goes to the far side and, after throwing the stuff onto the pyre, he looks up to wipe his brow. It's like a furious punch to my stomach, as I realise immediately who he is.

JP's usually charming, open face looks somehow distorted and devilish in the dancing candle light, as I hold on to the balcony to stop myself from fainting with shock. I'm still trying to process this information, when I realise that the three minutes must surely soon be up. I glance quickly at my watch and see that I have ten seconds to decide exactly what to say in these new circumstances.

I decide that I must sound unlike the police or security staff, as this might only scare him into immediately setting fire to the whole stage. I prepare my most formal lecturing voice and say, 'What on earth are you doing here?'

I can sense, rather than see, him stop what he's doing and, I imagine, gaze up at the balcony, in an effort to see who is speaking. I decide that, in these circumstances, Sam will have the best chance of disabling him, if I show myself and confront him directly. With luck, this should mentally confuse him for long enough.

'I know who you are JP. And I know what you've done,' I say, as I raise myself to my feet. He surely can see only a faint image of me, illuminated by the candlelight and he seems to squint into the semi darkness.

'Olivia? Is that you?' he croaks, in a voice that seems cracked and dry. 'But, how.... This shouldn't be happening...'

To my utter horror, he attempts to reconcile his confusion by turning round to face away from the pyre and towards Kirsty, just as Sam is entering the stage behind her. What happens next is so fast that I hardly take it in. JP reaches into his pocket, produces something and a very loud bang echoes through the auditorium. Sam falls and rolls over onto his side. With a sickening feeling, I realise that the shot was over a relatively short distance and fear that he could easily be dead. JP takes the most cursory of glances at the prone body, before rushing off the stage in my direction. Still shocked, I nevertheless realise that he's coming for me, so I scramble up the few stairs and out into the concourse. I can't go down the stairs, as I will most likely run straight into my pursuer, so I decide to run around the outside of the auditorium at first floor level. I'm just getting into my stride, when I see a dark shape hit the stairs from the main concourse and start up towards me.

I hope that when he gets to the top of the stairs, he won't know which way I've gone. If he chooses the wrong way, I might be able to get back downstairs towards the place where Sam and I came in. As soon as I think about Sam, my legs turn to jelly and I almost stumble. Surely he couldn't have survived a shot at such close quarters? I find all my thoughts directed towards the stricken policeman. I give surprisingly little further thought to the revelation of the killer's identity.

I think he's gone the other way, because I can hear some muffled cursing, when I'm halfway down the stairs which descend right by the ticket office. This is followed by a familiar voice, wheedling, 'Come on, Olivia. You know me. You needn't be afraid of me. Come and show yourself and we can work this whole thing out, OK?'

I decide that, if I try to reach the stairs, up which Sam and I came from the sub ground floor, I would have to cross an exposed part of the concourse and he'd almost certainly see me. Moreover, the clouds seem to have cleared and a bright moonshine bathes the whole area in an eerie silver light. My best chance is to hide myself away somewhere, in the hope that he soon decides that he doesn't have the time to spend on a search, before dawn breaks. If his grand finale is going to impress, it will have to be in, at worst, semi darkness. I creep into the ground floor mens' toilet and hide myself away in a cubicle. From here, I should be able to call 999 and get help. But where's my bloody phone? I had it in my jacket pocket when I wanted to make the call earlier. Christ! Why did I listen to Sam? Frantically, I search all my pockets and my shoulder bag, but there's nothing. The phone must have fallen out of my pocket when I scrambled up the balcony stairs. My stomach lurches as I realise that I'm entirely on my own.

Well, not quite. With horror, I hear successive cubicle doors being flung open. He's here! How the hell did he find me so quickly? It doesn't make sense. Finally, he pushes open the door and holds something out to me in his hand. 'This is yours, I guess,' he says showing, but not offering my phone. 'You must have dropped it on the

272

way in here. Nice signal, Olivia. I might almost think that you wanted me to find you.

He's remarkably strong and it doesn't take him long to drag me back into Sage One. Kirsty is still sitting, tied to the seat, her eyes swivelling madly above the crude cloth that is fastened around her mouth. Ominously, Sam hasn't moved at all. It looks very bad for him. In fact, it looks very bad for all of us. JP will obviously dispose of me quickly and then enact his insane plan to immolate both himself and Kirsty. I could kick myself for not realising that he'd almost certainly have a gun. Siegfried was, of course, dead when he was cremated. Clearly, that's what he intends to do to himself. Light the fire and then immediately shoot himself. Whether or not he'll spare Kirsty, as his Brünnhilde, an agonising death by fire, is anyone's guess. Why the hell didn't I warn Sam?

Numb, I realise that there's no way that I can survive the next fifteen minutes. But I think of my son, my life in Switzerland and all my friends and family and I decide that I will not give up without a fight. I've somehow got to do anything I can to shift his worldview. Get him to see this whole situation differently and maybe, just maybe, that might give me a chance. I've surely got to work on the fact that we already have something of a relationship.

Then it comes to me. Of course. He's given me the clue himself, by saying that he wonders if I wanted to be caught.

He's tied me up as well and is busying himself with the final preparations for lighting the fire, when, with as much confidence as I am able to muster, I speak. 'Let her go, JP. She's not your real Brünnhilde, is she? Look at her? Does she want to be here? Did she come here of her own free will? I did. And you said it yourself, it was almost like I wanted you to find me. Maybe I did.'

JP stops what he's doing and looks sideways at me. Good! I've got his attention. Now I must tread very carefully.

'Why did you say that perhaps I wanted to be found? Did you feel it too?'

'Feel what?' he asks.

'Oh come on, JP,' I'm taking a chance here, but if it works, I may at least delay the inevitable. And then, who knows what might happen? 'Admit it. You chose this woman here as your Brünnhilde, before you ever met me. Didn't you?'

'No,' he answers angrily. 'That's not true. I didn't select her. Fate did. We're all victims of our fate.' He turns back to his fiendish work with the pyre and I groan, as I confront the probability that my strategy has failed. Suddenly, he stops what he's doing and scratches his head.

Better! He's at least thinking about what I said. He then turns to face Kirsty, an expression of disappointment on his face. 'But, it's true that she hasn't responded in the way I would have expected. Maybe she's like a skitty horse, you know? Needs to be properly schooled.'

'A Brünnhilde needing to be schooled?' I ask incredulously. 'If you know anything about Brünnhilde, you must know that she's a powerful and brave woman who gives herself willingly to her Siegfried. Look at her. She's nothing like that. She's unworthy of you.'

This last appeal to his vanity seems to please him and it looks like he thinks this is worth thinking about. He says nothing, but strokes his chin reflectively. Finally, he walks across to me and says, in a cautious voice. 'I think I see what you mean, Olivia. When I explained what we were going to do, I thought she'd be ecstatic.'

'But she wasn't, was she, JP?' I interrupt. The more I'm in charge of the conversation, the more I can direct it, where I want it to go. 'She's been hysterical, hasn't she? She doesn't understand, JP. Let's face it. She's just a pretty face and a great voice. Oh, she might be very good at *playing* Brünnhilde. But you and I both know that she *isn't* Brünnhilde. Whereas you *are* Siegfried.'

'No,' I won't listen,' he shouts. 'I know what I'm doing. I'm not going to listen to you.' He strides across the stage and I prepare myself for the worst.

'Is this really how you imagined it?' I say sympathetically. 'You deserve a hero's end. I understand that. How do you think I got here? I understood, JP. I understood what the three others were all about. Why? Because I'm the same as you. We deserve something better, don't we? Not a sordid thing like this. Isn't all this a bit spoiled now?'

I'm playing a high risk game here and, initially, it looks like I've overplayed my hand. He raises his hand as if he is about to strike me, but holds it where it is. He then lowers it with what I can only describe as a loving, even awestruck smile on his face. It's amazing how he suddenly looks again like the handsome American I'd got to know and like.

'Wow, Olivia,' he says, sitting down on a vacant chair. 'Or should I call you Brünnhilde? I see it all now.' He waves his arm dismissively towards Kirsty, 'This woman isn't worthy of me. But you are. You, most certainly are.'

Full of restless energy, he stands quickly and begins to stride about the stage, taking only the most cursory glance at Sam's motionless body. Suddenly he stops and looks, with an expression of utter distaste, at the stage, Kirsty and Sam's body. 'This is unworthy of me now.' Pointing at Kirsty, he shouts, 'You are unworthy of me.' Indicating me, and evidently still addressing the sitting opera star, he says with adoration, 'But she most certainly is. Hail my real Brünnhilde!'

So far, he's done exactly what I wanted him to do. But now, he veers off piste alarmingly. He approaches me, kneels down before me and takes my bound hands into his. I swear that there's real love in his eyes, as he says, 'If fire is not to be our vehicle to everlasting fame and honour, my love, then let it be water.'

Unsurprisingly, Kirsty's shoulders slump at this news. Perhaps she is daring to hope that she might actually get out of this alive. I believe she might. But right now, I wouldn't give much for my chances.

Chapter Thirty

Olivia

I'm not sure whether it's my imagination, but I believe I can see the first glimmerings of the new dawn in the still dark, summer sky. It occurs to me that I may not live to see the full sunrise.

Back in Sage One, after my prompting, JP had certainly decided that I was going to enjoy the privilege of joining him for all eternity. He had quickly, and without ceremony, left Kirsty, and the almost certainly dead Sam, on the stage. I had thought he was going to set light to his pyre, but it was easy to convince him that this was a bad idea, as it would only attract the attention of the emergency services.

Now he has pulled me out into the concourse area, I'm not surprised that we don't initially make for his car. What he said about water gives me a pretty good idea of what he has in mind for us. We leave the building, by the entrance near to St Mary's Heritage Centre. He even has a set of keys which he uses to unlock the door and relock it. It's a shock to recall that, only hours previously, we had both stood more or less on this very spot, looking out across the Tyne. He briefly turns to look across to the city and I take the opportunity to remind him, 'Do you still think it looks like the Rhinemaidens are down there?'

He turns back to look at me with a conflicted expression. Almost as if some kind of internal battle is going on inside him for his mind and, even though I'm not particularly religious, it occurs to me even, perhaps for his very soul. This gives me hope.

The moment is soon gone, however, and his face is now a picture of suspicion. He's obviously very erratic and is now in a phase, during which he's not entirely convinced of my newly expressed devotion to him. He therefore keeps his gun pointed at me the whole time. He responds to my question with a terse, 'I won't hesitate to use this, Olivia. So, no funny business, OK?'

I note that he seems very keen to stay on the opposite side of the vehicle turning circle from The Heritage Centre and we hurry past the converted church without a second look. This was, of course, the scene of his first killing and his sensitive behaviour gives me a boost of encouragement.

I make a real effort to stop focusing on the shock of the killer's identity and, having got this far, concentrate on trying to work out how I might maximise my chances of surviving, at least for the next half hour. Right now, I'd settle for that, and take things from there.

So, as he pushes me along the deserted street, I desperately try to think of ways to keep him engaged with me. I decide that again, flattery might work best and say, 'But how did you manage to get her, JP? You were in the audience? I don't understand.'

He's obviously pleased that he can explain his own cleverness and stops to speak, 'I didn't go back in after the last interval, Olivia. It was as simple as that.' I remember looking for him, but being beaten by the dimming lights. If only I'd been a bit quicker back to my seat, I might have noticed and, perhaps, realised what was going on.

Satisfied that the conversation is over, he starts to move again. Desperate to work out another way to get his attention, I recall my thought about his evident reluctance, a moment ago, to get close to The Heritage Centre and what it might signify. I begin to ask myself, whether it's possible, that some part of him doesn't want to, or cannot accept what he did, both there and at the two other locations. Certainly, his first, brutal murder of a harmless old street person was hardly the work of a great hero in the making. Neither were the other two killings, for which he was responsible. As he pushes me further away from the entrance to The Sage, I reflect that his behaviour, when we met on the days of the performances, seemed entirely normal. While many psychopaths are perfectly able to behave absolutely normally sometimes, whilst at other times committing crimes of the utmost depravity, I somehow can't see JP as this type. I let my mind play around with this idea and am focusing so hard on this, that I don't notice that we are leaving a raised pavement. I stumble and almost fall, much to JP's irritation, before he pulls me upright again. I see that we have just   passed the junction of Oakwellgate and Brandling Street. I'm now pretty sure where we're headed. And it's not far away.

His reference to water, back in The Sage, strongly suggested a jump, either from The High Level Bridge or The Tyne Bridge itself. Both of these have, sadly, proved very effective for suicides down the years. JP's no fool. He's bound to realise that, although the early morning streets are still deserted, these conditions won't last forever. Even a newcomer to Newcastle, like JP, is going to be aware that The High Level Bridge is too far away and to get there on foot requires an awkward route. The Tyne Bridge, on the other hand, is much nearer.

Desperately, I try to focus on ways in which I can try to slow him down. I must find a way to reestablish the rapport, even perhaps the temporary control that I'd exercised over him in The Sage. As he pushes me at gunpoint past the locked up businesses, located underneath the railway arches on Brandling Street, I realise that, somehow, I've got to understand the essential reason for his descent into madness. All my professional instincts tell me that JP has been driven by some terrible experience into this behaviour and that some part of him cannot accept what he is doing and what he has become. Maybe that's why he left all the clues at the murder scenes. Certainly, that's why he wants to style himself as a hero. The alternative, that he is just a plain, sadistic killer,is just too unpalatable. I decide that this issue of how he sees himself must be my key, my way of acquiring some sort of means to influence him. Hopefully, even to stop him.

Then, I suddenly have it. My mind races as I think back to what I remembered earlier about Siegfried already being dead, by the time of his and Brünnhilde's immolation. I realise that, in some way, something happened to him which, in his mind, effectively 'killed' the old JP and set him off on this path of deranged behaviour. I think about our very first meeting, when he told me of the recent death of his wife. Could this have been the trigger that set everything in motion.? If so, maybe it will give me a lever to try to influence him.

We're at the end of the cobbled Brandling Street now and we turn right. The Tyne Bridge stands before us, about a hundred yards or so distant. I had hoped there might be some traffic, perhaps a passing police car, even at this time in the morning. But the road is eerily silent in both directions. JP starts to breathe more heavily and frequently, as he sees the bridge and contemplates what we are about to do.

'It doesn't have to end this way, JP,' I say, as I try to resist him pulling me towards my doom. 'I think I understand you. You don't really want to do this, but the loss of your wife...'

He suddenly stops and I think, maybe I've scored a direct hit. However, rather than respond with anger or sadness, as I expect, he simply stares at me and then guffaws with laughter. 'Oh, please, Dr Clavel. Spare the psychobabble. You have absolutely no idea what you're talking about.'

I feverishly try to re calibrate. I'm certain that my basic analysis is correct. I just have the precise trigger for his behaviour wrong. What else could it be?

I can see the tower of St Mary's, just ahead of us and to the right, as we walk past the green, wrought iron railings. I don't have much longer, before we'll be on the bridge itself and then over the Tyne. The castellated battlements of the keep are now visible, on the far bank of the river, and I stagger and grab hold of one of the old fashioned green wrought iron lamp posts. I'm desperate to stop him any way I can, now. But, of course, he's far too strong for me and simply pulls me away and drags me onto the bridge itself. The pavement narrows, as we pass the huge metal girder that curves down so magnificently into the pavement. I've walked across here many times, but the is the first time I've noticed the perfect lines of welded bolts, which help to give the bridge its strength.

We arrive at the first lamp post of the bridge proper and JP stops. He looks over the rail to verify that we are over the murky water of the Tyne. He's picked the spot well. Behind the lamp post is a kind of buttress which provides a small, flat surface, which I estimate at about 3 feet long and a maximum two feet wide. It's a perfect spot from which to make the jump and JP Pushes me up onto it. He still has his gun and I suppose that I calculate that my chances of surviving the jump, however slim, are better than those of surviving a point blank shot. I think again about my son, my work, my life and Sam in those couple of seconds, during which I clamber onto the platform. The concrete river bank is enticingly close, but an attempt to jump there would surely be impossible and, even if successful, fatal.

By this time he's up on the platform with me and I can feel the tension rising in him, as he prepares to jump and pull me with him. Almost unconsciously I say, 'It's you, isn't it, JP? It's not your wife at all, if you ever had one, that is.' He stops and stares at me. 'It's you who have been given a sentence of death. What is it? Cancer? Brain tumour? And you're such a little man that you can't take it bravely on the chin like so many, ordinary people have. You can't stand that this has happened to you, so you have to go out with a bang. Well, no one will remember you as a hero, JP, will they?'

He looks stricken, almost as if I have pulled the rug from under his very existence. His eyes are swivelling crazily from side to side and he drops his gun into the water. I really think that there's a tiny chance that he won't actually go through with his plan, that his saner half is struggling to reassert control.

Somehow, he is now the one standing furthest out on the platform and suddenly I feel something fast and determined, brushing past my legs. Two hands reach out and grab JP around the calves and push him hard, out towards thin air and the river below. As he loses his balance, whether intentionally or not, I will never know, but he lets go of me. He seems to stop, delicately perched, half on the platform and half in mid air over the Tyne and he stares directly into my eyes. His expression is one of such utter desolation, abandonment and sorrow, that I have to look away. He doesn't utter a sound, as he tumbles towards the water, which he hits with a huge splash. I feel as if I might faint, but find myself being pulled down onto the bridge, and back into my life, by a blood-soaked Sam. We look at one another for a second, before he pulls himself painfully up by the railing, holding his right side. Of course, ever the policeman, he wants to see whether JP surfaces. He stares at the water for some minutes, before turning back to me, muttering, 'The bastard's gone.' He collapses, unconscious, onto the pavement.

Chapter Thirty One

Wednesday 20th July, The Queen Elizabeth Hospital, Gateshead.

Olivia

I've waited almost ten days to see Sam. Ten days since the ambulance and the police cars sped onto The Tyne Bridge, sirens blaring and lights flashing. I didn't really understand how they could have appeared so quickly. But even so, during those desperate minutes, as the sky started to change to a lighter shade of blue, Sam had passed in and out of consciousness more than once. The paramedics pronounced me physically unharmed, so naturally they wouldn't let me go with him in the ambulance. That left me with the odious DI Harrison, who insisted that I go with him to the police station, to explain what had happened.

I refused to say anything, until they told me how they got there so fast. With little or no grace, Harrison reluctantly described how, as soon as Kirsty Cole Harding had calmed down after her rescue, she told the police that Sam had come round, just after JP had abducted me. She had told Sam that JP had taken me, rather than her, and that he would replace fire with water, for his final act. Sam had told her that the killer most probably intended to jump into the Tyne. He had also reasoned that the Tyne Bridge was the most likely spot and, although desperately wounded, he'd set off to follow us. But not before he'd given the American opera singer his mobile phone with clear instructions what to tell the police.

Of course, I've not really been involved in wrapping up the enquiry, though I have been interviewed several times by the police. But now, it's late afternoon and I'm standing in the reception area of the Queen Elizabeth Hospital. I've been put off time and again on previous days, but, today,I'm determined not to go away, until I have at least seen Sam. I've such a lot to tell him and, of course, to ask him. After I've thanked him properly for saving my life, that is. The staff at the reception desk seem unwilling to inform me of Sam's ward number and I'm just about to blow my top, when DC Jenkins comes striding into the hospital. She looks stunning, in her designer leather jacket and pencil slim black jeans. But worst of all, she is carrying an enormous box of Milk Tray. I, in contrast, have a small bar of Swiss chocolate . Shit, I mutter, as she approaches the reception desk. That's all I need. Another bloody row with this woman. To my surprise, as soon as she recognises me, she smiles warmly and shifts the box to enable her to shake hands. 'Dr Clavel! It's very good to see you. Did you get the all clear from the hospital too? Have you come to visit Sam?'

'Well, er, yes,' I say. 'But they don't seem keen to tell me where he is.'

'What?' she replies incredulously. 'I'll soon sort that out. Here, hold this for a minute, will you.' As soon as she's passed over the chocolates, she hurries over to the reception desk. I can't hear every word that is spoken, but the gist is clear. The receptionist blushes and looks directly at me, before DC Jenkins returns, takes the chocolates and leads me to Sam's room. 'Bloody jobsworths,' she says. 'Don't they have any common sense? Any way, call me Serena, please.'

'And call me Olivia,' I blurt out in reply, as we climb the stairs to the first floor. A middle aged, overweight nurse is guarding the entry to the ward, but as soon as Serena explains who we are, she smiles and directs us to Sam's room, 'He's had a hard time. Several operations and a lot of time asleep. But now he just has to give himself time to recover. In fact, for the last couple of days, he's been very cheesed off, what with being stuck in here for so long and not being allowed any visitors, other than his close family. But they all live in London, so it's been harder for them to get here.' She's obviously intent on giving us all the gossip and continues in, what I imagine she thinks is, a confidential tone, 'Would you believe it?   He even tried to check himself out this morning. But doctor's having none of it. In fact, you're his second lot of visitors this week. He wasn't so pleased with the lot that came yesterday, so I hope you two will cheer him up.'

I look at Serena and she whispers, 'Bloody Internal Enquiries. Can you believe they've been harassing him about what he did on the bridge.'

'I can imagine,' I say, 'they've seen me half a dozen times. They just don't seem to get that Sam's a hero. He saved my life. And Kirsty's'

We knock gently on Sam's door and open it. He is lying, half   propped up in bed, half watching Sky News on the TV. His chest and upper body are still heavily strapped and he's tied up to what looks like a blood drip and a couple of others that I don't recognise. He smiles weakly, as we enter and rasps, 'Christ Almighty! You two not been read and writing again, have you?'

We both laugh at his lapse into cockney rhyming slang, as Serena and I take it in turns to give him a peck on the cheek.

Unsurprisingly, Sam immediately asks, 'Has the body been found? Those bastards from Internal wouldn't say anything.'

Serena turns around from making space for his chocolates on the bedside cabinet to say, 'Nothing definite yet, Sam. The tide was going out when he went in. The experts say that, in such circumstances, it would almost certainly have been washed out to sea. It could be weeks, or even months before it washes up on the coast somewhere. Or, it might never. Good riddance, I'd say.' Sam nods stiffly, but it's obvious that he'd rather JP's body had been found. Closure, they call it.

'Don't worry,' I say reassuringly. 'He's gone. We both stared at where he went in for at least five minutes. No one could survive that.' It's easy to see that he's still thinking that it's not all over, so I try to change the subject. 'Anyway, forget him, Sam, how are you feeling?

'Oh the docs are always a bit careful,' he replies. 'They don't say too much. But it does appear that I was very badly wounded and that I didn't do myself much good, rushing around on the bridge.' I grimace and he quickly adds, 'But it was a good swap. Your life for a bit of blood.'

I squeeze his hand and note that Serena doesn't seem to object at all. 'But, you will make a full recovery?'

'Oh, I'm not in any danger now. But it's a bit early to know if there'll be any lasting damage.'

'You're young and fit,' Serena smiles at him. 'You'll be back on the job soon enough.'

'Crap,' retorts Sam. 'Those wankers from Internal want my Warrant Card. I can tell.'

'Well, there you're wrong, Sam,' says Serena. Her suddenly furtive manner suggests that she doesn't think she should be revealing this. But she continues anyway. 'They have to do their job. However, the DCI told me specially to let you know that you've been given a clean bill of health from them. In fact, for some reason, they have you down as some sort of hero and are recommending you for a medal.'

'Well, Quayle knows what she can do with that,' mutters Sam. 'Anyway, there's a lot I don't know about this bloke I shoved off the bridge. Who the hell was he? Why did he do it? And, hell, Olivia, why on earth did he take you?'

'You mean you don't know?' I ask incredulously. 'No one has told you.'

'No. They said I'd find out in good time. Well, I reckon that time's now. What's this all about, Olivia?'

I look at Serena and she nods in agreement, so I begin to explain. 'It's like this, Sam. I actually knew the perpetrator. Spent quite a lot of time with him, over the few days when it was all happening.'

His jaw drops in shock, 'Bloody hell! How can that be? It doesn't make sense.' Then he remembers something, 'Jesus! It wasn't that Leonard weirdo, was it? You know, the one you told me about , who was in your discussion group?'

Serena's looking sharply at me as well, and I can feel myself reddening. 'Er, no. It wasn't him. Another false trail, I guess.'

'So how did you know him?' Sam demands.

'Oh, it was just a coincidence really. We were sitting together on the same plane, coming over from Geneva before the operas. He was an American, working for a Swiss bank and we just got chatting. Turned out he was going to the Wagner Operas as well, so we both attended the pre opera discussion groups.' He squints at me, as if he knows there's more and I find myself saying, 'Actually, we spent most intervals together and had a couple of meals as well.'

'When he wasn't running around slaughtering people, you mean?' Sam asks caustically. 'Jesus! And you never suspected a thing?'

'No. He was always perfectly charming and pleasant with me.'

'Well, all I can say is that you sure keep some shady company, lady,' Sam jokes. 'Anyway, this Yank. Was he some sort of paranoid schizophrenic,then? Could you have been in danger? Why did he take you?'

'That's where I think I have to explain,' interrupts Serena. 'I doubt that Olivia would do herself justice.' Sam's eyebrows arch at the sound of my first name and a slight smile starts to play around his mouth.

'I see you two are all pals together now,' he says. 'So, come on Serena, explain.'

'Olivia recognised him when you were making your way to the other side of Sage One. Of course, she was shocked and nearly missed her job of distracting him.'

'That was a disaster,' I interrupt. 'As soon as he knew it was me, he became confused and turned around to look at Kirsty. That's when he saw you and shot you. I swear I thought you were dead.'

'Docs told me I was extremely lucky,' Sam says. 'Seems he was a pretty crap shot. And they said, if he'd shot towards that bloody petrol soaked pyre, we might all have gone up in smoke.'

'Well, I tried to hide from him so that I could phone the police, but I dropped my phone. He found it and caught me. That's about it, really.'

Sam looks confused and Serena immediately says, 'That's not it. That's not it by a bloody, long way. I knew Olivia wouldn't explain. Well this is what she did. She convinced this loony that Kirsty was basically just a pretty face and good singer and that she, Olivia, was his true Brünnhilde, his real soul mate.'

'So, that's why he let her go and took you? Christ, Olivia, that was brave. What the hell were you thinking?' Sam demands.

'I simply calculated that I'd have a better chance of reasoning with him and that he'd probably kill me anyway, if I'd done nothing. That, and I felt it was at least partly my fault that Kirsty was in that mess.'

'Crap!' shouts Sam.

'Well, anyway, it all turned out OK, ' I say, keen to move off a discussion of my role.

'But why did he do it, Olivia? You said that, by seeing himself as Siegfried, he in some way saw himself as already dead.'

'I did. Interestingly, Kerrigan, that's his name, by the way, had told me that he had just lost his wife to cancer. When I saw it was him, my first thought was that he felt that he'd 'died' in some way, with his loss of her. But that didn't really make sense. The first three murders, maybe, as some sort of anguished hitting back at a perceived cruel fate. But not his obsession with Ms Harding. How could that be consistent with his feelings for his dead wife? And it then occurred to me that he might, in a sense, see himself as already dead.'

'I don't understand.'

'Well, he might have been given a sentence of death.'

' And that's what we found out, when we contacted the Swiss police,' confirmed Serena. 'It turns out that he had never been married and that several months ago, he was diagnosed with an incurable and fatal condition. He wasn't expected to live out the year.'

'So he wanted to go out with a bang?'

'That's about the size of it, yes,' I say. 'It just pushed him into madness. In some ways, one has to feel a bit sorry for him.'

'No bleeding way!' insists Sam. 'The man was a psycho, pure and simple.'

'Who knows how any of us would react, in such circumstances, Sam?' I ask. 'I do believe that a part of him was disgusted and appalled at what he was doing. You remember that I wondered whether, in leaving all those clues at the crime scenes, part of him was actually wanting to be caught and stopped? I do think that he was waging a kind of inner battle for control.'

I don't say out loud, but I recall vividly that, right at the moment Sam pushed him off the bridge, I saw JP's face. If I'm being honest, I don't know, if he'd have just jumped himself, or taken me with him. But, of course, I could never say that to Sam. To kill a murderer and save a friend is a sufficient psychological burden to carry, without some unprovable hypothesis of mine confusing matters.

'But what about the others? He must have planned things for a long time,' Sam muses.

'Indeed he did,' explains Serena. 'We traced his movements and he'd visited Tyneside several times over the past few months, to choose his victims and set up suitable locations. We got some DNA from things he'd touched at The Sage and found traces at the place in Hymers Court where Mykel Stevenson was killed.'

'So you think he'd been a punter there?'

'That seems the most likely explanation. He was far too careful, when he was in killing mode. He'd even rented himself a flat on the Quayside, rather than risk staying in a hotel. And he'd taken out a short lease on a workshop, where he kept Ms Harding prisoner, before taking her back to The Sage. It was odd, though, when we searched his flat, we found the weapon that had killed Grantham, the gentle giant and the sword he'd used to kill Stevenson and Holden. He hadn't even cleaned them. We found loads of evidence to link them to the first three killings.'

Sam whistles softly and says, 'It really does sound like he wanted us to know what he'd done. After burning himself and Kirsty to a crisp, of course.'

'That's certainly what it looked like to us, Sam,' Serena says before before effectively drawing a line under the conversation. 'Anyway, Sam, who sent that huge card?'

For the first time since we'd arrived, Sam looks a bit embarrassed, 'Oh, it's from Opera North and The Sage ' he says. 'They've sent me a season ticket for every single performance at The Sage for the next five   years. Including the classical music and opera.'

Serena and I burst out laughing, but he's not finished yet. 'That's not all,' he adds. 'Kirsty Cole Harding is performing at The New York Metropolitan Opera next year. She's invited me to be her guest for two weeks in

The Big Apple, including tickets for something called 'Cosi Fan Tutte.'

'Couldn't have chosen a better introduction to opera for you, myself,' I say and, this time, all three of us laugh so loud, that the nurse comes rushing in, to see what's going on.

Author's Note

Sentence of Death is my first foray into crime fiction, my previous novels having both been spy stories, set in World War Two. In both cases, the books were adapted from little known, but fascinating and, most importantly, true stories.

In a funny sort of way, I have maintained that approach with this latest crime thriller. The basic structure of the plot is governed by events that really did take place in July 2016. From Tuesday 5th July to Sunday 10th July 2016, Opera North did, indeed, perform all four operas of Richard Wagner's 'Ring des Nibelungen' cycle at The Sage, on the bank of the River Tyne, in Gateshead. I was fortunate enough to experience the wonderful music and singing, during those days - something I will never forget. It was an absolute pleasure to be a small part of such an enthusiastic audience, drawn from many different countries.

I have tried to keep the setting as close to that, experienced by me, and have only changed names, when a character plays an active role in the plot. It goes without saying that, fortunately, the deaths and their investigation, which form the substance of Sentence of Death, are purely a product of my imagination.

I have no idea, whether or not a pre opera discussion group was hosted by Opera North. I certainly did not participate in anything like that and the group depicted in the book is, of course,purely fictional.

The completion of Sentence of Death has enabled me to fulfil a long held ambition to write a crime thriller.

While it was initially intended as a stand alone novel, I have since wondered about the possibility of Sam and Olivia working together, to solve further cases. I would be very interested in what you, my readers, think of that idea.

I can be contacted, by private message, on my website www.apmartin.co.uk , or on GoodReads.

I look forward to hearing from you.

31505516R00174

Printed in Poland
by Amazon Fulfillment
Poland Sp. z o.o., Wrocław